Islam's Fire

By

Joseph M. Pujals

Order this book online at www.trafford.com
or email orders@trafford.com

Most Trafford titles are also available at major online book retailers.

Printed in the United States of America.

ISBN: 978-1-4269-3494-0 (sc)

ISBN: 978-1-4269-3495-7 (hc)

ISBN: 978-1-4269-3496-4 (e-book)

Library of Congress Control Number: 2010909201

*Our mission is to efficiently provide the world's finest, most comprehensive book publishing
service, enabling every author to experience success. To find out how to publish your
book, your way, and have it available worldwide, visit us online at www.trafford.com*

Trafford rev. 8/31/2010

www.trafford.com

North America & international
toll-free: 1 888 232 4444 (USA & Canada)
phone: 250 383 6864 ✦ fax: 812 355 4082

1

Simon Rossman was eagerly waiting for the phone call that he knew would consume the rest of his life, possibly ending with his death. He was at home in Sacramento, California, playing with his two sons when the phone rang, answering it he heard the excited voice of Ken Barkley.

"It's done. The program worked. We're rich!"

"Where are you?"

"I'm in Washington at a fishing resort."

"Be specific, I want to come up and see you."

"I'm at the Ferguson Fishing resort, Cabin 12, just a few miles north of Belfair, just off State Highway 300--can we talk?"

"No. Not now. Not over the phone. I'll fly up this afternoon, just sit tight, don't talk to anybody, and don't call anybody. Got it?"

"Yeah, I got it."

Between the plane flight and the drive from the Seattle/Tacoma airport, it was late that evening before Simon drove onto the grounds of the fishing lodge.

When Ken had arrived at the fishing resort earlier he had asked for a cabin toward the back of the resort grounds saying he was a writer and wanted privacy. After he had parked and taken his one bag into the cabin, he used his cell phone to call Simon. Since then he had been pacing his room like a nervous cat.

By mid afternoon hunger got the best of him. He had to get out of the cabin that seemed to be closing in on him. He made a quick trip to a convenience store for junk food. Returning he resumed pacing the floor, watching game shows on TV, and munching on snacks. Finally, just as the 10 P.M. news came on he heard a knock at the door.

"Come on kid, open the door, it's me, Simon."

Ken yanked the door open and stood there with a wide grin on his face staring at his visitor. He reached out his hand to shake but Simon pushed past him and stood looking around the room.

Simon was in his late thirties, tall, with light brown skin and a strong muscular build. He had a well groomed appearance but he was not what you would call memorable in appearance. Yet there was something about him that made people uncomfortable. His dark eyes seemed to bore right into you.

He carried a twelve pack of beer into the kitchenette and placed it on the short counter. He took off his hat and black leather coat, threw them on the bed and looked around, his eyes taking in every detail. The room was clean with a rustic décor you would expect at a fishing lodge.

He pulled two cans of beer from the carton, and smiling, tossed one to Ken. After putting the remainder of the beer in the refrigerator, he popped the tab on his can and took a drink. "Alright Ken, let's hear all about it."

"What do you want to know?" Ken asked, after opening his can, taking a drink, and slumping into a chair.

"Everything Ken. Start from the beginning and don't leave anything out," said Simon, taking a sip from his can of beer.

Ken began telling Simon about the computer program he had written and how he had recruited a friend, Al Genovese, from the production review section to run the program through the bank's testing procedures, and then install it in the Wire Transfer System.

At the mention of Al Genovese Simon grew tense but did not interrupt Ken.

As Ken gave his detailed account, Simon kept the supply of beer coming. After another two beers, Ken described how they could transfer the money from the account in Panama to anyplace in the world that he and Simon wanted to go. They would have all the money they would ever need.

Simon was familiar with the account at Banko de Panama since he had established it. He had already left instructions with the Panamanian bank to re-transmit the funds to an account he had set up in Bahrain. Ken would never know about this part of the plan. He forced himself to relax and let Ken continue telling his story.

Simon patiently listened. He got Ken another beer and when he finished his story Simon began asking questions.

"Tell me more about this person, Al Genovese?"

"He's the bank manager in charge of the production Wire Transfer System. He's the guy who has the password that you need in order to upload a program into the production stream. I couldn't make this work without his help."

"Is Genovese the only one at the bank who is helping you?" asked Simon in a tight voice.

"Yeah, he's the only one. Nobody else knows about this plan or the program I put together."

"How much did you promise to pay him?"

"I promised him ten million dollars when we finally get settled someplace."

Simon studied Ken with unyielding eyes that sent shivers up Ken's spine. Then he said, "I hope this guy can be trusted."

For the next two hours Simon asked questions, and prodded for details when Ken faltered. He took notes, asking more questions when necessary. He verified the account number Ken had sent the money to, and the bank's location. As the questioning continued, Simon encouraged Ken to drink more beer.

When Simon felt sure that he had an understanding of the banking details and how the system worked he went on to other subjects.

"So exactly where does Genovese live? Do you have his address?

"Yeah, sure," replied Ken as he scribbled Genovese's address on a note pad and handed it to Simon.

"How about we have one more beer and call it a night?" He leaned back, folding the note with Genovese's address and putting it in his shirt pocket.

Ken got up and unsteadily walked to the refrigerator. He did not notice that Simon had also risen and was just behind him.

Simon pulled a snub nosed .22 caliber revolver from his jacket pocket and, walking up behind Ken shot him in the back of the head. Ken slumped to the floor. Simon leaned over and placed the muzzle of the gun in Ken's ear and pulled the trigger a second time. Neither bullet left an exit wound. Death was instantaneous.

Simon returned to the table and sat down heavily, his hands trembling and his forehead glistening with beads of sweat.

The training camp he attended twenty years ago, where he had been taught how to kill a person a dozen different ways, did not really prepare him for actually killing another human being. They did not teach him how it would feel to kill a friend. Maybe he had been in America too long and grown soft.

He knew it had to be done. His plan was proceeding flawlessly. He could not allow emotions to get in the way now.

Simon felt good about his plans to set bombs across the country that would kill hundreds, but that was different. Just strangers, never looking into their eyes or knowing their names, not friends, just people in the wrong place at the wrong time. He took a deep breath and willed his body to relax.

Killing Ken was personal. They had been friends since Ken was a teenager living next door to him in Sacramento. Ken was a geeky kid, a nerd, and a loner, and Simon had just come to the United States from Pakistan, and didn't know anybody. They had become friends through a mutual need for companionship.

Simon's orders had always been to get the money that was so badly needed. And now his friend was out of school and working for the largest bank in the country. Planting ideas in Ken's mind wasn't too difficult, he was easily manipulated. He began planting ideas about taking a very large amount of money and travelling the world. It started as a game to see if they could devise a plan to steal a billion dollars but over time they both realized that it could actually be done.

They began talking over their different ideas, discarding some, further refining others until they had perfected a plan.

Writing a program to steal the money while it was being sent over the Wire Transfer System would be difficult but not impossible. By the time anyone had discovered the theft they would have already moved the money to many different banks all over the world, making it impossible to trace. Ken was a genius programmer and he knew it, and here was his chance to prove it.

Simon sat for a while thinking about Ken and the years they had known each other. He deeply regretted killing his friend but there was no other way.

He would call Parviz Jalili, may Allah bless him, tomorrow afternoon and let him know the plan had been carried out. He would receive the money soon.

After a few minutes, Simon began to search the cabin. Every scrap of paper, empty beer can, cell phone, magazine, or piece of clothing was thrown into a travel case. Then he began to wipe down all the surfaces that might hold his fingerprints. When he was sure that he had cleaned up thoroughly, he took an extra blanket from the closet and rolled Ken's body onto it.

Turning off the lights, he stood in the dark room until his eyes adjusted, then, opening the door, he scanned the area. By this time it was two-thirty in the morning and there did not seem to be anyone still up. The moon was just a slender crescent in the Western sky, making the night extremely dark.

It required some effort for Simon to pick up the body. Ken was tall and lanky, but still carried some solid muscle. Simon was a strong man but Ken was not as light as he appeared. As Simon carried the body out, he lurched to one side and scraped his arm on the door jamb.

Carrying Ken to the dock gave a whole new meaning to the term "dead weight." Out of breath when he reached the dock, he dumped the body into a rowboat. He rowed to what he thought was the middle of the Hood Canal. Tying the anchor chain around Ken's legs, he tried to throw Ken and the anchor overboard. Throwing a body overboard while in a small boat was difficult. The boat kept rocking as he tried to lift the body over the side. He finally had to kneel in the bottom of the boat to get enough leverage to throw the body over the side. After the body had sunk out of sight, Simon waited silently for a few minutes as he caught his breath, then he rowed back to the dock and tied up.

Before leaving the boat, Simon wiped his fingerprints from the oar handles. Back at the cabin he carried the travel case with Ken's clothing and personal items to his car then went back to the cabin for a last check. Satisfied with his work, he left the cabin, wiping off the door knob as he closed the door behind him.

He went to Ken's car and tried to remove the license plates but he needed a screwdriver. He went back to the cabin and found a knife that would serve the purpose. Working in the dark he was able to loosen the screws. He put the knife on the ground and used his fingers to finish removing the screws. He looked at his watch, it was getting late, he had to hurry. He added the license plate to the travel case.

Using Ken's car keys he started the car, looked out the rear window as he backed into the narrow driveway that circled through the fishing resort. He didn't see the flash when the headlights reflected off of the knife blade.

About a mile from the fishing resort Simon found a deserted

road. Using magazines and newspapers he had found in the cabin he set the car on fire. He didn't worry about fingerprints here, he knew the fire would take care of them.

Simon ran back to the fishing resort to get to his car and drive to Bremerton, to catch the 6:00 AM ferry to Seattle. He arrived at the ferry terminal early and had time to go through the items in the travel case. When he was done he threw the travel case and its contents into a dumpster.

Simon was tired but he would nap an hour and a half on the flight to San Francisco, where he would find out how much Mr. Al Genovese knew. He removed the paper with the address from his shirt pocket and studied it, then put it back. I'll call Professor Jalili when I'm through with Mr. Genovese.

It would be a week before the bank knew they had a very serious problem.

2

Carl Lukin rolled onto one elbow, yawned, stretched, and looked down at Ann. Ann lay on her stomach with the sheets pulled up to her waist. Her auburn hair cascaded over her face and down her back. Carl looked at her tanned, well toned back as she breathed softly, still asleep.

Carl enjoyed watching her. As he watched he felt himself becoming aroused. He leaned over and kissed the back of her neck. He ran his finger lightly up and down her spine until she slowly rolled over. Her large breasts moved up and down with each sleepy, shallow breath. He kissed her lightly on the lips, then on each breast, running his tongue lightly over her nipples until they started to become hard and erect as Ann awakened.

Without opening her eyes she reached up and pulled Carl down to her. With his elbows on each side of her body they began to move rhythmically until they both climaxed and a warm relaxed feeling swept over their bodies. They lay there a few minutes more enjoying the moment and the warmth of each other's body. Only then did

Ann open her eyes and smiling, looked at Carl. In a sleepy voice she said, "Oh, it's you!"

"Are you in the habit of making love to strangers when you wake up?"

"Not since I met you." After a long and tender kiss Carl rolled onto his back. Ann rolled onto her side and slid her leg across his body. With her head on his shoulder she nuzzled and kissed his neck. Sometime later, Carl said, "You snooze I'm going to make coffee."

After showering, Carl entered the kitchen, and turned on the coffeemaker. It was just 7:00 A.M. and the sun was up but the house was still in the shadow of the Olympic Mountains. While the coffee was brewing he walked out onto the deck. The sun was bright and the air felt cool to his skin. Taking a deep breath, he could smell the salt water from the Hood Canal. He grabbed an old towel to wipe the morning dew from the deck furniture, and then brought out the cushions from the storage area.

The Hood Canal is a seventy-mile long waterway in the state of Washington. It begins at Puget Sound and ends near the town of Belfair on the Olympic peninsula. The canal is shaped like a backwards "J." The very end of the canal becomes a mud flat when the tide is out. The vast majority of the Hood Canal is a navigable waterway. The house where Carl and Ann were staying was just past the curve at the bottom of the "J," the canal at this point is over a mile wide, a deep blue green, and only about 200 feet deep at its deepest point.

On this day there was no wind and the surface of the canal was so smooth that the far shoreline was clearly reflected on its surface. The tide was in and the oyster bed just below the deck was under water. He thought about picking up some oysters for lunch when the tide ebbed. From the time they were picked up off the beach, shucked, breaded, and dropped into the frying pan with butter where they would turn a golden brown was just a few minutes. It just didn't get any better than that.

The red light on the coffeemaker blinked off. After pouring

himself a cup, Carl sat down to enjoy what promised to be a great morning. As he did each morning, he watched for the river otters that always came swimming, playing, and diving for their breakfast. There were six otters that lived in a den on the hillside behind the house. Their morning adventures were always entertaining to watch. Their routine was to use the drainage pipe under the highway to reach the beach then swim out into the canal to get their breakfast. Once they caught a fish they would climb onto the swim float moored sixty yards from shore to enjoy their meal and play. They always left a mess of fish scraps and defecations, forcing Carl to clean the swim float daily because of the smell.

Carl had drunk about half his coffee when he spotted the six otters. As they neared the swim float one otter surfaced with a large fish in its mouth. But instead of going toward the swim float as they usually did, they swam around the float, giving it a wide berth, and headed toward the beach in front of the neighbor's house where blackberry bushes offered cover. The other otters followed closely hoping for a share of the first catch of the day.

Carl was surprised by the otters' actions in avoiding the swim float, this was not part of their morning routine. He looked at the float again and noticed something caught near one of the corners. He picked up a pair of binoculars and looked again. Whatever it was it appeared to be snagged on one of the grab ropes that hung from the sides of the float.

Curious, he went down the steps to the beach and pushed the row boat into the water. When he reached the float he could see that it was an arm that had become tangled in a loop in the grab rope, the upper half of a body just visible under the water, its arms stretched out. The lower half of the body was under the swim float. Using a rope that was normally tied to the boat's anchor, he tried to cinch a loop around the exposed arm but it was difficult to get the rope to hold because the body had been in the canal long enough to cause the skin to tear when he tried to tighten the loop. He finally moved the loop farther up the arm until he reached a point where the shirt sleeve still covered the upper arm. He then tied the rope to a cleat on the float.

Although he had been a Naval Criminal Investigator for five years, and had to kill in defending his life, and had seen dead and decomposing bodies, he began to feel nauseous.He headed back to the house to call 911.

While he waited for the sheriff's officers, he went to the bedroom to find Ann still curled up in bed. He sat on the bed and told her he had found a body and had called the sheriff.

Ann rolled up on one elbow and said, "If there are going to be cops coming around, I guess I had better get up. I'll take my shower and be right out, would you mind pouring me a cup of coffee?"

"Coming right up. You may want to wait until the cops finish moving the body before getting anything to eat. The smell is not going to be pleasant."

Fifteen minutes later two Mason County sheriff's cars pulled up in front of the house. When Carl opened the door one of the officers said, "Are you the person who reported finding a body?"

"Yeah, I called 911 this morning about a body snagged on our swim float. Come on in and I'll show you."

When they reached the back deck Carl pointed out the swim float, saying, "I used the anchor rope to tie the body to the float."

One of the officers took the boat out to the float for a look while the other officer took a statement from Carl. They radioed the Sheriff's office and forty five minutes later the coroner and a team of divers arrived to retrieve the body.

A few minutes after the sheriff's officers had arrived Ann had finished her shower and dressed in shorts and a tee shirt. She stepped out of the house holding a coffee mug. Ann was tall with auburn hair to her shoulders, dark blue eyes, with a figure that most women only dream about. She was in her late twenties and a beautiful woman by any standard. She would draw the admiration of both men and women, although women had a tendency to step in front of the men they were with when she appeared.

The Sheriff's officers instantly stopped talking as they stared at Ann.

Carl finally turned around, saw Ann, and made introductions.

"Mr. Lukin, can you tell me again what drew your attention to the body?"

Carl recounted the story of the otters and explained the difficulty he had in tying the rope to the body. He wanted to make sure the coroner understood where the damage to the arm came from.

Carl finished answering all the officers' questions, which were not many, since from all appearances it looked like it was an accidental drowning.

They stood on the deck watching the divers put the body into a basket. They covered the body with a rubber sheet and attached restraining straps. A short time later the body was pulled to shore, loaded onto a gurney, and placed in the coroner's van. The van and the patrol cars were soon gone.

Ann said, "I'll never get used to the smell of a decomposing body. The smell seems to cling to your clothes and hair. I think I'll take another shower."

"Okay, in the meantime I'll take my swim."

"How can you swim when they just pulled a decomposing body out of there?"

As Carl turned to go put his swim suit on he said, "There are all kinds of dead things in the canal, and besides, I don't intend to swim where the body was."

Carl was used to long open ocean swims. He enjoyed the physical effort of a three or four mile swim, but today he would take only one lap, take a quick shower to rinse off the salt water, and then join Ann on the deck for some sun.

3

After her shower Ann put on a swimsuit, found a book she had been reading and pulled up a lounge chair and stretched out to enjoy the sun. Occasionally she would pick up the binoculars and watch Carl stroke cleanly through the water. After a short time she put the book down, leaned back enjoying the warmth of the sun, and closed her eyes. She thought about her life and realized that she was thoroughly contented.

Ann was not only Carl's fiancée whom he loved deeply, but she was his assistant, his partner and his best friend. She was an integral part of the investigation agency Carl owned. She was a beautiful woman of many talents.

She spoke four languages fluently. Frequently she and Carl would carry on their conversations in French, German, or Russian in order to maintain their fluency. She had degrees in linguistics and computer sciences. She was smart, capable, and in love with Carl. She was truly happy.

They had met at the beach in Southern California when Carl

was in high school. The attraction between them was immediate, one could say it was love at first sight. They were both good looking, highly intelligent, had a deep interest in foreign languages, and had very compatible personalities.

Ann learned French from her parents, and growing up in Los Angeles, speaking Spanish was a necessity for getting along with the other kids in school. Her neighbors, the Bacigalluppi family, had five children who all spoke Italian so it was not long before she also spoke fluent Italian. In high school her interest was in mathematics and sciences consequently she decided to take German to meet her language requirement. When Carl came into the picture she realized that he also had a keen interest in languages, which increased her interest in him.

After high school Carl joined the Navy and Ann went to Stanford University, getting an advanced degree in computer sciences and a degree in linguistics. Carl tried to maintain contact with her but As the years went by and duty assignments took him out of the country he began to lose track of her.

Ann did not entirely forget Carl but he had faded in her memory as the workload and the challenges of her classes sapped her energy. In spite of the pressure she still managed to learn to speak Russian. She graduated at the top of her class in both majors. Just prior to graduation she was recruited by the Central Intelligence Agency and after a short vacation she moved to Washington, D.C.

When she reported for work at the CIA and had gone through her orientation she was assigned to the Russian desk to analyze documents. At first she enjoyed it but after reading market reports on wheat futures and steel production forecasts for months on end, she found the work had become boring and lacked any challenge. To give herself a break from the endless supply of reports she would bring in highly technical books on computer science to break the monotony.

Her interest in computer technology soon caught the attention of Chet Gibson, the man she had been dating. Although they dated frequently and enjoyed each other's company, Ann was not in love with him, but she was getting older and thoughts of marriage would occasionally surface at the back of her mind, only to be banished a short time later. Chet was a nice guy and he was convenient but their relationship could never seem to make the leap to a deep love with thoughts of a lifelong partnership.

Chet offered to help her get transferred to the technology office in the Special Operations Branch, which she jumped at. While there she was exposed to the latest technology and was taught all the tricks of computer espionage. Within a short time she was recognized as an expert in the field and the person to go to when a tough computer problem came up.

Ann could have been happy with her life, it certainly matched her technical curiosity, but it was less than satisfying on an emotional level. She would have probably drifted along in emotional limbo had it not be been for a fateful meeting Chet attended in the New York World Trade Center on September 11, 2001.

After Chet's death, Ann wanted to get away for awhile and visit her parents in Seattle. She had been in Seattle only a short time when she decided to do a little shopping and have lunch downtown. She was wandering through the crowd at Pike's Market when she was jostled by a tall man. When he turned to apologize she recognized Carl and a flood of fond memories came rushing back.

After a few awkward seconds, recognition dawned on Carl and he simply hugged her. When he released her he said, "God, I've missed you," and hugged her again.

When he released her the second time he asked, "Can we find someplace to sit and talk, maybe have lunch? We have a lot of catching up to do."

"I'd really like that. There must be a restaurant away from the tourist crowd."

Dinners followed, sail-boating on Puget Sound, and long walks where conversation was not necessary. They simply enjoyed each other's company.

Over the following week they found that their feelings for each other had not diminished. At the end of the week Carl asked if she would be interested in working for his private investigation firm based in San Francisco. That night she called her boss at the CIA and quit her job. She joined Carl's firm and had been his partner, friend, and lover ever since. She had never regretted her decision to leave the CIA.

Carl soon returned dripping from his swim and interrupted her reminiscing about her past.

Later that afternoon a black sedan pulled up in front of the house and two men got out. They introduced themselves as homicide Detectives Murry and Davis then went on to say, "We have a few more questions concerning the body you found in the canal. Do you have a couple of minutes?"

"What did the coroner determine was the cause of death?"

"I'm sorry, Mr. Lukin, I can't discuss that, the only thing I can say is that it was an unnatural death. Are you and Ms. Curlin the only occupants of the house or do you have guests?"

"No, we are the only two staying here."

"Do you know if any of the neighbors had house guests or have you seen any strangers in the neighborhood?"

"No, we haven't spoken to any of the people in the area so I don't know the answer to your question. As far as strangers are concerned, I haven't seen any."

"I didn't think so but I had to ask. The tides could have washed that body here from anywhere but, then again, maybe not. I'll need addresses and telephone numbers for both of you in case we need to contact you.

"By the way, divers will be here shortly to search the area around the float for evidence. It's doubtful they will find anything because tidal action would have scattered any evidence over a wide area by now, but we have to look."

The following day, Carl and Ann were sitting on the deck reading when the phone rang. Carl answered and heard the voice of Alex Pribich, the President of World Bank and a personal friend. Alex was in his fifties, had a full head of graying hair, and was lean and muscular despite the fact that most of his day was spent behind a desk. He had degrees in economics and business from the best business school in the nation. The combination had allowed him to advance rapidly through the management ranks of World Bank to the top position of Bank President. Alex was tough and not prone to panic. But when he called Carl there was an edge to his voice that caught Carl's attention.

Speaking rapidly, Alex asked if Carl would come to San Francisco immediately, saying, "We have a big problem and I really need your help."

"Slow down, Alex, Ann and I are on vacation in Washington, there is no way we can get to San Francisco today. What's the problem?"

"I can't discuss it over the phone. What's the name of the nearest airport and I'll have the company jet pick you up." said Alex, in a tense voice.

"Okay, okay, the Bremerton National Airport is about thirty minutes from here, it's a small airport but I think it handles business jets."

"Be there in two hours." Without another word Alex hung up. Carl listened to the dial tone for a second or two then hung up the phone and turned to Ann. "Pack up, we're flying to San Francisco in two hours."

"What did Alex want?"

"I don't know, he didn't want to discuss it over the phone, but it must be serious because he's sending the company jet to pick us up at the Bremerton airport in two hours. He sounded nervous, which is not at all like Alex, he was really worked up."

4

It was mid afternoon when Carl and Ann walked into the reception area of the office of the President of World Bank. The secretary, an attractive woman in her early forties with ash blond hair, walked around her desk, saying, "Mr. Lukin, Ms. Curlin, good to see you again, Mr. Pribich is waiting for you. Please step this way." Without waiting for a response she turned on her heel and walked to a large oak door, then opening the door she stepped aside, allowing Carl and Ann to enter.

Alex came around his desk and shook hands saying how glad he was that they could come on such short notice and apologized for interrupting their vacation.

Carl said, "Come on, Alex, you didn't interrupt our vacation and fly us down here on the corporate jet just for small talk, what's going on?"

Alex leaned forward, saying, "What I have to tell you must remain between us. If word of this should get out it could have a disastrous affect on this bank."

Pausing to think, he continued, "Two days ago we started receiving calls from a number of companies, such as Jenkins Aircraft, Armon Shipping, and others, both small and large organizations. They all said the same thing. That money wired to them never arrived. Not just sent to the wrong address but that it had been diverted to another bank someplace in the world. As you know, World Bank has the largest wire service in the world. Billions of dollars are transferred between banks every day using our system. For instance, if China's Panda Airline buys five 747's they would be required to wire installment payments at various stages of the orders' completion. Many of these payments can be for tens or hundreds of millions of dollars.

"As of today we estimate that a little over $985 million dollars has disappeared. Each sender received a receipt from World Bank indicating that the money had been delivered. It took a couple of days for each company to realize they had not received payment as promised, research their records, and then call the sender to complain that they had not received the expected funds. The sender then had to research their records, and of course they had a World Bank confirmation that the money had been delivered. Then another couple of days of conversation back and forth until finally both companies called World Bank. We, of course, had to research the problem and another day was lost. Our best estimate is that the funds were stolen seven days ago.

"To make matters even more difficult our best system's programmer was on vacation. Today I received a call from a detective Murry in Silverdale, Washington saying that they had pulled a man out of the Hood Canal whom they believe worked for us. You guessed it, our best programmer, Ken Barkley.

"Our IT manager believes that the only way the theft could have occurred is that one or more system programs were replaced with duplicate programs containing bad code. We haven't found any bogus programs yet but that is the only way the money could have been rerouted and the dummy receipts sent out.

"Our IT manager tells me that Ken Barkley was smart enough

to develop such a program but he would still have to put it into the production stream and he did not have access to that part of the system. With all the checks that have been involved in the changes to our system it would have taken a genius to pull this off, but then, Ken was a genius.

"Without the bogus programs it will be virtually impossible to trace the money to the bank account where it was sent. In any case, by now the money could be anyplace in the world."

"This appears to be a banking operations problem, where do we come in?" asked Carl.

"We want you to learn everything you can about Ken Barkley, and help us in recovering the money. We can cover the loss for a short time but if word of this gets out the bank could be ruined. You will of course be paid your usual fee and expenses plus a bonus on all recovered funds.

"And one other thing, this type of loss has to be reported to the FBI. We can probably hold them off until tomorrow afternoon because we are still in the process of conducting our internal investigation. Once the Feds get involved I don't know how much latitude you will have in your investigation, but I'll open the door for you and support your investigation as far as possible."

"If you want us to investigate of course we will. Ann will handle the investigation at the bank and I'll take on the field work."

Ann said, "Tomorrow morning I want to begin by meeting all of the DP managers, and I'll be giving them assignments. If they have any problem taking instructions from me or don't respond quickly I'm going to send them to you."

Carl continued, "You are going to have to call the Sheriff, and district attorney of Mason County, Washington, and tell them I am investigating a major crime and ask them to cooperate fully with my investigation. If they aren't willing to cooperate call the governor but get me access to all the investigative material.

"Ann will be staying here in San Francisco tonight but I need to get back to Washington as soon as possible. Can your plane fly me back to Washington tonight and bring me back tomorrow afternoon? I'll need to speak to detective Murry as soon as possible.

"Lastly, both Ann and I will need to be in on the meeting with the FBI. If they have a problem with our involvement we'll want to know what it is."

"The plane will be ready for you within the hour and I'll call the Washington authorities right now."

5

Alex looked at the two men sitting in front of his desk and said. "As you two know we have had a serious theft. I've hired the Lukin Investigation Agency to help us. Ann Curling will be in charge of the investigation here at the bank until they are done. You will follow all instructions she may have with respect to the investigation. If you have any serious concerns with following her instructions see me. Any instruction she issues will have the highest priority, is that clear?"

Vice President for Security, Jim Gordon, and the Vice President for Information Technology, Phillip Wise both nodded their understanding.

"Ann, do you have any comments?"

"Not at this time."

Alex continued by making it clear that the theft was not to be discussed with anyone. They had less than twenty-four hours before the theft had to be reported to the FBI and he wanted answers before then.

After the meeting with Alex, Ann met with Philip Wise and Jim Gordon to get a briefing on the banks operation. Ann was a world class computer systems analyst who could quickly grasp the essential elements of a complex computer system and devise a plan to find a problem. Phillip Wise outlined the operation of the banking network and suggested that the problem most likely occurred in the modules of the production stream that handled wire transfers.

Ann said, "I agree, the problem is in programs supporting the Wire Transfer. We need to isolate that section of the system. Do you have a backup available?"

Phillip said "We take a backup of the entire system once each week. More often if we are going to make significant changes."

Ann said, "Ok, let's go back about five weeks. It's doubtful that the phony program was introduced that far back, there would be too much risk that a Trojan Horse program would be discovered."

Philip said, "It'll take about an hour to update the system with the back-up tape."

"We'll also use the backup tape to do a bit by bit comparison against the existing system. Once we have identified the bad code have two of your best system programmers begin to backward engineer the phony code."

Ann said "Jim, can you get me a roster of all employees who had access to the production and testing systems?"

"Sure, there are very few employees that have the authority to access the production system and special authority is also required to use the testing system. It's only used for testing changes to the production system. Development work is done on a totally different computer in another part of the building and it's not connected to the testing or production system."

"Okay, tell me how you control access to the production system."

"The process requires that after a new program has been developed or any changes made to the existing system, the new program, or modified program must undergo weeks of testing.

Testing uses a set of specifically developed test data as well as live production data. After the testing is complete, Department managers must approve the changes and test results before any changes are placed in the production stream.

Development programmers are not allowed to do final testing. All testing is done by a special team on a separate computer. After all the approvals have been received only one production manager has the authority and password to update the production stream.

The production and testing are even in a separate part of the building behind locked doors. Development people are not allowed to enter this area, violation of this rule is sufficient reason for dismissal.

"Which production manager has the authority to make changes to the production system?"

"Al Genovese has had the authority for the past few years but he is on vacation. While Al is gone John Cary has the authorization to make any necessary changes."

"By the way, the managers' passwords are changed every sixty days. When Al gets back it will be changed again even though it will not have been sixty days."

6

"Are all four managers available for an interview?" asked Ann.

"No. One is on vacation but the rest are working or can be called in. The manager who is on vacation, Al Genovese, is planning a few local area hiking trips and might be at home."

Within two hours all the production managers had been questioned, with the exception of Al Genovese, who could not be reached. Both Ann and Jim felt it was necessary to talk to Genovese immediately and the place to start was at his apartment. They tried to reach Genovese by phone again but received no answer.

When Ann and Jim arrived at the Genovese apartment they knocked on the door but there was no answer. There was a faint odor that seemed to be coming from the apartment. Ann stepped back, she had smelled that odor only two days ago and it made her nauseous. "I hope this is not what I think it is. We need to find the apartment manager and get him to open the door, there's something dead in there."

Five minutes later the apartment manager was inserting a key into the door lock. When the door opened a wave of the foul odor came floating out. The shocked manager put a hand over his mouth and nose saying, "Oh my God!"

Ann grabbed the apartment manager by the arm and said, "Call 911, tell them we have a dead body." With that, Jim and Ann cautiously entered the apartment.

The front room had obviously been ransacked, desk drawers had been pulled open and dumped, books pulled from the bookshelves and dropped, pictures pulled from the walls and smashed.

The kitchen was also a mess, all the cabinets were open and the contents strewn about the room, drawers had been dumped on the floor.

There were two bedrooms, one of which was apparently used as an office. It had been thoroughly searched, the desk that once held a computer had been ransacked and the computer taken, all that was left was the dust imprint where it once sat.

The door to the other bedroom stood open. What they saw sickened both of them. Al Genovese was tied to a chair and had obviously been tortured then killed. The chair he was seated on was turned to face the bed on which there was a woman whose hands had been tied to the head of the bed and her legs spread and tied to the corners at the foot of the bed. She had tape over her mouth and her clothes had been ripped off. She had also been tortured and it appeared as if she had been raped. She was obviously dead.

Ann heard Jim say, "Oh shit."

They carefully backed out of the apartment and waited for the police to arrive. While they waited Ann called Carl and told him in detail about what they had found and what they were doing at the bank to find how the money had been stolen. She told him that they expected to have some answers by that afternoon.

The police arrived within a few minutes. Both Ann and Jim were asked to give statements.

They overheard the forensic team tell one of the detectives it appeared that the cause of death for both bodies was a gunshot wound to the head from a small caliber weapon, probably a .22, revolver since no shell casings were found.

7

Carl approached the front desk of the Sheriff's Office in Silverdale, a town about twenty minutes north of Bremerton, Washington. He asked for Detective Murry.

"May I say who wants to see him?" asked the middle-age receptionist, as she pushed a visitor's logbook toward him.

Carl told her his name and signed the log book, then sat down to wait.

A few minutes later the Detective who Carl had met at the Hood Canal house came through the door, said hello and shook hands with him. "We'll use one of the interview rooms, that way we won't be disturbed."

They entered a small interview room and Detective Murry gestured for Carl to sit in a chair across the table from him. He said, "I don't know who you know in this state but I received a call from both the Sheriff and the District Attorney, and they each received a call from the State Attorney General with orders to fill you in on everything we know about the body you found in the Hood Canal."

"I'm investigating a large scale robbery for a major bank in San Francisco and the dead man appears to have played a key role in the robbery. We're trying to find out as much information as we can about Ken Barkley and hopefully recover the money."

"How much was taken?"

"The bank has requested that I not disclose that figure. The only thing I am permitted to say is that it was substantial. I suggest that you talk to Detective Jomblonski of the San Francisco Police Department."

There were a few seconds of silence as Detective Murry thought about Carl's answer, obviously not happy with it, he shrugged, and said, "Okay, I'll tell you all I know, which isn't a whole hell of a lot at this time.

"When we fished the body out of the canal we thought it was another drunk who had been fishing, fell out of a boat, and drowned. We had a hard time identifying him because of the damage from the crabs that had fed on him so it was not evident that he had been murdered until he was examined by the coroner, who found a small bullet hole in the back of the head. He had also been shot in the right ear. The bullets were recovered. The killer used a .22 caliber gun, from the groves on the bullet it was determined to be a Smith and Wesson, snub nose, revolver, which explains why we didn't find any shell casings. The bullet in the back of the head went through the brain stem then rattled around inside the skull, turning his brain to mush. The second shot wasn't really necessary, but it too just rattled around in the Vic's head, further damaging the brain. We haven't found the gun yet. The killer probably dumped it in the canal or took it with him.

"There was a tattooing around the entry wounds on the back of the head as well as singed hair from the muzzle blast. There was also tattooing on the ear as well indicating that the gun was held very close to the victims head. There was too much narcosis and damage to the brain to provide any directionality information about the bullet path. But from the position of the entry wound I would guess that the victim was bending over for the first shot and prone on the floor for the second shot.

"The first shot damaged the brain stem so much that all bodily movement would have stopped instantly. The heart would also have stopped pumping blood immediately. That's probably why we didn't find much blood at the crime scene. He would have simply fallen to the floor after the first shot.

"It took us a while to identify him because the crabs had pretty much destroyed his face and fingerprints but there was enough on the right hand thumb to get a six-point match for an ID, which as you know is not enough to take to court but it pointed us to a DMV record. Hair color, weight, and height matched the body we found so we're pretty sure we have the right ID.

"How did you find the crime scene?"

"A couple of days earlier we received a call from a fishing resort manager who was concerned about one of their guests. A resort housekeeper had reported that when she went to clean up his cabin she didn't see any personal items or clothes. She noticed that a pillowcase, blanket, and some towels were missing. She also found what looked like blood on the door jamb. The housekeeper reported her findings to the manager who called the sheriff's office. Since Mr. Barkley hadn't checked out he was concerned. DNA tests show the blood didn't belong to Mr. Barkley.

"We didn't think much about it at the time, just another guest who skipped out without paying his bill.

"At about the same time a patrol officer found a burned out car about a mile from the resort. The license plates were gone but we found ID numbers on the motor block and chassis that led to a car rental company at the SEA/TAC airport. The reading on the odometer matched the distance from the airport to the fishing resort. The car had been rented to a Ken Barkley from San Francisco. A check with the airlines indicated that Mr. Barkley had arrived early the previous morning. It turns out it's the same guy that skipped out on the resort.

"That's about all I can tell you, if we find anything else I'll give you a call."

"Did your divers find any evidence in the canal?"

"No, either there wasn't any or the tides washed it away.

"We did find a kitchen knife on the ground where cars are usually parked. And it had a fingerprint on it that we ran through AFIS. It came back as belonging to a Simon Rossman of Sacramento, California. We checked with the manager and there has never been a Simon Rossman registered there. Rossman probably used it to take off the license plates and forgot it. Of course we have the blood on the door jamb, it didn't belong to Barkley, and it doesn't show up on the Criminal Justice DNA File. We'll check it against Rossman when we find him.

"It looks like the killer took the time to clean up. That's probably why the towels are gone. The cabin had been wiped down, we didn't find any fingerprints in any of the normal places that you would expect to find them, Ken Barkley's, or anyone else's. It was a little too clean, if you know what I mean.

"There was a complaint from one of the other people staying at the resort that someone had stolen the anchor from their boat that had been tied up at the dock. It looks as if the body might have been carried to the boat, rowed out and thrown overboard tied to an anchor. Which makes me think the killer was a man. A woman would have had a hard time carrying the body. We checked the oars for fingerprints, there weren't any, they had been wiped clean.

"That about covers it, I don't know what else I can tell you."

"Thanks, I guess that's it for now. I have to get back to San Francisco in the morning but I would like to look around the cabin before I go."

"I'll meet you at the cabin in the morning. We intend to release it back to the resort sometime tomorrow unless you find something that we missed."

Carl arrived at the Ferguson fishing resort a few minutes early. While he waited for Detective Murry he looked around the resort grounds. He found that someone could have carried a body to the dock without being seen, particularly if it was late at night and dark. Nothing else caught his attention.

When Detective Murry arrived they examined the inside of the cabin, found nothing, and were standing outside when Carl asked, "Do you know if there was a full moon when Barkley disappeared?"

"I don't know, why do you ask?"

"The cabin is at the back side of the resort. If the moon was dark it would have been almost impossible to see the killer, but if it was full it might be worthwhile to check with the other guests."

"Good point. I'll check it out."

Carl said he had to return to San Francisco. He thanked Detective Murry for his help and left.

8

Carl had just landed at San Francisco when he received a call from Ann telling him about the discovery at the Genovese apartment.

A short time later he met with Ann and Alex at Tadich Grill for lunch. They discussed their findings and were back at the bank conference room when the FBI and Detective Jomblonski arrived.

"The FBI and police are not going to like having Ann and me at this meeting, Alex. You're going to get a lot of flak from law enforcement about our involvement in the investigation. If you want us to continue with the investigation you are going to have to stand firm."

Agent Harris of the FBI and Detective Jomblonski from the San Francisco Police Department were ushered into the conference room. Phillip Wise and Jim Gordon were already there. After introductions were made Agent Harris nodded toward Carl and asked, "Why are Carl and Ann invited to this meeting?"

Alex said, "This bank is liable for a $985 million dollar loss and if the FBI or anyone else doesn't like their involvement I'll damn well call everyone in D.C. from the President on down if necessary. Is that clear?" Agent Harris frowned but said nothing.

Phillip Wise opened the discussion by saying, "In any twenty-four hour period about 175 billion dollars, give or take a few billion, is sent over our wire system. The transferred funds that were stolen were probably small transactions but they totaled $985 million. Large transactions, of $50 or $100 million, would have immediately raised a red flag."

"You sound like you haven't found the fake program," said Agent Harris."

"We only found out that we had a problem less than twenty-four hours ago. Since that time we have removed the Wire Transfer System from the production stream and replaced it with a backup taken five weeks ago on the assumption that the bogus programs had not yet been introduced. We are now in the process of doing a bit by bit comparison of the code with our backup production system and we should be able to identify the bogus programs within a few hours. Since we are working with machine code we'll have to backward engineer the machine code to find the details of how it worked, and that will take time. It's not an easy job."

"When will this process be completed?" asked Harris.

"I don't know, it depends on how much computer code we're dealing with."

"I'll go and check on its progress," Phillip said, when the subject of the conversation turned to other matters.

"Have you questioned the production managers and supervisors yet?" asked Harris.

"We have interviewed them all but Al Genovese. Ms. Curlin and I found Al and his wife this morning, they had been tortured and murdered," answered Jim Gordon.

Detective Jomblonski brought everyone up to speed on their investigation of the murders. "It looks as if Mr. Genovese was tortured for information and murdered approximately six days ago. Wallets belonging to both he and his wife were found with cash and credit cards still in them, and it appears that none of the normal stuff that a thief would want was taken except for a computer.

"Mr. Genovese was tied to a chair facing the bed so that he could watch his wife being tortured and possibly raped, When whoever killed them got what they wanted they shot him in the back of the head and in the right ear with a small caliber weapon and then shot his wife in the eye and ear with possibly the same gun. We'll know more when the post is done. The killer then ransacked the apartment."

Carl said, "Detective, you might want to check with Detective Murry of the Sheriff's Office in Silverdale, Washington." He went on to describe finding Ken Barkley's body and what he knew of that murder, and that Ken was a programmer with the bank, and he was probably an acquaintance of Al Genovese.

When Carl was finished, it was obvious to everyone that there was a tie-in between the murders.

At the end of the meeting, Agent Harris made it clear that Carl and his associates were to do nothing without talking to him first. Their actions could jeopardize the FBI's investigation and jeopardize the admission of any evidence that they might find.

Carl leaned over to Ann, and in Russian muttered, "Like that's going to happen."

The door of the conference room opened and Phillip Wise re-entered. He walked over to Alex and whispered something to him. Alex asked Phillip to share his information with the group.

Phillip said, "The money has been diverted to an account in the Banko de Panama in Panama City, and as suspected, only amounts of $5,000,000 dollars or less had been stolen."

There was a groan from Harris. As everyone turned to look at him, he said, "I'm sorry, if the money had been sent to a bank in the U.S. we would be able to get a subpoena tomorrow morning for a search of bank records and be there when the bank opened. But it could take several days or weeks to get a subpoena that the Panamanian government will honor. The banking confidentiality laws in Panama are strict and notoriously difficult to work with."

After another thirty minutes of discussion the meeting broke up. As Alex walked out he asked Carl, Ann, Jim and Phil to join him in his office.

When Alex walked into his office he threw his notebook on his desk. Papers on the edge of the desk were blown to the floor.

Turning to face the others he said, "We can't afford to wait for the FBI to jump through all the hoops to make sure they have a watertight legal case. It will take the FBI weeks, and by that time, the money will have disappeared with little or no chance for recovery. This bank will fail if we can't get the money back. We're going to have to find out where the money is and fast. Once we find out where it is, Carl, you are going to find a way to get it back."

"How do you intend to find it quickly?"

"We are going to rely on the banking industries fondness for secrecy and its innate greed or we may have to use a little blackmail, that's where you come in Carl. You are going to have to find a way to apply pressure on the banks to cooperate with me.

"There are only three large banking computer networks that operate nationally and internationally, and of course the feds have their own network. There are a few more regional networks that feed into the international networks. Both local and international networks supply wire services to local banks. The one truth of the past thirty years is that banks and their customers have come to depend on wire services to move money locally and globally. In this day and age a bank would slowly wither until it ceased to exist if it did not have access to a wire service, and they know it.

"It so happens that we provide the wire service to Banko de Panama. Jim and I will meet the President of the bank tomorrow morning. If we do a little arm twisting I think we can find out the name of the account holder, and where the money is or where it has been sent, or the bank will find that they can't send funds by wire. I think they will see the light rather quickly. When we have that information we can figure out our next step."

Leaning over to Ann, Carl said, "We'll go have a talk with Dan later and you had better limber up your fingers, honey, I think you are going to do a little hacking."

"Once you have located the money do you have any suggestions as to how we're going to get it back?"

Ann looked at Carl and said, "Don't worry about that. I can handle it."

When the meeting broke up Carl and Ann headed for the Oakland hills to visit Dan.

9

Dan Nakamura had graduated with a PhD in computer sciences from the Massachusetts Institute of Technology at the age of twenty-two. Tired of academia, he had gone to work for the Central Intelligence Agency.

At the CIA, he had a chance to hone his skills in cracking the latest operating systems. He also found that he had a real skill in breaking encryption systems. It was not long before his skills were recognized and he was asked to support the Special Operations Unit. While there, he met Ann Curlin and they became good friends.

One night, a year after joining the Special Operations Unit, Dan was at a party in Georgetown near the university. There were a few graduate students and professors plus a number of young co-eds. It was a very pleasant evening with good music and lots of beer.

Soon someone opened a baggy of marijuana and began to roll a few reefers. Dan was not a smoker, much less a marijuana user, but after a few beers he was coaxed into trying one. The rest of the evening was a very warm, fuzzy blur. He thought he had spent the night with a young blond co-ed but he was not really sure. His tolerance for beer and drugs was exceedingly low and left him with a huge hangover and a nauseous stomach.

The following afternoon his supervisor informed him that they were doing random drug tests and it was his turn to, as he put it, pee in a cup. Since testing was a common occurrence within the agency he did not think anything of it, but he had failed once before after he attended a party where marijuana was used. He had been warned that he would be fired if he was caught using again. He was told to report to the clinic within the hour for his test. There was nothing he could do except go and hope that he had not smoked enough marijuana to show up in his test but with all the beer he had drunk he was not too sure how much he had smoked.

The next morning he was called to his department manager's office.

"Dan, you were warned once before not to indulge in drugs and you were told that if you failed the drug test again you would be fired. Since you failed the test, I have no choice but to terminate you in accordance with CIA policy. Please sign these termination papers and give me your agency identification. Your personal items have been collected from your desk and will be waiting for you as you leave. I am really sorry to have to do this. You are one of the best technical people I have working for me.

"Do not discuss your employment at the agency with anyone. If you do, you will face criminal penalties."

Dan walked out of the office in shock, he had never been fired before. Two very big guards were waiting to escort him to the front desk where he was handed a box filled with his personal items.

Carl Lukin called Dan two days later. After introducing himself he said, "I have a job you might be interested in and I would like to meet with you to discuss it. I'm in Washington for the day and I am hoping that we might be able to meet this afternoon, somewhere where we can talk in private."

Dan asked, "Who is this again? And who recommended me to you?"

"My name is Carl Lukin of the Lukin Investigation Agency. Ann Curlin, whom I believe you know, said that you might be able to help me with a problem I need to resolve."

"If Ann says you're okay that's good enough for me. Where do you want to meet?"

"How about on the steps of the Lincoln Memorial at four this afternoon? I'll be on the bottom step looking lost."

When Dan Arrived, he saw a tall, rugged looking individual standing on the bottom step to the left of the memorial. He did not appear to be lost but then again he did not look like a tourist either. Dan watched him for a few minutes as Carl scanned the crowed. When their eyes met he smiled and walked over to Dan to introduce himself.

After meeting and shaking hands, Carl suggested that they buy an ice cream bar from a street vendor and walk along the reflecting pool.

"What's this job you want me to do?"

"I have been hired by a small bank to find a person who has hacked into their computer system. While in the system he managed to destroy some records. The hacker caused some minor damage but it leads us to believe he has been on the system more than once. Ann would normally handle this type of job for the firm but she's on another assignment. She suggested that you would be the guy she would choose for the job. She made a few calls and found out you were no longer working for the agency and might be available."

They finally veered away from the reflecting pool toward a bench near the Vietnam War Memorial and sat down. Carl handed a file to Dan. After reading the file Dan agreed to do the job and they agreed on a price.

Within two days Dan was able to find the hacker and the trap door the hacker used to enter the bank's system. He also suggested a number of security measures that the bank should take.

During the course of the next two years and a number of jobs,

Dan and Carl became close friends. Carl suggested that they start a computer security company together. Dan would run the computer security company and Carl would put up the financing and be a silent partner in the business. They decided to call the new company Scriptorium Guards.

Dan eventually moved to California and within a few years had enough money to build a house in the Oakland hills. It was a beautiful ranch-style set on two acres. The décor of the home was the result of a home decorator Dan had hired. The walls were soft beige, the floors were covered with a plush beige carpet that had dark flecks running through it. The first floor was decorated in comfortable modern furniture, artwork on the walls. The kitchen was modern with stained ash hard wood floors, all the cabinets had stained glass doors, and drawers instead of shelves were used in lower cabinets. The countertops were covered with granite.

Although it was not obvious to anyone visiting the house, there was a sophisticated computer lab in the basement. Dan was solely responsible for the basement, which was totally the opposite of the rest of the house, it was decorated in pure geek.

The entry to the basement was behind a bookcase located in the master bedroom. When the bookcase was swung to one side, a flight of stairs leading to the basement appeared. The basement had an eight-inch raised floor that allowed cables to run in any direction without obstruction. The remainder of the basement consisted of a workbench and an array of computers and communication equipment.

In a far corner of the property sat an auxiliary power supply. The entire system was engineered to automatically maintain electrical power in the event commercial power was lost.

Other than Dan, Carl, and Ann, very few people were aware of the computer lab.

They sat at the kitchen table drinking coffee while Carl filled Dan in on the World Bank fiasco. When Carl was finished, Dan asked what he was expected to do.

"I'm going to ask that both you and Ann work on this together.

We will be dealing with a number of banks across several time zones and I have a feeling that I'm going to need two people who are familiar with the technical aspects of this operation in addition to having good language skills."

Smiling widely Dan said in a seductive voice, "That's okay by me. I always enjoy working with Ann...alone...in my dark basement...just the two of us."

After the laughter died down Carl continued, saying, "The likelihood that the money is still in the Banko de Panama is remote but you guys will have to check it out. If the money is still there and Alex is not successful in convincing the bank to give it back, then you two will have to find a way to transfer it back to World Bank.

"In the event the money has been transferred out and Alex is not successful in finding where the money was sent, you two will have to find it and find a way to get it back." Carl handed Dan the bank name and account number to which the money had been sent.

"If a bank is reluctant to give Alex the information he wants then we may have to help convince the bank to be cooperative."

"Ann will be the point of contact when I have information or need help in giving a bank president a real headache."

10

After getting a few hours sleep and having breakfast, Alex and Jim walked into the Banko de Panama's headquarter offices in Panama City. As they approached the reception desk, the receptionist, a tall, beautiful dark-eyed young woman with black hair looked up and asked, "What may I do for you gentlemen?"

"We would like to see Senõr de Palma please."

"Do you have an appointment?"

"No, we don't, but I believe Senõr de Palma will see us."

"I am sorry, but Senõr de Palma is in a meeting and cannot be disturbed," said the secretary, smiling.

"I think he will make an exception and see me."

The receptionist studied the card and said, "I'll see if he can leave his meeting."

She returned a few minutes later. "Would you please follow me?" Turning on her heel she led the way to an elevator. When they reached the second floor she showed them into a wood-paneled conference room. "Senôr de Palma will be with you in a moment. Would you like some coffee?"

Alex and Jim declined. The secretary left the room, softly closing the door behind her.

They took a seat at the conference table and waited. A few moments later, in walked a tall heavyset man with a graying fringe of hair, smiling, he eyed his visitors.

Extending his hand, he said, "I am Senôr de Palma, how may I help you gentlemen?"

Not wasting any time, Alex got right to the point. He explained that a large theft had occurred at World Bank and they needed information to track the thief. "We would like to know who set up an account in your bank and what his or her instructions were for the dispersal of funds." He then passed a slip of paper to Senôr de Palma with the account number.

The smile faded from Senôr de Palma's face. "As you know it is the bank's policy to provide complete confidentiality regarding client information, it is a foundation on which the bank was built, additionally, divulging such information is illegal in our country. It would be a violation that had serious consequences were the bank to provide such information."

"I assure you that any information you provide will go no further than this room and your assistance would be of great service to the World Bank."

Smiling, Senôr de Palma said, "I am very sorry but I cannot help you."

There was a moment of silence then Alex nodded at Jim.

Jim pulled out his cell phone and dialed. When the call was answered he said only three words "repair the system," and hung up.

"What is the meaning of this?" asked Senôr de Palma, with a puzzled look on his face.

"The wire service we provide to your banking system has been shut down because of technical difficulties. It is difficult to say when it will be restored."

Senõr de Palma's jaw dropped as he began to grasp the significance of what Alex had said. He sat quietly for a moment then got up and went to a telephone on a credenza at the side of the room and dialed a number. He spoke in very rapid Spanish to the man who answered. With the phone to his ear he listened, a few minutes later he hung up the phone. He stood there with his back to Alex and Jim thinking then slowly turned and walked back to Alex and hissed, "This is blackmail!"

"Blackmail is a very harsh term, Senõr de Palma. We prefer to think of it as system maintenance, a necessary task to keep the system running."

Without another word Senõr de Palma left the room.

A short time later he was back with a folder. Seating himself, he opened the folder and read for a minute. Finally he said, "The account was opened by a Mr. Simon Rossman of the United States. Mr. Rossman said that he was in the import/export business, that he was in the process of selling used aircraft in South America and the Middle East, and that any funds in excess of the fifty thousand dollars he used to open the account should be forwarded to an account at the Ithmaar Bank in Bahrain. A few weeks later a large amount of money was sent to the new account, and as instructed, we forwarded the money in smaller increments to an account in the Ithmaar Bank in Bahrain. This account now only holds the original $50,000 that was used to open the account." Senõr de Palma then wrote the bank name and account number of the bank in Bahrain on a piece of paper and handed it to Alex.

Alex looked at the information and then turned to Jim and nodded. Jim took out his cell phone and dialed a number. He waited a moment then said, "Bring up the system."

Alex and Jim both stood and shook hands with Senõr de Palma saying, "This conversation did not take place. I am sorry that we had to take such harsh measures."

They walked out the door and forty minutes later they were at the airport climbing aboard the Gulfstream-G5 on their way to Bahrain.

When they were airborne and had a chance to relax with a drink Alex said, "I think this is going to be a long trip. It looks like the money is being transferred from bank to bank in countries with strict privacy laws making it difficult for law enforcement to follow quickly. It looks like the thief wants time to drain the accounts by drawing it out in cash or converting it to another form of currency. We are going to have to follow the money as quickly as we can and convince each bank that it passes through that it would be in their best interest to provide the information that we need. Luckily World Bank has some influence and coupled with the greed of bankers we might just be lucky enough to find the money before the thief has had much of an opportunity to take it out of the banking system.

The next few days were a whirlwind trip through five foreign countries ending in Zurich, Switzerland.

The evening before flying to Zurich, Alex called Carl and gave him the name of the account number and the name of the bank in Zurich. "The Swiss are not going to be as easy as the first five banks, do you have any ideas that could help me?"

"I have to talk to Ann first and I'll give you a call back later this evening or before your meeting tomorrow."

11

Alex and Jim were seated in front of the desk of the President of the Credit Suisse Bank in Zurich. Alex had just completed telling Herr Garneer the story of the theft from World Bank and its implications. He asked for Herr Garneer's help in identifying the culprits and recovering the funds.

Herr Garneer clasped his hands in front of him on the desk and with a look of smug superiority on his face he stared across his large desk at Alex and said, "I understand your problem, and I have great sympathy for your predicament, but it is of no concern to this bank. The Swiss banking system was built on a foundation of confidentiality for its customers. If I were to provide the information that you have requested I would be undermining the entire Swiss banking system and betraying the confidence of its customers."

"I am sorry you feel that way, I hope you are never in the position where you will need my help."

While Alex continued to plead his case one last time Jim pulled out his telephone and sent a single word text message. It read, "Now."

When there seemed little else to say, Herr Garneer stood up. He broke the silence by saying, "I am afraid I can't do anything to help you gentleman, I hope that you catch the thief."

As Alex stood he handed Herr Garneer his business card and said, "Thank you for listening to us, it has been a long day for us. Mr. Gordon and I will be across the street at the coffee shop in the Ambassador Hotel should you reconsider."

As they walked through the lobby of the bank both Alex and Jim noticed the worried look on the faces of the tellers and the managers. Managers began to go from teller to teller examining their computer screens. By the time they reached the front door several managers had phones to their ears.

Alex and Jim exited the bank and strolled toward the Ambassador Hotel.

As they headed down the street Alex looked over at Jim with a wry smile said, "So far, we have relied on blackmail, greed, and now breaking and entering. Don't you just love the banking business?"

All Jim could do was chuckle, saying, "I have never seen you play hardball like this before."

"I have never had to do this before and I hope I never have to do it again, but I'll do anything to keep the bank from collapse."

Herr Garneer picked up his ringing phone, said hello, and listened. After a few seconds his head jerked up and he said, "Repair it quickly."

Twenty minutes later Herr Garneer crossed the street and entered the small hotel coffee shop. He stood in front of Alex and yelled, "What did you do to my computing system?"

Alex smiled and in a soft voice said, "What do you mean, Herr Garneer? We have been sitting here enjoying this excellent coffee. Would you care for a cup?"

Herr Garneer, sputtering, said, "You made the bank's computer system crash!"

"Herr Garneer, please sit down, we don't want to make a scene, now, do we?"

The smile on Alex's face disappeared and his features took on a cold, hard appearance. He said, "Please order a cup of coffee and we can talk about your problem like reasonable men."

Reluctantly Herr Garneer sat down. Soon a waitress appeared and took his order.

After the coffee had been served, Alex said, "First of all, I have done nothing to your computers, but I understand how these problems can have very serious effects on a bank. Loss of customer confidence often grows to the point that the bank is forced to close its doors. When these problems arise one has to ask for help or they will happen over and over again. And heaven forbid should the newspapers report that your bank has computer problems." He paused and looked over his cup. "You should really try one of these sweet rolls, they're excellent."

Herr Garneer took a minute to think. "Precisely what information do you need?"

Alex passed him a slip of paper with the account number. "I need all instructions, passwords, activities, and the names associated with the account."

Herr Garneer got up, saying, "I will be back shortly," and stormed out of the coffee shop. He returned a short time later with the account information, and the accounts to which some of the funds had been disbursed, which included one to a bank in Sacramento, California. "I rely on your discretion as to where and how you got this information." Then he simply stood up and walked out.

When Garneer left, Jim dialed his phone, listened, then said, "We have what we need."

Returning to the bank, Herr Garneer called his Information Security Manager into the office and said, "We cannot tolerate further computer failure, find the best information security firm that you can, I don't care what it costs. Have them do an audit of our system and insure that no one can break in again."

Four days later the Security Information manager returned to the office saying that they had hired a company with a first rate reputation called Scriptorium Guards and they would start work the following day.

12

Carl, Ann, and Dan Nakamura spent a few hours examining the account information they had received from Alex, and the information that had been retrieved from the banks that had been penetrated. It was abundantly clear that the money was slowly being drained from the Credit Suisse Banks and being sent to Pakistan, Chechnya, Iran and one account in the U.S. The U.S. account had received half a million dollars, the rest received amounts ranging from fifty to a few hundred thousand dollars. The money was being wired to the accounts in other countries and therefore the money trail could be followed. With one exception, there was one cash withdrawal from the Zurich Bank. Since it was a numbered account no name was recorded. The only information regarding the person making the withdrawal was his image recorded by a hidden surveillance camera.

Carl thought about the flow of money, saying, "This one really worries me, I think we should tell the agency about it. What do you think?"

Both Dan and Ann thought about the implication of that much money being used by terrorists in the U.S. and agreed.

Carl picked up his phone and called Alex, who was on his Gulfstream-G5 on his way back to San Francisco. He asked Alex if they could meet the minute he got back, adding that it was important. Alex put him on hold. When he returned he said his flight would be landing at San Francisco at 1:30 AM and that Carl could meet him at the airport.

Carl was outside the private aircraft terminal waiting as Alex landed, ten minutes later they were in Carl's car on Highway 101north headed into San Francisco.

"Okay Carl, what is so important that we had to meet tonight?"

"My associates and I have examined the information we received and we believe the money was stolen by a terrorist organization to fund their operations. We are particularly concerned about the money that was wired to a bank located in Sacramento, California, since that would indicate an operation was planned against a target in one of the Western states, most likely California.

"My company has done a few jobs for government organizations that don't have the investigatory resources or don't want to be connected to any investigation. I have seen this kind of money movement before. One of the organizations I have done work for would find this information extremely interesting and I intend to brief them on it. Since I collected part of the information from you, and the rest as the result of the work I and my associates have done, I felt that I had to tell you what I planned on doing. I'm sure that the people I will be talking to will want to see you immediately.

"If you think that what I am planning to do is not in your or the bank's best interest, I will terminate my contract with the World Bank and minimize the bank's involvement with this situation as much as possible."

"Carl you know what this theft means to the bank. Do you trust this organization to keep this confidential and not leak the information to the press?"

"Yes sir, I do."

"Okay Carl, I trust your judgment. If it looks like it's going to leak to the press, call me immediately."

Later that morning Alex received a call from Carl asking for a meeting for himself and a Mr. John Gray at three that afternoon. He did not indicate whom Mr. Gray worked for, only that he was a friend.

At three, Carl and Mr. Gray were ushered into Alex's office. When the secretary left, Carl introduced Mr. Gray as Deputy Director of the Central Intelligence Agency.

The secretary soon returned with a carafe of coffee and a tray of cookies.

"Gentlemen, please help yourself to the coffee, and tell me what this is all about."

"When Carl called this morning with what he suspected, we did a little checking of our own and we concur with Carl's assessment. As a result, I am here to ask for your assistance. Anything that I say is off the record and is confidential, agreed?" said Mr. Gray.

"I agree."

"By law, our intelligence investigations can only be carried on outside of the United States. However, from time to time an investigation that began in a foreign country may lead us to this country. If an investigation is required here to essentially close the loop or fill in the gaps in our information, we ask the FBI to investigate. In a very few rare cases, we might use a private investigator, as we have in the past with Carl.

"Carl has told me how you managed to follow the money trail from Panama to Zurich, and how you retrieved the information that Carl has shared with us." Mr. Gray paused, then smiling, said, "If you ever need a job please give me a call, the CIA can use you."

"Thanks, I will, but for now I'll stick with banking." said Alex with a chuckle.

"I suspect that you are thinking of ways to get the stolen money back into your bank. I am here to ask you to leave the money where it is for the moment. Because we know the names of the banks and the account numbers, we are in a position to follow the movement of the money to its final destination, and hopefully, we will be able to identify the people who try to use it. We are particularly concerned about the organization here in the U.S."

Alex thought about the request for a minute. "What you are asking me to do would place this bank and its customers in serious jeopardy. Depriving the owners of the use of their money would soon lead to a closure of this bank and seriously bring into question the safety of sending money by wire. But more importantly, the money belongs to specific customers who need it to operate. Because of that I must get the money back as soon as possible. If we were to leave the money where it is now, it would be tantamount to World Bank making a loan to the CIA with stolen money. In essence, the bank would be participating in the theft and the owners of the money would be making interest free loans. The bank can't be a party to that. This bank cannot loan you $985 million. We would be willing to help you by putting up five million of our own operating capital for a short period of time."

Mr. Gray was quiet a moment before speaking. "That may be enough to keep them coming in for more funds. It appears that the money is wired to individuals, the recipient doesn't get to see the account balance. Only the person who owns the account knows the balance remaining. And he is the only person who is going to recognize that the money has disappeared and he is also the person we are most interested in. We may get lucky if he doesn't look at the balance for a few days."

There was a short pause then Gray said, "Thank you for helping out and don't worry, the CIA will cover any loss up to five million dollars. By the time the accounts are drawn down to that level we'll have most of the information we need." With that promise the meeting ended.

When they left the office, Carl called Ann to tell her to move all World Bank money, except for five million, from the Credit Suisse to an account at the World Bank. Then turning to John he said, "I hope this works."

Thirty minutes after leaving the bank, Carl and John were walking alongside the ocean surf. The sound of the ocean waves crashing on the shore would cover their discussion in the event someone was trying to listen in with a parabolic microphone. And they could see anyone within half a mile approaching them. Besides, it was a pleasant afternoon for a stroll on the beach.

Carl filled John in on new information they had discovered since their last conversation and on what he was planning to do later that night. He also told him that he and Ann were going to Zurich, Switzerland the next day to try to identify the persons involved in the theft since that was part of what his World Bank contract required.

John was silent for a moment then said, "Carl, your plan will fit in nicely with what we would like you to do for us. The Director also wants you to look at Rossman Import/Export and find out why he should be receiving money from an account we believe is a fund for terrorist activities. If it is what we think it is, we will let Special Agent Jean Peters of the FBI's Task Force on Terrorism handle this end while you try to find out who is withdrawing cash directly from the Credit Suisse Bank account. Our friends at NSA and our people can follow the electronic money trail. Since you will be working for us you will have all the support you need."

"I don't think that will be a problem. My office will also be watching the account from here and hopefully we will see how that money is being used. I'll keep you posted on anything we find."

"Director Rice would like you to brief him in D.C. tomorrow afternoon if you can make it.

"One other thing, we will have to update your security clearance since you last worked with the CIA. It's just a formality since you may have access to classified information and may be using CIA resources. If you can update your personal history it will make the process go faster."

"That shouldn't be a problem if I can get a flight to D.C. We can reschedule our flight to Zurich."

The Director of the CIA was Richard Rice, although most people who knew him called him Dick. Dick had retired from the army as a two-star general then joined the CIA. He had a talent for analysis of issues and the ability to communicate problem areas to Congress and the President. He was trusted by both the Legislative and the Executive Branch because he did not play politics. He was considered a straight shooter who could be trusted. When the previous director, Richard Grace retired, Richard Rice was appointed Director with little opposition.

"How is the director doing since he broke his leg playing soccer? Tell him I'll take him on for a game of one-on-one on the basketball court if he is up to it. I might have a chance to win this time."

As they returned to the car the conversation immediately turned to football and who was going to be in the Super Bowl.

13

The wire transfer of half a million dollars to the U.S. went to a Simon Rossman, who had an account at a branch located in the Natomas area of Sacramento, California, where he and his family lived. His home in Natomas was a two-story four bedroom model on a quiet suburban street. It was just a ten-minute drive from his warehouse near the port in West Sacramento, and five minutes from the Sacramento International Airport, and only ninety minutes from the San Francisco and Oakland airports and ports. All in all, it was an ideal location from which to run his business.

There were also half a dozen or so colleges and universities within ninety miles in which he could search for students to recruit into his terrorist cells. That is not to say that all students that were Islamic would be interested in striking at the United States, but a number of these students had attended madrassa in Pakistan and had been noted for their radical beliefs. Students with radical leanings were encouraged to attend a camp where they received military training. Following training camp the brightest students from more wealthy families were then encouraged to go to a university in the West. The headmasters of madrassas would forward the names of students that had been accepted to Western universities to a Mr. Chowla, an Islamic cleric in Islamabad. Those that would not do well at a college or university, or were from families of modest means, were encouraged to join Al Qaeda or similar organizations. Mr. Chowla would supply a list of the names of students that went to colleges or universities and the schools that they attended to Parviz Jalili, who would then pass it on to Simon Rossman and other recruiters. Simon used the lists to comb the west coast universities with great success.

Ann Curlin had been able use her social engineering skills to bluff her way into the telephone company offices, and posing as a telephone company accounting employee managed to get a copy of Rossman's personal and import/export business telephone records. With that information, Dan Nakamura was able to hack into the warehouse computer and Rossman's personal computer at his home. In each case he left traps that would forward a copy of all activity that took place on either computer.

When Dan downloaded the contents of Rossman's personal computer he found a number of encrypted files. He immediately sent copies of everything he collected to the CIA. As he looked through the files he copied those files he thought would be of most interest to Carl. Information that was related to company operations, business correspondence, and a few pieces of personal correspondence were placed in a separate file for later review. Since Carl could read, write, and speak Arabic he could quickly determine if there was any information of value in files that were written in Arabic.

Dan also found a second computer in the house but it appeared to be used by Rossman's wife and children. The correspondence on this computer was to his wife's family and written in English. The rest of the information was the kids' homework, or games.

Ann had set up operation in Sacramento and began to keep tabs on Simon's activities. Using several cars and disguises she was able to follow him unnoticed for three days. On each day he visited nearby university campuses where he spent his time talking to students. On one afternoon he visited a local mosque for prayer. Ann was able to take photographs of the people he met, but she was not able to record any conversations. She was unable to follow Simon into the mosque but using a parabolic microphone she was able to record some of his conversations as he walked out.

Copies of the recordings, photographs, and records of his travels were sent to the CIA.

14

Carl started to lower himself down from the skylight when he heard the entry door opening. He let himself drop the last ten feet to the top of a loaded pallet. There was a bright flash as the lights were turned on and were magnified by the night vision goggles. He was momentarily blinded. He pulled the night vision goggles off his face and waited for his vision to return. Carl had no alternative but to lay flat and hope no one noticed the cable hanging down from the skylight. A few minutes passed before he was able to see again. All he could do now was remain motionless until whoever had come into the building left.

Earlier, Carl had parked at an all night café a block from the Rossman Import / Export warehouse in West Sacramento. The café was fairly busy with truck drivers and shift workers but it had a clear view of the warehouse. He had the appearance of a truck driver who was not anxious to get back on the road. From his table where he lingered over pie and coffee he was able to see any activity around the warehouse, and time how long it took for the security patrol to make rounds.

It was a short walk to the loading dock where a truck was parked ready to be loaded the next morning. He had been watching the warehouse for the past hour and was fairly certain that there was no one there, although a security patrol drove by once every forty minutes.

Carl walked to his car and removed a backpack then he headed over to the Rossman warehouse. Climbing onto the roof of the truck that had been parked at the loading dock, Carl was able to pull himself onto the roof of the building. He quietly made his way to a skylight near the rear of the building where he could not be seen from the street.

Using night vision goggles he examined the skylight and found what he was looking for, the latch and the alarm wires. Using a glass cutter and a suction cup, he cut a hole in the glass that would allow him to reach the alarm wires. Using two alligator clips and a length of wire, he was able to bridge around the alarm. He then unlatched the skylight and gently raised it. He attached a very thin hoist cable and a ratchet climbing device to the skylight frame then climbed through the open skylight and started to lower himself when he heard the front door opening. Now all he could do was lay flat on a pallet of carpets and hope that he would not be noticed by whoever came in the building.

When his eyesight returned to normal he could see Rossman and two young men who appeared to be in their early twenties. Speaking in Arabic, Rossman instructed the two men to remove the boxes from five pallets that were against the wall of the building near the front office. When that was done, they dragged the pallets to a better lighted area near the work bench. Rossman had found two crowbars. He instructed the two men to remove the boards from the 4x4s that formed the pallet. Then he told them to move the center 4x4s to a pair of sawhorses.

Rossman examined the 4x4s carefully, then using a skill saw he cut one in half along a glue line that he found. When the two halves of the 4x4 were pulled apart he lifted one half and turned it vertically and shook it gently. A one and a half inch PVC pipe slipped out of a hole that had been drilled into the end of the board. Laying the 4x4 down he pulled the pipe out of the hole and gently handed it to one of the men. He followed the same procedure with the remaining 4x4s. When they were done they had ten eighteen-inch long PVC pipes. From the way the men were handling the pipes it looked like they were probably filled with explosives.

Rossman opened the end of one of the pipes and pulled out a paper-wrapped cylinder of orange material. From the back of the building where Carl was, it looked as if the material was similar in consistency to bread dough only it was orange in color, it was a pliable material, probably semtex-A. Rossman passed it around for the others to examine and then reinserted it into the PVC pipe.

Rossman and the students talked for a few minutes but Carl was too far away to hear what was being said.

The entry door rattled as someone tried to pull it open. Simon said something to the students and they hurriedly put the two tubes of explosive in the office while Simon went to the door. The security guard making his rounds was standing there. There was a short conversation that satisfied the security guard's curiosity and he left.

After they finished removing the explosives from the four remaining pallets they cleaned up the wood and sawdust and placed it in a dumpster at the side of the building, then turned off the lights and left the building, taking the explosives with them.

When Carl was sure they had gone he climbed back onto the roof, removed his cable, closed the skylight and removed his alarm bypass. He positioned the glass cut-out back into the hole it had come from and used super-glue to hold the piece of glass in place.

15

Carl caught an early morning flight to Washington D.C. He drove up to the main gate of the CIA and handed the guard his identification, saying he had an appointment with the Director. After the guard had checked the trunk, underneath the car, and confirmed the appointment, Carl was told to drive to a second gate.

At the second gate, his ID was checked again and his appointment confirmed again, he was told to drive to the visitor area in the basement of the building where a guard would be waiting for him.

Carl got out of the car and approached the elevator where a guard in plain clothes stood waiting. They entered the elevator and the guard pushed the button for the seventh floor then asked if he was carrying a gun. Carl said no. The guard spoke softly into a small microphone pinned to his lapel. When they reached the seventh floor he was led to a big office where Director Rice sat behind a large desk reading.

Director Richard Rice rose to greet Carl, and after shaking his hand asked him to sit at a small conference table. He said, "Would you care for some coffee?"

"Yes please, I'm a little tired and coffee sounds great."

"John has filled me in on a little of what you've been doing and I agree that it looks like you have uncovered a terrorist cell. I thought it best if we brought a few others up to date. I have asked Special Agent Jean Peters from the FBI to join us. I believe you know her, Jean heads up the FBI's Task Force on Terrorism. Aaron Kodak, who is in charge of Special Operations for me, and of course John Gray, whom you already know, will be joining us. They should be here in a minute."

"Yeah, I've known Jean for a few years, she is one of the brightest people I know and she is one tough cookie. I have met Aaron before but I really don't know him."

Five minutes later the others had arrived, introductions were made, and everyone was seated. Director Rice asked Carl to start at the very beginning to ensure that everyone was on the same page.

Carl started with finding the body at the Hood Canal, the call from World Bank, the meeting at the bank with law enforcement, Ann finding the bodies of the bank manager and his wife in San Francisco, Alex's whirlwind trip to Panama, Bahrain, Spain, Vienna and Switzerland, the hacking of the Credit Suisse Banking systems, the transfer of money to suspected terrorist accounts, Ann's surveillance of Rossman, and his breaking into Rossman's warehouse. He described how Rossman was shipping explosives into the country. He finished by saying that the bank's funds had been recovered although the bank had agreed to leave five million dollars in the Credit Suisse bank as bait.

"I didn't hear anything about blackmail, hacking, or break-ins, but the part about smuggling explosives caught my attention," said Jean smiling.

The Director addressed Jean with, "The activities that have taken place in California are squarely within the FBI's jurisdiction.

We will of course keep you informed on any new information we uncover."

"The San Francisco office will not like it, but I am going to fly out there and take over their investigation."

"Jean, I'll give you my direct line and ask that you keep me or Aaron informed on anything new."

Turning to Carl he said, "I understand that your contract with the bank is to, one, recover the money, and two, see if you can find who the person was who drew out the cash, is that correct?"

"Yes sir."

"We also want to know who took out the cash. Anybody who wanders into a bank and takes out half a million in terrorist cash must be rather high up in the organization.

"We would like to hire you to find out all you can about this organization, but be careful. If the Swiss Government finds out you're working with the CIA you will have a real problem on your hands. You won't have any diplomatic status and officially we have not heard of you."

"Yes sir, John mentioned that I might have an opportunity to do some work for the agency and be asked for my personal history to help the FBI in updating my security clearance. I have it with me."

"Aaron's Operation's group with the help of NSA will be able to follow the disbursement of funds electronically, but following funds taken out in cash requires feet on the ground. His people may be able to help you. We'll alert him to expect you. Based on the information we've already gotten from following the disbursement of funds, we think we've already identified two more terrorist training camps."

The Director concluded that that was all the information available at the moment. "I believe what we have so far is enough to warrant pulling out all the stops. I'll fill the President in on our current status. Thank you for coming. And by the way, Carl, anytime you want to play one-on-one I'll be glad to kick your ass for you." There were smiles and chuckles, but they would not last long.

16

Jean Peters walked into the San Francisco FBI office and immediately called a staff meeting. She informed them that they now had evidence that the robbery that took place at World Bank was connected to a terrorist organization operating on the West Coast and that it was being funded from the proceeds of the World Bank theft. The money trail had been followed to Zurich, Switzerland. The money was being disbursed to terrorist organizations operating in the Middle East and half a million dollars had been sent to a bank account in Sacramento, California held by a Mr. Simon Rossman. It was now believed that Mr. Rossman is the organizer and leader of one or more terrorist cells operating in California and possibly others around the country.

Fingerprints found at the crime scene in the State of Washington were identified as belonging to Mr. Simon Rossman. Ballistics data confirms that the same weapon was used to kill Ken Barkley in Washington and the murder of the World Bank employee in San Francisco. Mr. Rossman's past was being researched and it appeared he had no history prior to twenty years ago. A review of immigration records, visa applications, and passports prior to the time that Mr. Rossman first appeared on the scene is currently underway, but it was an enormous task and will take some time to complete unless we get very lucky.

"Mr. Rossman's activities are currently under review by the FBI's Sacramento office. Preliminary reports are that he has been living in Sacramento and runs an import/export business from his home where he has his office and from a local warehouse. Rossman appears to be Muslim and attends prayer meetings at the Islamic Center in Sacramento.

"It seems that Mr. Rossman had sought out friendships with a number of university students and other people who appear to have close ties to the Middle East. Because of this information Mr. Rossman is to be taken into custody this evening and all his facilities searched.

"Following the raid in Sacramento this evening, the San Francisco office will interview all of Rossman's contacts in the Bay area. Other field offices will conduct interviews of Rossman's contacts in their jurisdictions. We expect to find many more contacts in our search of Rossman's business and home and they will all have to be interviewed."

Jean went on to say that she would be meeting with the local police following the staff meeting to fill them in on any information they might need to know.

8:00 PM Sacramento, California. Two Black suburban SUV's pulled up to Mr. Rossman's home. Agents knocked on the door and when it was answered by Mrs. Rossman, they announced who they were, and brushed past her with guns drawn. Within a minute they had searched the house, finding only her two very frightened children.

"Where is your husband, Mrs. Rossman?"

In a frightened voice she stammered, "He's out of town on a business trip and he won't be back for several days. What do you want?"

"Where did he go?"

"I don't know, he said it was a business trip. Why do you want him?"

"Mrs. Rossman, we are going to take you to the Sacramento FBI office for questioning and we have a warrant to search your house. Is there anyone who can take care of the children while you are gone?"

"I'll see if my neighbor can take them for a few hours."

The search did not provide any clues as to Rossman's whereabouts. A check of airlines, busses, and trains yielded nothing. A description of his car and an all points bulletin for the arrest of Rossman was sent to all law enforcement agencies.

Bank records indicated that Rossman had withdrawn over a half million from his account in cash. He also erased all of the data from his computer at his home. What Rossman didn't know was that Dan Nakamura had hacked into his system earlier and that the CIA had copies of all his files.

The search of the dumpster behind the warehouse uncovered ten 4x4 pieces of wood, each two feet long, indicating that five pallets were used to ship the explosives. Each of the pieces of 4x4 timber had a one and a half inch hole drilled in one end. There were traces of semtex-A, a plastic explosive, on each of the pieces of wood.

The semtex-A was determined to have been manufactured in Libya. What the forensic experts could not tell was how many explosive-laden pallets had been shipped over the years prior to this shipment.

Agents fanned out across the state to find the students and others who were acquaintances of Mr. Rossman. All but nineteen were located and interviewed. The rest had simply disappeared.

17

There are two 500,000 KV power lines that run from the State of Washington to Southern California. Both power lines carry the huge amounts of electrical power that supply California, Arizona, Nevada, Oregon and parts of Idaho. Jamil Kassir and Aza Hamza had been walking under the power lines for most of the night and they were tired and thirsty. In another half hour they would be at their car and they could get something to eat and drink, and then drive to San Francisco. They had placed a quarter pound of orange semtex-A on two legs on each of twelve two hundred-foot tall steel towers holding the power line. The charges were set to go off at 7:00 A.M.

Two other teams were doing the same at two other locations in Central and Southern California. The bombs were timed to go off in the south first and minutes later in Central and Northern California.

At the same time small holes were being cut in the chain link fences that surrounded the substations that convert the high voltage power to a lower voltage, which utility companies could use. Huge oil-filled transformers stood inside a chain link-fenced enclosure. Power companies would further reduce the voltage and distribute it to homes, businesses, hospitals, and the thousands of other entities that were dependent on electrical power.

A man crawled through the hole he had cut in the chain link fence. He carried a backpack filled with explosives. He went to each of the huge transformers and placed an explosive charge near the base of the transformer. The nearby high voltage lines caused the hair on his arms and head to stand straight causing a tingling sensation. After he finished he went back out the way he came in. He was not concerned about the day crew finding him. They would not make their inspection rounds for another hour.

The charges were set to go off five minutes before the charges on the towers. The resulting explosions would rupture the transformers, spilling the hundreds of gallons of cooling oil within each transformer. Without the cooling oil the transformer coils would become hot enough to fuse into a lump of molten metal, and then ignite any remaining oil and the oil that had spilled onto the ground. Once the transformer short circuited, the circuit breaker that protects the utility companies would trip, cutting power to thousands of homes and businesses. The heat from the burning oil would cause further damage to the facility by softening the steel legs of the towers that support electrical cables leading to and from the transformers, and they would crumple to the ground.

Huge transformers such as those that handle extremely high voltages are not shelf items maintained at a storage depot, they are manufactured as required, and would take weeks or months to replace.

Within minutes of the explosions that ruptured the transformers, the Semtex-A charges placed on the power transmission towers exploded. The transmission towers fell into a mass of twisted steel, the power cables snapped, touched steel towers, and began to arc, or touched other cables with a resulting shower of sparks starting grass fires. In the northern part of the state the fires spread to the dry surrounding forests, setting them ablaze. The forest fires spread rapidly and within a short time threatened nearby towns. To make matters worse, many of the areas surrounding California's larger cities had not seen forest fires for decades, resulting in huge quantities of fuel available to feed the flames. The California Department of Forestry and local fire departments were overwhelmed. Soon a call went out to other states for assistance.

In rural farming areas of the state, the fires spread to the nearby grain fields, then on to farm buildings, and then moved toward farming communities.

With the sudden drop in power, circuit breakers that are designed to protect the power grid and utility companies began to trip all over the eleven Western states, plunging cities into darkness. The Diablo Canyon nuclear power plant near San Luis Obispo, could not sustain the sudden power demands made on it, and began to shut itself down, as did the state's hydroelectric generators. The Western states went black except for the flicker here and there from lights powered by emergency generators that immediately kicked in. But they too would start to flicker out as diesel and gasoline fuels used by the generators began to run out.

The sudden loss of power on the grid supplying the Western states caused a sudden demand for power from adjacent power grids. When demand for power could not be met the adjoining power grid also collapsed causing an additional demand for power. The effect was a cascade of power failures that moved steadily eastward and did not stop until it reached the industrial Midwest where breakers tripped before the power grid failed. In less than a minute approximately two thirds of the Country was without electrical power.

Gas stations without emergency power supplies to operate the pumps could not service the cars that were running out of gas. Within a short time streets became dotted with stranded vehicles. City bus companies that had the foresight to convert to natural gas would continue to operate until their fuel storage tanks ran dry.

The eight terrorists from the northern part of the state drove to San Francisco where they found a motel and spent the rest of the day sightseeing like thousands of other tourists. Tourists were inconvenienced by the loss of electrical power but continued their vacations, thinking that the power would be restored any minute. For tourists, the power loss became a serious problem when restaurants had to close and they had to find their way around darkened streets and hotels. The city's residents became worried when refrigerators and freezers began to warm up and frozen food began to thaw.

The terrorist' did not enjoy the sights like other tourists. Their nerves were on edge, they were too keyed up and unable to relax. They kept looking over their shoulders, sure that they would be recognized as being responsible for the bombings. Because of the loss of power, there was no light in their room so they had to use the flashlights they had brought to see, and of course there was no T.V. so they had no way of knowing what was going on in the rest of the city. Only the radio stations that had standby generators were able to broadcast any information.

Unlike tourists, the eight terrorists had planned ahead and brought enough bread, cheese and bottled water to last until the following day when they would leave the city.

Early the following morning the terrorists caught a cab to Pier 34 where they boarded a cruise ship bound for Mexican port cities. The terrorists in the southern part of the state posing as tourists attempted to cross into Mexico by car but were detained at the border. The FBI's warning to be on the lookout for young men travelling on student visas or on foreign passports from Middle Eastern countries had been received and read just hours before the students arrived at the border crossing. Simon Rossman was nowhere to be found.

Alarm horns began to sound all over the state as elevator and burglar alarms in stores lost power. In homes, burglar alarms chirped and buzzed as they shifted to battery power. Alarms attached to thermostats that controlled freezers and refrigerators in meat markets and grocery stores began to ring. Added to the noise of alarms was the sound of hundreds of sirens from police cars and fire engines as traffic accidents were reported, or emergency calls for help were received.

A number of people died as a result of traffic accidents that occurred when traffic lights stopped working. Some died when medical equipment failed. Others became very ill when dialysis centers could not open. A few of these later died. A few had heart attacks as a result of the panic that occurred when elevators stopped between floors. In some cases, it would take emergency personnel more than eighteen hours to reach them.

The attack could not have happened at a worse time of year. The Western states were experiencing the worst heat wave that they had seen in decades. The temperature at midday would reach a high of 119 degrees in the California central valley, with some cities reaching even higher temperatures. Arizona and Nevada were in even worse shape since temperatures in the desert areas would be much hotter, some places exceeding 125 degrees. When the power failed, every air conditioner in the eleven Western states stopped running. Many of the elderly residents became dehydrated and died before help arrived.

There was not even a breeze to cool things down. Wind generators could only provide a trickle of the power that was normally produced and it could not be added to the system because all the circuit breakers had tripped.

The economy of the Western states came to a standstill as factories, offices and stores closed their doors. It would take weeks before the power grid supplying the Western states could return to normal. Power grids that had collapsed as a result of the demand of power from adjacent power grids began to rebuild quickly but it would still be days before full power was restored to all of their users. The impact to the United States was enormous as factories stopped production, construction projects halted, and retail business came to a standstill in two thirds of the country as they lost power.

Law enforcement became overwhelmed as thieves realized that they had an opportunity to take whatever they wanted without being caught. In many areas of some cities there were riots and looting. Police could only stand by and watch.

When the enormity of the power loss was realized, calls went out to every trucking company west of the Mississippi to rent semi truck trailers with refrigeration capacity. The trailers would be used to store the frozen food located in stores and storage facilities that did not have a backup power supply. Keeping refrigerated trailers supplied with diesel fuel would become a severe problem in the following weeks.

The next day the Governors of the Western states mobilized the National Guard to keep order and provide assistance wherever they could. Governors in other states pleaded for calm saying that they expected full power to be restored in a matter of days

While the economy of the Western states ground to a halt, the terrorists on the cruise ship ate breakfast and drank tea, and read about the chaos they had created in the ship's newspaper. They later gathered on the deck in a largely vacant area where they would not be overheard and began to talk about their attack and what it meant to them. For the past two days they had been on an adrenalin high and had not really thought of the personal consequences of their actions. Now the adrenalin had dissipated and they had time to reflect on the past two days.

They had given up an opportunity to improve their lives through education, they were no longer welcome in the Western world, and they had undoubtedly been identified and were wanted by police in every Western country.

Two of the men decided that when they got back to Pakistan, they would make their way to one of the training camps where they would teach others how to operate effectively in a Western culture. Jamil and Aza had decided to change their identity and re-enter the U.S., and with financial help from Islam's Fire they would try to establish new terrorist cells. The remaining four had decided that they would go to France, England, or Denmark, countries that had large Muslim communities where they could continue their education and also try to establish terrorist cells. They would be the first of the embers created by Islam's Fire.

18

Ellen Rico, Attorney General, called President Clyde Andrews and told him that more than half of the country had experienced an electrical power blackout as a result of a terrorist attack on the Western power grid.

"I've just seen the news on CNN but they said nothing about it being the result of a terrorist attack."

"The FBI has not made that information public yet, Mr. President, but it will only be a matter of time before the news is leaked to the press. I think it would be beneficial for you to have a briefing with the CIA and the FBI before you start dealing with the press."

"Thank you Ellen, I'll have Margaret set up a meeting immediately."

The President was a handsome man. He was six feet two inches tall with deep blue eyes, and a full head of black hair. He had the lean rugged muscular build of a man who has done hard labor for a good portion of his life. Many said that he reminded them of the Marlboro man often seen in cigarette advertising.

President Clyde Andrews was a democrat from Colorado. He had held various State offices, finally being elected to Governor of the State of Colorado. Elected to the Presidency when he was only forty-eight years of age, he brought with him the exuberance of youth and the pragmatism of a Western rancher. His approach to world problems was straight forward. He would talk to anyone if there was an opportunity for a mutually beneficial solution. But he had no tolerance for those who negotiated and failed to live up to their commitments. He had an absolute abhorrence for those organizations that ignored international law or common human decency. Terrorist organizations fell into the latter group.

He enjoyed good health and was very fit for a man his age. He liked outdoor activities when he had the opportunity to participate in them, which was not too often since he was elected to office. After his election, the secret service had to search its ranks for agents who were fit enough to keep up with the President.

Forty-five minutes later the Attorney General, Ellen Rico, the Director of the CIA, Richard Rice, the Director of the FBI, Mike Riley, and the Press Secretary, Lois Castillo were in the oval office with the President.

The President welcomed everybody and nodded at Director Rice, saying, "Why don't you tell us what's going on, Dick."

Director Rice spoke by telling the President how Mr. Carl Lukin, a private investigator whom the agency had worked with in the past, had been hired by World Bank to trace the money from a $985 million dollar theft. "In the process of doing so he recognized that the money was being funneled into accounts that, in all likelihood, were being used to fund terrorist activities, and brought it to our attention. We asked him to verify the information if he could. In the course of his investigation for the bank, he found that the people involved were smuggling explosives into the country. Since this is a domestic issue we immediately called the FBI. Mr.

Lukin is continuing to investigate the banking connections and is keeping the FBI and CIA informed of his findings."

"Is this the same Carl Lukin that helped us with the issue of stolen missile technology a year ago?"

"Yes sir, it is."

"When this meeting is over, I would like you to stay a few minutes and give me some background information on this man."

"Certainly sir."

The Director of the FBI, Mike Riley continued the story. "The target of our investigation, a Mr. Simon Rossman, is the owner of an import/export company that deals in pottery, home decoration items, and carpets from the Middle East. We now have evidence that in addition to merchandise for resale he was smuggling explosives into the country. Mr. Rossman is also believed to have murdered three people who were involved in the theft from the World Bank. The Bank and Carl Lukin also identified him as the man who established the overseas bank accounts to which the money was sent.

Special Agent Jean Peters who heads our Terrorist Task Force flew out to San Francisco to head up the investigation. She immediately conducted a raid of the home and business warehouse of Mr. Rossman, but by that time Rossman was gone and so were the explosives. She also issued warrants to pick up Rossman and his associates. The following morning the explosives were used to destroy power transmission lines and substations, the result of which was the total blackout of more than half the country. It will take three or four days to get power back to most of the states affected and it maybe several weeks before power can be fully restored to California, Nevada, Arizona, and Utah. We will have better information on the duration of the blackout when the power companies have finished their assessment. We have alerted the Border Patrol to be on the lookout for the suspects who may be trying to leave the country. Mr. Rossman still has not been found.

So far there have been one hundred thirty-six deaths that have been attributed to this incident and we expect many more."

"Okay, what are we doing now?"

"The CIA is following the money in Europe and the Middle East. We have identified several training camps and individuals who are involved with terrorist activities. Mr. Lukin is under contract to the bank to get the money back and he has agreed to keep us informed of his findings. A portion of the stolen money was wired to an account in Sacramento, California held by Mr. Rossman. Mr. Rossman withdrew it in cash three days ago," said Director Rice.

"The FBI is continuing to investigate Rossman and his activities. We are also working with local law enforcement on the murders that have taken place in connection with this case. We are working to get the assistance of foreign countries where the training camps are located in tracing movement of money and identifying the people running the camps, but that will take time," added Director Riley.

"Gentlemen, I want the people who did this caught, no matter what it takes. Thank you for the briefing. Please keep me posted. Lois, please develop a press release."

Everyone stood, saying, "Thank you, Mr. President," then walked out, except Director Rice who stayed to brief the President on Carl Lukin.

19

The others had left and the president had refilled his coffee cup and resettled himself on the sofa saying, "Ok, Dick what can you tell me about Carl Lukin?"

"The information we have on Carl Lukin comes from information obtained by the Navy when they investigated him for a security clearance at the time he became a member of NCIS. That information had been updated as a result of his involvement in the missile case and again updated to a higher level to a higher degree of detail in order to obtain a current CIA security clearance."

"Carl is a rather unique man. As you will recall, he came to our attention when he was hired by the Martin Munitions Company to find out how missile parts they had manufactured ended up being used by pirates off the Somalia Coast. When he found out how the parts were being smuggled out of the manufacturing plant, he followed them to Algeria where he located the factory that modified rockets that were later being used by the pirates. He notified Martin Munitions of his findings and Martin told the FBI, and the FBI told us of his work. We contacted Carl and offered him a consulting contract to keep us in the loop. At that time we also ran a background check on him.

"He's the son of French-Algerian immigrants who settled in Los Angeles. Carl was born in 1977, his parents moved to Los Angeles when he was six. The section of Los Angeles where they settled was composed largely of middle-eastern immigrants, mainly Iranian, Iraqis, Pakistanis and a few families from Turkey. There was always an assortment of languages on the street. Languages fascinated Carl. As you know, kids learn fast from other kids so it was not long before he could understand and speak a few words in Farsi, Arabic, Urdu and several other languages. A large part of his vocabulary at that time was curse words and oaths.

"When he was ten, Carl walked into a grocery store owned by an Iranian family and asked for a job but was told he was too young. After trying several other stores and being turned down, he decided to take matters into his own hands. He would go into the grocery store and wait until a shopper had her shopping bags full then he would walk up and ask if he could help her with the bags. If the woman had a car he would say that he would help her carry the bags to the car. If she lived nearby he would offer to help carry her bags to her home. Many would take him up on his offer then offer a small tip at the end of the chore.

"He learned that if he said thank you in the language that the woman spoke he would often receive a larger tip. He soon saw the value of knowing various languages, and began to learn the predominant languages of the area, Farsi, Arabic, and Urdu. Within a few years he was fluent in all three languages plus he possessed a passable ability to speak Punjabi. As his fluency in the languages increased so did the amounts of the tips. He soon became a favorite of the customers who would ask the owner of the store to have groceries delivered to their home by Carl.

"Carl was not particularly aware of it but his experience at the grocery store had developed an entrepreneurial spirit within him and a greater self reliance in achieving the things that he wanted.

"When Carl reached high school he tried to figure out what courses he wanted to take, finally deciding on French and German plus the normal fare of math, history and literature. It was a heavy workload but with his talent for languages he breezed through French and German. None of the other courses he took seemed to present him any difficulty.

"In the middle of his freshman year the school gave the new students a battery of IQ tests to help student counselors assess the students' ability to handle workloads. Carl scored above 158, not quite a genius but significantly higher than any other kid in school or for that matter the school district.

"It wasn't all work for Carl, he liked open water swimming and snorkel diving. He spent as much time as he could at the beach in the summer. It was his last year of school when he met the girl of his dreams at the beach. She was tall with auburn hair, from all accounts a raving beauty. Her name was Ann Curlin. She was intelligent and like himself, could speak four languages.

"When Carl was just over eighteen and about ready to graduate from high school he walked into a recruiting office and signed up with the Navy. While in his basic training he was given a battery of tests to see what he was best suited for. The testers were sure that the test had been scored wrong. In the interviews he surprised them further with his fluency in languages.

"His physical tests scored equally high. Carl stood 6' 2" and weighed 190, he was solid muscle from all the swimming he had been doing. In addition to Carl's physical characteristics the interviewers were impressed with Carls intelligence and noted their thoughts on his records. At the end of his basic training cycle Carl was interviewed by an officer who thought his academic achievement, language, and high IQ made him well suited to become an intelligence analyst. After completing four months of training he was assigned to the Naval Intelligence Division at the Pentagon.

After three years sitting behind a desk analyzing data he decided to apply to Offices Candidate School. When he submitted his request he received endorsements and glowing recommendations from the officers in his command. He was accepted to OCS provided he was willing to extend his enlistment for four years. On his graduation as an Officer he was sent to five months training in Criminal Investigation and later assigned to Naval Criminal Investigation Services.

During his tour of duty with the Navy he had practiced martial arts as a means of keeping fit and fighting boredom. In spite of his training as an Intelligence analyst and his tour with NCIS he was still able to get a Masters degree in Business from Georgetown University. While Carl was in the Navy he saved as much money as he could, or more accurately, he did not have the time to spend any money. After his discharge, his savings enabled him to attend UCLA as a full time student where he earned a Masters degree in Foreign Affairs.

A few months after completing his education he started his investigation business. It was not long after that that he ran into Ann in Seattle and hired her, she was working for the CIA at the time. She is his fiancée, runs the office for him, and is also a very competent investigator.

"We were very impressed with Carl the first time we met him, so when he contacted us about finding a terrorist cell we took him seriously. Although he is under contract with World Bank to recover the stolen money, we have offered him a consulting contract to keep us informed of any information he finds regarding how the stolen money is being funneled to the terrorists."

"He sounds like quite a man. When this is over you will have to introduce him to me."

"Yes sir. That will be my pleasure."

"Have you given any consideration to hiring him to work for the Agency full time?"

"Not yet, sir, I thought I would wait to see how this project worked out."

"Keep me posted."

20

Carl and Ann stepped out of customs and into the Zurich, Switzerland airport baggage pickup area where a man held a card that read, "Mr. Lukin, World Bank, Inc."

"I'm Carl Lukin." said Carl with a smile."

"This way, sir."

"Where to, sir?" said the driver as he put their two carryon bags in the trunk and climbed into the driver's seat."

When the limo was underway the driver glanced back and said, "My name is Hans Muller, I work for the same organization that you do. I've been told to give you and Ms. Curlin all the assistance that you may require while you're here. I have taken the liberty of providing some equipment that you may need while you are in Zurich. If you require anything else just let me know."

"Thank you, Hans, please give me an hour or so to think about your offer. I have to make a few phone calls before I'll know what our next step will be."

"My phone number and a secure cell phone are in your blue

case, as well as a satellite phone and a few other items that you may need."

"Thank you, Hans."

When they reached their hotel, Hans handed Carl the two carryon bags and one small blue overnight case. Smiling, Hans said, "The limo is courtesy of the Agency."

When they got to their room, Carl opened the blue overnight case and found two Beretta pistols, extra clips of ammunition, two cell phones, a satellite phone, and an envelope with four words written on it, "Welcome to Zurich. Muller." and a telephone number.

Carl picked up the satellite phone and dialed the secure phone at Dan's home. When the phone connected he flipped a switch to make the connection secure. When Dan came on the line Carl asked, "Anything new on your end?"

"Yeah, there is, Scriptorium Guards received a call from Credit Suisse Bank in Zurich, and they want to contract with us for a security review of their computer systems. It seems someone broke into their computers. Of course, we assured them we would be happy to help. They said they would pay a premium if we could start tomorrow. We told them that we would be happy to assist them and that our premium rate would be substantial. We are having our representative from the German office meet with them in the morning."

"Dan, do you think you could put a trap in their system that would notify us if anyone accesses the account?"

"Yeah, no problem, we'll get a message the instant someone opens the account and a blow-by-blow description of what they're doing."

Carl next called the number that he found in the blue overnight case, and when a woman answered, Carl gave her his name and asked for Herr Muller. He flipped the switch to create a secure connection and waited, a few seconds later a voice came on the line and said, "What can I do for you, Carl?"

"I need some help in planting a few bugs but I am not sure just where yet. Unfortunately it may be a few days or more before we will know who the target is and where he lives."

"Yes, I can help you. I'll get a team together and wait for your call."

As he put the phone down Carl turned to Ann and said, "We need to rent two cars and grab some lunch."

After lunch Carl and Ann began to study street maps to familiarize themselves with Zurich. The main avenues were laid out in a somewhat semi circular pattern with each end of the avenue ending at a bridge that crossed the Limmat River. In the downtown area four other bridges crossed the river from Limmat-Quai Strasse that ran along the bank on the north, and Banhof-Quai Strasse, which followed the river on the south. It was not a large city and using a map they could find their way around relatively easy.

For three days the routine was both boring and, conversely, an opportunity to enjoy their time together. Each morning they would drive both cars to the bank and park close enough to keep an eye on those entering and leaving. The rest of the day they would wait. While one went for coffee, or to pick up something to eat, the other would watch the bank. When the one taking a break returned, the other could take a few minutes to stretch. They would occasionally move the cars to a different location to avoid the curiosity of the police or the people in the local shops. Their cell phones were always on, waiting for the expected call. At the end of the second day they returned the cars to the rental agency and rented two others. It would not do to have the same two cars become a familiar sight on the street.

After the Credit Suisse Bank had closed for the day, they returned to the hotel to freshen up then they drove around the city becoming familiar with the streets and the various sections of the city. As expected, near the universities there were many apartment buildings, coffee houses, a few nightclubs that offered dancing, and inexpensive restaurants. Later in the evening they would have a late dinner then return to the hotel. If it had not been for the tedium of watching the bank they could almost have considered their stay in Zurich a vacation.

On the third day the routine changed.

Carl and Ann were parked and sitting in their cars when Dan called and said, "The account is being accessed as we speak. It looks like a cash withdrawal for four hundred and fifty thousand dollars."

Putting down the satellite phone used to talk to Dan, Carl picked up a cell phone to call Ann, saying, "It looks like we are on. The account is being accessed as we speak. Sit tight and we'll see what develops."

Inside the bank, Parviz Jalili had just received his cash and a teller receipt, which showed an account balance of $4,550,000.

"There must be some mistake the balance should be over $985 million?"

The teller checked his computer and said, "There is no mistake, there is only $4,550,000 in the account.

Parviz voice began to rise as he asked to see the manager.

The manager came up and Parviz in a loud voice said, "There is $985 million missing from my account, and this idiot is telling me that the balance is correct when I know it is not."

Examining the computer screen the manager finally said, "No sir, the balance is correct, $4,550,000."

In a voice that rasped with total disbelief he said, "This bank is trying to cheat me out of $985 million."

"I can assure you the bank is not trying to cheat you. For confirmation, I'll have your account audited, but I can assure you that the balance is correct."

Parviz was now sweating, his hands were trembling, and in a shaky voice said, "I will be in tomorrow for the rest of my money."

He collected his briefcase with the four hundred and fifty thousand and walked unsteadily to the door. He exited the bank, going to a bus stop at the corner.

As Parviz walked to the bus stop, Carl took photographs.

The shocked look on Parviz's face was clearly visible through the camera's viewfinder.

Carl called Ann and described the man, saying, "I have him, he looks like he's about to have a stroke. He must have seen the balance in his account. I'll take the lead."

Following a person on a bus without being spotted is difficult. A bus has a stop and go rhythm of its own that normal car traffic does not follow. Cars will pass buses when they stop or they will turn into side streets, but they rarely stay behind a bus for long periods of time. Anyone watching to see if they are being followed will notice that a particular car is simply staying put behind the bus. However, two or more cars can follow someone riding a bus by leapfrogging the bus or changing positions in the traffic stream, one car pulling up and the other car dropping far back. Occasionally the first car will pass a bus and turn into a side street where it can easily turn around and then fall back in the traffic behind the bus or go around the block to once again merge into traffic behind the bus.

When the bus came along, Carl and Ann fell in behind it and followed. When the bus stopped, Carl simply pulled around it, drove a few blocks, found a parking place and waited. Ann in the second car would continue to follow behind the bus for several blocks then make a right turn. Carl and Ann kept changing positions behind the bus until the man got off at a stop on Bahnhofplatz, two blocks from the University. He walked a half block down Lowenstrasse and entered an apartment building.

Carl waited ten minutes and then walked to the door and entered a vestibule where he examined the names on the mailboxes. Three of the names were obviously Swiss and the last name was Parviz Jalili, definitely not Swiss.

Carl called Muller saying, "Hans, I have the name of the man we talked about, it is Parviz Jalili. He lives at 1150 Lowenstrasse."

"Ok I have it, Jalili at 1150 Lowenstrasse. Our man will be there in about 30 minutes."

"Thank you Hans."

A short time later a small van with "SwissComm" on the

side pulled up to the address on Lowenstrasse. A man dressed in a telephone company uniform and carrying a bag of tools got out of the van, walked to the door, and pressed the bell for the manager. When the manager, an elderly woman opened the door, the telephone repairman said. "Good afternoon, I have a report of some telephone problems in this building and I will need to see the telephone terminals in the basement."

"I have not been told of any telephone problems. But that is not a surprise, no one tells me anything. The door to the basement is at the end of the hall."

Fifteen minutes later he was back saying that he had found the problem and it had been repaired. In a van parked on the next street another man listened, ready to record any calls that were made from the phone in Mr. Parviz Jalili's apartment.

Mr. Parviz Jalili's name was also forwarded to the CIA in Washington with a request for all information available on this individual. A request from the FBI was made to the Swiss police and to Interpol for information. A search of the directories of cell phone companies did not yield a cell phone number. A check of his telephone history indicated that aside from local calls he occasionally called a number in Islamabad, Pakistan belonging to a Yusef Azziz.

The first report to come in was from Interpol indicating that Mr. Parviz Jalili's name had never surfaced in Interpol files. The second report to arrive was from the Zurich police. They said that Mr. Parviz Jalili was a guest worker from Iran. That he had been in Switzerland for the past twenty-five years, and that he was a professor of economics at Zurich University. He had not been involved in any activities that warranted the attention of the police, not even so much as getting a parking ticket.

It seemed that Mr. Jalili did his job and just blended into the background. Mr. Jalili's perfect record would soon be shattered.

21

Parviz had received a call from Simon Rossman earlier saying that the plan had worked perfectly. The money would be in the Suisse Credit Bank shortly and that all loose ends had been eliminated. When he checked the bank two days later indeed the money had arrived. Parviz was anxious to tell Yusef about it. He caught a flight to Islamabad the next day.

Yusef Azziz and Parviz Jalili sat at opposite ends of a large gold-embroided sofa facing each other. The room was in a small house located in a modest neighborhood on the west side of Islamabad, Pakistan. The room had one window over which drapes could be pulled to keep out the heat of the day as well as any prying eyes. Two of the walls were hung with small intricately patterned carpets. The floor had a Persian carpet with a geometric design and an edging that contained a pattern of crosses with bent arms reminiscent of the Nazi swastika. The only other furnishing was a coffee table on which sat a small bowl of fruit and two cups of hot sweet tea with milk.

Both men were professors, Yusef, a Professor of Government and Culture at the International Islamic University in Islamabad, and Parviz, a Professor of Economics at the University of Zurich, Switzerland. They had met at a conference as young men just entering their fields of study. As they got to know each other they realized that they held many views in common. Both were devout Islamists and both considered those in the West as crusaders bent on destroying Islam through the plundering of their national resources and the taking of their lands through conquest or by controlling their governments. A prime example of Western arrogance was the taking of the fertile land in Palestine and giving it to the Jews in which to establish a Jewish state. Both felt that the Jewish State had to be totally destroyed, much as one would destroy a cancer in the body.

Yusef favored the more direct route to punish the West through the use of force. He believed that when people in the West suffered enough pain and fear they would force their governments to respect the sovereignty of Islamic lands. Meanwhile, Islam would continue to grow throughout the world and eventually become the dominant religion in Western culture.

For years Yusef had participated in planning attacks against Israel by the Arab states and the Palestinians. He did not want to be in the limelight but preferred to play a less prominent role. He involved himself in long term planning. Always operating in the background, planting seeds of ideas, and watching them take root. He was known to Arab leaders as an intellectual who understood the relationships that existed between the West and Middle East. He was not a fighter in the sense that he carried a gun but he could see opportunities to strike at Israel and the West. Yusef learned that he could manipulate situations to move in directions that he preferred without becoming directly involved.

The Israelis had had their suspicions about Yusef for some time but to date had no direct evidence linking him to acts of terrorism yet his name seemed to come up now and then as a person of interest.

Parviz held the same long term vision as Yusef but he was more of a realist, rather than an action-oriented antagonist. Parviz believed that the natural resources of Islamic nations were finite. That one day their resources would run out leaving the Islamic lands a dried up husk, and the government unable to take care of its people, then they would be dependent on the West for their very survival. A case in point was the petroleum that the West thirsted after as essential to its continued economic growth. If the West could not buy the oil from the Islamic states they would one day simply take it.

Unfortunately, the petroleum was expected to last only another thirty-five years or so before it would fall into a steep decline, then Islamic states would become one of the world's beggars. For Parviz the answer was to invest Middle East petro dollars in the Western economic machine and to drive Western interest out of Islamic lands through political means or they would simply devour Islam's remaining resources. He saw the Western economy and greed as its greatest weakness. He would use those fatal flaws to weaken their governments and bring about a greater respect for the Islamic people.

He further hated the West, in particular America, for the way their CIA had engineered the overthrow of the first legitimately elected government of Iran in 1941, the government of Mohammad Mossadegh, and for putting the Shah Mohammed Reza Pahlavi on the peacock throne. The Shah and his hated secret police, the Savak, ruled Iran until 1979, when he was overthrown. When the Shah sought asylum in the United States he was welcomed by the President, which further inflamed anti-American feeling in the Iranian people. When the story of how American agents engineered the overthrow of the democratically elected Iranian government of Mossadegh came out, it was viewed by many as a direct attack on Islam, furthering the rift between Iran and America that exists today.

Parviz understood the history of Iran and the American involvement in the overthrow of its democratic government and it fed his hatred of the Americans for meddling in Iran's internal affairs. He understood that the overthrow of the Mossadegh government was to facilitate the West's efforts to plunder Iran's oil.

By working together, Yusef and Parviz wanted to bring chaos to America. America and her partners in the war against Islam would feel pain and with that pain the crusaders would rethink their position and grant the Islamic nations the respect they deserve.

They had discussed their philosophy regarding the Western ideological crusade against Islam, the corruption of Islamic governments, and the plundering of Islam's resources many times over the years and were well aware of each other's views. After a few pleasantries the conversation came around to the theft from World Bank.

Yusef looked pleased, asking, "The operation went as expected?"

Parviz smiled, his Persian-accented voice crisp, as he said, "Much better than expected. We now have $985 million dollars to run our training camps and finance the Bali, India, and U.S. operations as well as the one planned for Islamabad. We will also have sufficient funds to begin planning other operations. The money is now in the Credit Suisse Bank in Zurich. I will begin distribution as soon as I return.

"There were no problems. Simon has been in America for over twenty years, he is trusted and capable. He's married and is fully involved in American society. He and his wife have two children. He also owns his own import/export business, which gives him the freedom of movement that he needs.

"Simon has what the Americans call 'a typical American family.' His wife's parents are Saudi and she was raised to follow Arabic customs regarding her relationship to her husband. She does not know that Simon supports Islam's Fire and that he is a firm believer in our objectives. All that she is aware of is that he is a devout Muslim who prays five times a day. As a good Saudi wife she does not question her husband's activities or absences.

"Is there any evidence that the authorities can follow the money to Islam's Fire or take back their money?"

"Simon has eliminated anyone who was connected to the theft. There are no loose threads for the authorities to follow.

"Over the past twenty years Simon has recruited believers in Islam on both the East and West Coasts of America. All are Arabic students from the Middle East and a few are Arabic men born in America who are in agreement with our goals, and all are willing to take part in bringing destruction to American cities. Our attack on the power grid on the West Coast will be costly to the Americans. Other Western countries have seen our attack and will fear that their country will be next unless they leave Islamic lands."

"Excellent Parviz. Each time we strike others will flock to us to help in our great battle with the infidel. Allah will surely smile upon us. Islam's Fire will create such infernos that the infidels will shake with fear and the embers from those flames will float on Allah's wind starting other fires all over the world that cannot be ignored."

22

When Mr. Jalili arrived home from the Suisse Credit Bank he was badly shaken. How could $985 million disappear? When the deposit was made he had seen the account. Now two weeks later the money was gone except for five million.

How had the Americans followed the money so quickly and how had they taken the money without leaving a record? And why had they not taken all of money, why leave five million dollars in the account?

The only answer he could come up with was that they wanted to see who came to pick up the money or where it was sent. The realization that the Americans were looking for him made him sick to his stomach. He could feel the tension in his body, his hands shook and his head ached. When the others found out what had happened he would be a dead man. There was little tolerance for failure. He would not tell anyone until the bank audit of his account was finished, maybe there was a mistake.

The rest of the night was agony, with every sound he heard he expected the police to break in and arrest him or the Americans to kill him. He lay there in the dark trying to plan his next move. The only thing he was sure of was that he had to disappear. As he lay there a plan began to form in his mind. He would simply walk out in the morning with the money, and go to a large city where he would disappear. He would eventually tell the others but not until he had created a new identity. In the meantime there was still $4,550,000 million in the account.

Later that evening Muller called Carl, saying, "Parviz knows that we have the money and that we're after him. He's been checking the accounts in all the banks that were involved in the movement of the money."

"Has he told anyone else that the money is missing?

"No. Not yet. He's probably afraid. When they find out, he's a dead man and he knows it."

"Keep an eye on him, he'll probably try to run," said Carl.

The following morning Mr. Jalili left his home promptly at seven-thirty, as was his custom, and walked to the University. He carried only his briefcase with him.

Within a few minutes of Jalili's entering Zurich University, apparently going to work, Muller called Carl again, saying, "Either Parviz doesn't know that we have identified him or he's trying to bluff his way through this problem. He has gone to his job at the University. We have a few hours if you want to take a look at his apartment."

"Can we get in without being seen?"

"I think that's possible, the building is empty during the day. The only person there is the landlady and she lives in the basement apartment."

The front door was open to a vestibule that held the mailboxes. It took Muller only a few seconds to slip a credit card between the door lock and the jamb to open the inner door. On the second floor Muller picked the lock to the apartment. They entered the living area and looked around. There was a desk and telephone against the wall with a window, a search of the desk turned up nothing of interest.

On one wall there was a sofa with a coffee table in front of it. On the coffee table was a well used copy of the Quran and several magazines. Across from the sofa was a small television set. There were no photographs in the room. Two small carpets with intricate designs hung on the walls. Two side chairs sat in the corners of the room. Everything appeared to be undisturbed.

Adjacent to the living room was a kitchen, with a small stove with a teakettle on it. The cupboards held some canned goods and other staple items. A small refrigerator held milk, soft drinks, vegetables and two small steaks. On the drain board there was a half full coffee cup beside a French coffee press.

In the bedroom the sheets and covers were pulled up. Clothes were hanging on the closet rod. There were a few boxes on the shelf and a suitcase on the floor along with three pairs of shoes. The dresser was full of underclothes. The bookcase held a hundred different books on economics and a dozen on travel in France and Spain.

Nothing seemed to be disturbed, in fact, it looked as if Parviz would return at four in the afternoon to simply continue his normal routine.

They placed a few bugs that would pick up any conversation in the living room and one in the bedroom.

They quietly left the building and waited for Mr. Parviz Jalili to return. It would be a long wait.

After entering his building at the University, Parviz simply walked out the back door instead of going to the faculty lounge for his morning coffee as was his custom. He left the campus and walked five blocks, stopping often to look in the reflection in store windows to see if anybody was following him.

He entered a coffeehouse filled with people having breakfast before going to work. He elbowed his way through the crowd to the back and walked through the kitchen and out the back door. When he reached the next street he hailed a taxi, directing the driver to take him to the train station where he bought a newspaper and a ticket to Paris.

He went straight to the train that was already boarding. As he sat in his compartment he held his newspaper up shielding his face, pretending to read, scanning the passengers as they boarded. He would have a layover of about two hours in Geneva where he would switch trains. He would find a coffeehouse near the station where he could wait until it was time to board the connecting train. His train was scheduled to arrive in Paris at eight that evening.

He was so nervous that he started to perspire. He could not harness his thoughts to focus on the newsprint. How had the Americans traced the money so fast? The money had been passed through five banks on three continents using numbered accounts. And to make it more difficult he had chosen countries noted for their banking confidentiality laws. Yet they had managed to take $985 million and make it look as if the money had never been deposited.

As the train made its way toward Geneva, no one seemed to pay any attention to him. As time slowly passed he began to relax. When the trained pulled into the Geneva station he folded the newspaper and put it under his arm. He held the briefcase in his right hand and when he walked onto the platform and through the terminal building he looked like the hundreds of other businessmen leaving the station.

He walked several blocks from the Geneva station until he found a coffeehouse that suited his purpose. It had large windows through which he could watch the street. He selected a table in the back where he could see the front door and still have a view out of the front window. He ordered coffee and a hot breakfast. He had been too nervous to eat anything earlier but now he was ravenous. An hour and a half later he left the coffeehouse and made his way back to the train station where he boarded his train.

Arriving in Paris he walked out of the station and caught a taxi, asking the driver to take him to a modest-priced hotel. After checking in under a different name he went to his room where he collapsed onto the bed. He was exhausted from the trip and his nerves were raw. He would call Yusef in the morning when he could think more clearly.

At five that evening Muller called Carl and told him that Parviz had not returned. He said, "I've called the University and a department secretary said Professor Jalili had not shown up for classes that day. It looks as if he walked off and left everything."

"Get a team in there and give that place a thorough going over. Photograph every scrap of paper and get them to Langley."

Over dinner that evening Carl said, "Unless we can get a lead on where he has gone we might as well head home. Tomorrow we'll check buses, airlines, trains and car rentals agencies."

Ann said, "I hope we can find him, I don't want to go back so soon. This trip has been like a vacation."

"Yeah, I know, it's been rather pleasant. Unfortunately, if he got away we may never find him, he's carrying enough money that he can go anyplace he wants."

"If he is going to run I hope he chooses an island with nice beaches someplace in the tropics."

The following morning Carl and Ann went to the bus station and showed Parviz Jalili's photograph to the ticket agents without luck. The next stop was the Zurich Airport where they went through the same procedure. Again the answer was the same, no one had seen him. By that time it was mid afternoon and the final stop was the train station. After showing the photograph and getting a negative answer, the last ticket agent they talked to said that they had just changed shifts and they might want to come back in the morning and speak with the early shift. If the morning shift of ticket agents hadn't seen him then they would have to check all of the car rental agencies.

Muller joined Carl and Ann for dinner that evening. After ordering a bottle of wine Carl asked, "Did you find anything useful in Parviz's apartment."

"Not much, just an impression about the man. For instance, he had a well used Quran, there were no icons or photographs visible in the any of the rooms, and there was a prayer rug on a side table in the living room, I would guess that Parviz is a devout Islamic believer.

"There were a number of magazines on a coffee table but they were all news magazines that dealt with economics. He was well read. His bookcase held books mostly on Middle East history, economics, and Western Culture, plus a few travel books on France, Spain, or Portugal. He was neat a person, you know, everything in its place, neat closet and dresser drawers.

"We did find one thing that was out of character with the rest of the apartment. On top of the dresser was a women's scarf that had a hint of perfume on it. He apparently had a girlfriend but there was no indication that she spent much time there or who she might be. In his desk there was business correspondence from his publisher but no personal letters or notes from a girl friend.

"All in all, I would say he's a religious man who pretty much kept to himself and did not have many close friends. He may have had a girlfriend but, if so, their relationship does not appear to be intense since the only indication that she existed at all was the scarf."

Carl said, "That doesn't give us many clues as to where he might have gone. Let's hope we can find out how he left town tomorrow."

The conversation moved to the steps that would have to be taken if they could not get a lead on where Parviz had gone.

The following morning, Carl and Ann showed the photograph to the early shift ticket agents at the train station. One man said that he thought he had sold the man a ticket to Paris the previous day. "If he was the man you are looking for he would have arrived in Paris at eight last night."

They drove back to the hotel and called Muller to let him know what they had found and thank him for his help. Carl told Muller that they were good for a meal that night if he cared to join them. Muller said that he would like that and would meet them in their hotel lobby at eight. Carl put the Beretta pistols, extra clips of ammunition, two cell phones, and satellite phone back in the blue case then he and Ann headed to the hotel bar for a beer.

Tomorrow they would be back in D.C. and a meeting with the Director but tonight, they had a few hours left for a few drinks and a good meal.

23

Carl called Director Rice from the plane and arranged an appointment for late that afternoon and added that Ann would be with him.

"Great, that will me a give a chance to meet her, but there is something I need to discuss with you in private if Ann doesn't mind waiting in the outer office, or if that's not acceptable you can come back tomorrow."

"Wait and I'll check with her."

When Carl came back on the line he said, "Ann said that she has been looking forward to meeting you as well, and that she is quite willing to wait if it doesn't take more than a few hours."

Late that afternoon, Carl and Ann arrived at the CIA and after showing their IDs and the guards going through the car check routine, Carl was directed to the basement visitors parking under the building. They were met at the elevator and again asked if either of them were carrying weapons. When they reached the seventh floor they were led to the Director's conference room where

Director Rice, Deputy Director Gray, and Mr. Kovak were waiting. They were invited to sit at the conference table.

The Director welcomed Ann, saying, "Normally I would ask a visitor to wait outside during a briefing but since you were an integral part of the investigation in Zurich, please do stay and feel free to contribute to the briefing. If you decide to stay I must ask you to sign a security statement that states anything you hear during the briefing will not be discussed with anyone other than those present at this meeting."

"Thank you, Director Rice. I'll sign the security statement."

Carl gave them a briefing of the events that occurred since their last meeting and what he believed needed to be done if the leaders of Islam's Fire were to be found.

During the briefing the Director as well as Aaron Kovak and John Gray asked questions of both Carl and Ann.

Carl said, "Our involvement in this investigation has ended. World Bank's contract required me to find the money and the people who stole it, which we've done. The money has been returned less the amount that the CIA asked be left in the accounts and the person responsible for the cash withdrawal has been identified and, unfortunately, has disappeared. So unless the bank wants me to keep tracking him, I have completed my contractual requirements."

After Carl had finished speaking, Director Rice asked if the others had any questions, when they did not he said that he would like to have a word alone with Carl. The others left the room. Ann waited in the outer office reading a magazine she found there.

"Carl, it's after five, would you care for a drink? I'm going to have one." With that Director Rice got up and went to a credenza behind his desk and opened a cabinet door, taking out two glasses and a bottle.

"I don't think so, sir, after all the travel, lack of sleep, and jet lag, I would probably fall asleep at the wheel driving home if I did."

"The President is very impressed with you and has said that I should hire you. I tend to agree with him, and not because he is my boss, but I too am impressed with your insights and abilities.

So I would like to offer you a job with the agency in our special operations division, are you interested?"

"I am flattered sir, but I prefer to run my own show. I have to admit that I am intrigued by some of the work your people do, but I'm not cut out to sit behind a desk and do analyses all day. I'm afraid I tend to be more action-oriented. In my investigation agency I am the boss, and I can direct other people to do the grunt work. It may not be as glamorous as working for the agency but it pays the bills and gives me a great deal of freedom."

"That is not the answer I would like to have heard but I understand where you're coming from. Let me make another proposal. How would you feel about working for me as a special consultant? You would report directly to me. When I don't have a job for you, your time will be your own to pursue your other interests. Of course, your consulting retainer would be paid yearly whether you were on a job or not. This arrangement could be terminated by either of us at any time.

"You would be required to attend our training farm for six months so that you could become familiar with the agency, the tools that are available, and how the agency operates. After six months you can either leave or continue your consulting contract with me."

"That's quite an offer. Can I have a little time to think about it? Say, until tomorrow morning?"

The Director held up his finger indicating he wanted Carl to wait one moment, then reached for the phone and pushed the red button. When the phone rang he said, "Hello, Mr. President, I would like a moment of your time tomorrow morning and I would like to bring the guest you said you wanted to meet. Yes sir, I believe we can be there then. Thank you, sir.

"Be here at eleven-fifteen tomorrow, we'll have lunch with the President at noon. You can give me your answer after lunch."

That evening, after dinner, Carl and Ann went for a stroll by the Vietnam War Memorial, ending up at the Lincoln Memorial. They sat on the steps enjoying the cool of the evening and he told her about the offer and the luncheon with the President. He said he would like to take the offer but wanted to discuss it with her first.

Ann asked why he wanted to do that kind of work. His only answer was, "Investigating fraud and embezzling is becoming a little boring. After the time I spent with NCIS and then working on the missile case, I miss the excitement that comes with that type of work. Consulting for the Director of the CIA might provide the excitement I miss and also give me the freedom to look at other kinds of work for our firm.

"But there are two things that have to happen first," he said. "You would have to become the CEO of the Lukin agency and when I'm not consulting for the Director I will be working for you. Do you think you can or would even want to handle that? To make that thought a little sweeter for you, if we were to get married tomorrow you could boss me around at home as well."

She threw her arms around his neck, kissed him several times and said yes to both ideas.

24

The following morning Director Rice and Carl entered the White House and were led to the residence floor where the President met them, and after introductions he led them to a small dining room saying, "I'm sorry gentleman, but my wife will not be joining us today as she has a previous engagement.

"But she is here in spirit. She and the cook have conspired in an effort to make me lose weight, but you two can have anything you would like." Carl and the Director both chuckled and said the salad would be fine.

After a few minutes of polite conversation the President said, "I want to thank you for your service in the past and your help in identifying this terrorist organization. It's unfortunate that we were unable to catch the leaders, but we will.

And I understand that you've managed to recover the money for the bank. That kind of loss would have shaken confidence in World Bank or even caused it to collapse. The collapse of the Country's biggest bank plus the economic loss from a terrorist attack and the subsequent power blackout would have shaken our faith in the Country's economy.

"Yes sir. World Bank is whole again, and has been helpful by making five million available as bait so that the intelligence services can continue to identify and track members of Islam's Fire

"Then, of course, there is the loss of life here and in other countries as a result of the terrorist attacks. At last count, over two hundred-thirty people have died as a result of the power failure in this country plus an additional fifty-six from the bombing of the Marriot in Pakistan, and over two hundred in the Bali bombing. Organizations like Islam's Fire cannot be tolerated, they must be stopped.

"We were able to use some transformers that were scheduled to be installed at another location, and borrow some power line towers from a Canadian firm that is constructing a new power line across Canada, or the problems could have been much worse."

The President continued, "I understand Director Rice has made you an offer. Have you given it consideration? I would like to have your help in identifying the people that have attacked us and bring them to justice or eliminate them."

"If we can reach a deal along the lines that Director Rice has proposed I would like to be on board and do what I can to help."

Looking at Director Rice the President said, "Great. Dick, make getting the bastards who attacked us a priority."

On the way back to Langley, Director Rice said, "I'll have the necessary paperwork ready for you in the morning, and we can set up a schedule for your training then. You and Aaron can begin to put together a plan to stop Islam's Fire."

"I would be happy to meet with Aaron tomorrow if he has the time."

25

The following morning Carl was led to the Director's conference room where Aaron Kovak and John Gray were seated at the table.

"Grab some coffee and have a seat," said the Director as he pushed a folder over to Carl. "Inside are non-disclosure forms, a contract, your ID, and several other pieces of formality that you will need to sign."

Carl signed the various documents and slid the file back to the Director.

"Now I would like to hear your ideas on how we are going to catch these guys, Carl. Any thoughts?"

"A few. Since this started we have acquired a number of different telephone numbers. It's possible to eliminate a few of them. For instance, the numbers for the Zurich University, which are more than likely work related, and numbers that belong to students. The vast majority of these students are eighteen to twenty-two years old and unlikely to be handling the money, and they are not in his peer group. We'll keep a watch on the rest of the numbers.

"Since he is on the run, calls from elsewhere in the world, particularly those calls made from throwaway phones, would be suspect. Over the course of six or seven months we should be able to put together a fairly good picture of phone usage, highlight phone calls that are unusual, and record some voice that can be used for voice print identification. If he is using a cell phone with GPS capability, so much the better, we will be able to locate him. If not, we can at least get a general location by seeing what cell phone towers he is using. It may not give us an address, but it will give us a place to start looking.

"Obviously his mail might give us a clue where he might be, it might have taken his contacts a few days to find out that he is on the run. Mail that was in the postal system and didn't arrive before he left might be interesting.

"The search of his apartment gave us the impression that he was a religious man which means that he probably said his prayers at a mosque frequently. With the information that the phone program should generate, we'll get a good idea of where to start looking. From then on it's a matter of watching mosques in the area. It is doubtful that a religious man will change his prayer habits.

"Of course since he was involved in a bank robbery, having the FBI send pictures and fingerprints to Interpol could generate a lead. As far as law enforcement is concerned the person we are looking for is wanted for bank robbery, not terrorism."

Aaron spoke up, saying, "We are in the process of checking passport records but it seems that he has not travelled much out of Europe, although he has made a number of trips to Pakistan. He appears to have spent considerable amount of time in France. It would be my guess that he's in Europe, most likely France. After forty years immersed in the Western culture he has probably grown accustomed to our Western decadence. We have examined all the papers and books in his apartment in addition to a number of travel brochures, maps, and books on French history, and when he left Zurich, he bought a train ticket to Paris. My guess is that he has gone into hiding in France, possibly Belgium or Spain, but again, my best guess would be France."

"One of the numbers that he occasionally called was in Pakistan, from what you are saying, it's a little out of line with his character. It might be worthwhile to take a closer look at the person that has that number. It could be a friend that he met through his university work or much more." said John Gray.

"We should also go over the evidence from Rossman's home and business, particularly his phone records. Considering what we now know something may pop out at us."

Carl announced that all of the work they had been talking about would take five or six months to accumulate and analyze, so he was taking the next four weeks off to take Ann back to Seattle and get married. He would be back after a few weeks of honeymooning.

"I'll be damned! He signs a consulting contract with me then has the balls to tell me he's going to take the next four weeks off!"

When the laughter died down everyone offered their congratulations and wished Carl and Ann well.

The door opened and the Director's secretary entered and handed a sheet of paper to the Director saying, "I think you might want to see this."

He read the message and handed it to Aaron. "One of your people brought up a message that just popped up on Al Jazeera regarding the bombing in Islamabad."

Islam's Fire has struck another blow at the arrogant American infidels who bring their hotels and factories to Islamic lands to strip the wealth and natural resources in order to enrich themselves at the expense of the people of Islam. This was a reminder to Pakistan that foreign Infidels are not welcome. If you continue to harbor the infidel's additional actions will be taken.

The Infidels continue to tread on Islamic land with their military bases in Afghanistan, Turkistan, Qatar, Iraq, and Kuwait. They send arms to the Jews so that they can continue to subjugate the Palestinian people. The Jews threaten the Iranians with attack if the government of the sovereign state of Iran attempts to provide electrical power to their people using atomic energy, as is their right.

Islam's Fire will continue to fight for the rights of Islamic people all over the world. The Western aggressors will pay for their arrogance and their continued support to the illegal Jewish state until it is wiped from the face of the earth and the Palestinian people regain their ancestral land taken from them by the Jews.

Join Islam's Fire in jihad.

"That's it, gentlemen, let's get to work. Carl, please give Ann a hug for me. Enjoy your honeymoon and best wishes to you both for a long, happy, and prosperous marriage." When they had stepped out of the office the Director went to his desk where he began to write an item to be included in the President's morning briefing paper.

26

Carl and Ann left for Seattle the next morning. They called Ann's parents who lived in Issaquah, Washington to let them know that they would be having house guests for a week. When they arrived at the house and had a chance to say hello, Ann told her parents the news. Her mother broke down in tears and her father said, through a big smile, "It's about time." When they said they planned on a civil ceremony the following week, all her mother could say was, "No way, we'll get the church in Issaquah or one in Kirkland. We can pick a wedding dress tomorrow, begin to notify people. . . ." The planning went on until two in the morning when everyone realized they were exhausted.

While the wedding plans moved forward in Issaquah, Carl decided to make a quick trip to his office in San Francisco, he was just in the way anyway. Ann's father looked as if he wanted to go with Carl, but after a quick glance from his wife he decided he had better stay at the house.

Late the following morning Carl entered his San Francisco

office and he told the staff that Ann was the new CEO of Lukin Investigations and that while he would still be available his new role would be as an investigator, not the boss. He went on to say that he was working on another project and may be away for long periods of time, he did not elaborate further. He told them of his plans to open a second office somewhere in the D.C. area, "If anyone is interested in moving to the Washington D.C. area let Ann know when she comes into the office or send her an email."

He phoned the local FBI office to see if Jean Peters was back in San Francisco. He was told that she had just flown in that morning. He asked to be transferred to her extension.

When Jean answered he said, "Hi Jean, this is Carl Lukin. I am in San Francisco tonight and I was hoping that we might get together for drinks and dinner if you have the time. I would like to find out how things are going with the Rossman case and fill you in on a few things that I have been doing."

"Sure, I would love that. Is Ann in town with you?"

"No, she is in Issaquah, Washington and I'll be going back up there tomorrow morning. I'll try to get a reservation at the restaurant 'Acqurello' for eight o'clock. If I can't I'll let you know."

After Jean arrived, they were shown to their table and had ordered cocktails, Carl told her of the wedding plans.

Jean congratulated Carl, adding, "I know that you and Ann will be very happy together." The conversation then drifted to finding a house in D.C. She suggested that they might want to look for an office in Reston, Virginia instead of D.C., the prices might be a little cheaper.

The conversation finally turned to the Rossman case and the California terrorist attack investigation. "We found out that after eight of the group had planted their bombs, they boarded a cruise ship in San Francisco that was bound for Mexico. When they got to Mazatlan they jumped ship and flew to Mexico City, then on to London, and Islamabad where they disappeared. The ten that were caught at the Mexican border were between the ages of twenty-two and twenty-six. All were students, two were Jordanians, two Egyptians, and six Pakistanis.

The conversation was interrupted by the waiter asking if they had made their dinner selection.

After Carl and Jean ordered and the waiter left Jean continued, "From what we can tell, all the terrorists had received early training at madrassas in Pakistan. Those students that showed real promise were sent to a training camp for military training and then to universities in the U.S. on student visas. With their extremist form of Islamic religious and military training they were prime targets for a local cell recruiter, and eventually made part of a terrorist cell.

"It's our opinion that the madrassas are the basic level of indoctrination. They provide the raw material under the guise of being religious training centers, and undoubtedly some are, but if you have a headmaster who is a terrorist at heart it is a great place to cull out the candidates for a terrorist army. It is my opinion that Pakistan one day will find that the danger that madrassas present to the Country are not worth the benefits they provide.

"Rossman was the pied piper who did the recruiting and cell organization. He had probably been given a list of names to contact and the names of the universities that the students were attending. He has apparently organized two other cells in the U.S. that we are aware of. Both appear to be on the East Coast. There is no indication as to who the people are or where the other cells are located. We are trying our best to find them, but Rossman kept his information about his organization compartmentalized.

"The members we caught knew nothing about the other cells. The information we have was gained from remnants of deleted files on his computer. He did a pretty good job of cleaning up his disk so we were not able to reclaim much.

"As for Rossman himself, well, he cleaned out his bank account of half a million dollars and disappeared, and we don't have a clue yet as to where he went.

"We are in the process of looking at his business contacts but that hasn't yielded anything either, but we will keep looking. It's our belief that he is somewhere on the East Coast living under an assumed name. He has too much of an investment in putting together two other terrorist cells to simply walk away."

"Do you have anything on the explosives that were used?"

"Yes, as you suspected, it was semtex-A, and it was manufactured in Libya. It's used extensively in construction projects in Libya and throughout the Middle East, China, and Korea. The Libyans didn't keep very good records of who got the explosive material or how it was to be used, or at least they are not sharing that information with us. The import/export business that Rossman put together was an ideal business to have when you are smuggling explosives into the country. And using the hollowed out pallets as the method of moving the explosives to different locations was clever, considering the thousands of pallets that go through a port.

"The import/export business is a great cover if you want to distribute bombs around the Country, just stuff the bombs in clay pots put the pots on a pallet, and then send them off."

"Have copies of Rossman's personal and business phone records been given to the CIA?"

"Yes, we've copied everything we found to the Agency."

"Is there anything new on the murders in Washington and San Francisco?"

"Both the San Francisco and Washington police have reached the same conclusion that Rossman committed the murders alone. As a result, they have quit looking for anyone else. We've reached the same conclusion. We think the murders were committed to clean up any loose ends and make tracking the money more difficult."

"Now it's your turn, Carl, what's happening on your end?"

"After the wedding next week we're off to Hawaii for a two week honeymoon. When we get back we are moving to Washington D.C. After we've had a chance to find a home, we'll start up our East Coast office for the investigation agency."

The waiter again interrupted with their meal. Before leaving he asked if they wanted another drink or a bottle of wine. Both Carl and Jean declined.

"Hey, that's great, let me know when you have settled in and we can all get together for dinner."

"We'll do that. The other thing is that I have signed a consulting contract reporting directly to Director Rice for projects we can both agree that I can help with. I will not be part of the regular agency staff but I will have access to agency resources if I'm working on one of their projects. I'll have to go to the CIA training farm for six months to become familiar with CIA procedures, but other than that there is nothing else new. My first assignment is the organization that Rossman worked for. My second project is finding good office space and an inexpensive house to buy or rent."

Chuckling, Jean said, "Good luck with the house and office, you may be in for a shock when you look at prices."

The following morning Carl returned to Issaquah to help out where he could with the wedding plans, which was to basically keep out of the way. The following Tuesday, the wedding took place at a small church in Kirkland, Washington. Following the ceremony was a dinner at the Woodmark Hotel on Lake Washington. Then the couple was off to Hawaii for two weeks.

27

Aaron looked in his rolodex and called Special Agent Jean Peters. When she answered he said, "Hi Jean, this is Aaron Kovak, I think we have something that you might be interested in, can you come by for a briefing?"

"Sure, I'll be there in an hour."

When Jean arrived she was shown to a conference room where Aaron and Deputy Director John Gray were waiting. After a few minutes of casual conversation Aaron said, "You know the drill Jean, this is for your ears only. We have been running a program that has given us information that might interest you.

"With the help of the Zurich police we have developed a list of telephone numbers that the money man for Islam's Fire used or were used to call him. For the past six months we have been tracking those numbers and we have come across a few numbers that look promising." Aaron passed over a sheet of suspect numbers that originated from or received calls in the U.S., and their locations.

Jean picked up the summary report and focused on the phone

calls that originated in New Jersey since that fit with her theory that Rossman had other terrorist cells on the East Coast and that he had merely moved to the East Coast following the attack on the Western power grid. "My God, that fits with what I have felt for some time. This is good information. Now we can focus our search."

Within hours of Jean's return to her office, photographs of Rossman that were copied from family albums found by the FBI in their Sacramento raid were circulated to law enforcement agencies in New Jersey and New York without any results. Some photographs showed him without any alteration, others had been altered to show him with a beard, mustache or goatee. The FBI focused its manpower on the Princeton area and began showing the photographs to the Imams in the surrounding area mosques, but again the answer was the same, no one recognized him.

When the FBI began interviewing students from Islamic countries at the local colleges and universities who had entered the Country on student visas, the sharply increased FBI activity triggered Rossman to make a move.

Rossman didn't know how the FBI knew he was in the Princeton area, but he was not going to take any chances. His next attack, which had been planned for the holiday shopping season, was moved up to the following week.

New York City would never forget his attack or the mandate from Islam's Fire.

28

Ann had been in New York for the past three days finalizing a contract with Carlson National Bank to perform security audits of their New York headquarters and East Coast branches. She had taken the subway to reach her hotel. The train was crowded and she stood near the door. Her thoughts were on the contract and what it meant to Lukin Investigations when the train pulled into the station.

The last thing that Ann saw as she stepped through the door exiting the train was a bright flash. The exposed parts of her body were seared beyond recognition by the intense heat. Leather belts and buckles were torn into small shrapnel that sank into her flesh. The concussive force of the blast ripped her internal organs from connective tissue, veins and arteries. Some of the seared flesh was separated from the bones beneath and ripped from her body. Her right arm and the lower part of her right leg were torn away. She hit the opposite side of the car and fell to the floor in a heap of smoldering flesh and bone. The train car that Ann was in and three others were blown off the track and lay crumpled against the far wall of the station.

It would take authorities more than a week to identify Ann and notify her parents. It took an additional two days for word of Ann's death to reach Carl at the CIA training farm.

The effects of the explosion were significantly increased by the confinement of the underground subway station. The concrete walls and ceilings served to focus and amplify the blast and heat resulting in even greater destruction and a larger number of deaths. Hundreds were killed with the initial blast concussion and many more were injured.

Others were killed by the searing heat or received serious burns from the added heat generated by the aluminum powder. Scores of first responders were killed twenty minutes later when the second explosion occurred. Because of the destruction, it took two days to get a reasonably accurate count and identify the dead and injured. The total for all ten subway stations was announced as 431 deaths and 871 injured. The death count was sure to increase because there were so many with severe injuries.

No one had noticed the university-age students carrying shopping bags and backpacks that had entered the New York subway at different stops just minutes before 5:00 P.M. Each carried a book and pretended to be reading. At 5:00 P.M. the afternoon rush was in full swing, the platforms were crowded. The students were instructed to leave the backpacks against the back wall, preferably against a trash can or some other object where it was less likely to be noticed. One student left his backpack next to a drunk sprawled against the back wall of the platform. Each backpack held forty pounds of semtex-A, and ten pounds of aluminum powder. The timing mechanism in each backpack had an added feature, a microphone attached to a device that made a connection when the noise reached a preset level. The next train to reach the station after five would make sufficient noise to reach the necessary level.

To increase the death toll and hamper rescue efforts, the shopping bags that the students carried were left near turnstiles or in trash bins located near the subway entry. They had similar explosive charges set to go off at 5:40 P.M., when emergency responders were expected to be in the area tending to the injured. Twenty eight emergency responders were killed in the blast and an additional thirty six injured,

The people of New York were terrified, as were most people in metropolitan areas that rely on public transportation. The Mayor of New York City and the U.S. Congress were demanding answers and action. The FBI pulled agents from all over the country to add to the manpower in New York and again Jean Peters was put in charge of the investigation.

Four of the students who had planted the bombs panicked and were caught at JFK airport trying to get out of the country. The rest of the students simply returned to their universities as if nothing had happened, but were later identified and arrested. When interrogated, they all said that they were Islamic combatants engaged in a jihad called for by Islam's Fire. None had remorse for their actions. They said the killing of infidels was sanctioned by the Quran and would continue until the Western invaders had left Islamic lands, stopped corrupting their governments and no longer plundered Islamic natural resources.

Research into their pasts revealed that three of the ten were Saudi, two Iranian and five Pakistani. All had received years of training at Pakistani madrassas before receiving military training in a camp located in the mountains of Pakistan, near the town of Gilitt and then being sent to the U.S. They were dedicated and prepared to die for Islam.

Most of the victims of the blast were identified within days. Those directly in front and in the immediate proximity of the blast took much longer to identity. For many the only means of identification was DNA, Ann fell into this category.

29

When Carl learned of Ann's death his immediate reaction was disbelief. His denial heightened when he called Ann's parents and they told him they were planning a closed casket funeral because her body was too badly damaged to be recognizable. On hearing that, Carl's hopes rose that Ann had not died. Carl said that he was on his way to Dulles and would be on a plane in a few hours, he would see them later that night.

After takeoff he immediately called Jean Peters, saying, "What can you tell me about the attack and the investigation?"

"I'm sorry Carl. I just found out that Ann's name was on the list of victims."

"Yeah, I found out about three hours ago myself and I'm on a plane to Seattle now. Are they sure it was Ann? I understand that the bodies were so badly damaged that identification was difficult, maybe they made a mistake."

"Carl, these are the same people who have identified the victims of 9-11, they have had a lot of practice. I don't believe they would have said it was Ann if there was any doubt."

"Have you identified the group who planted the bombs?"

"We caught four people trying to get out of the Country and they are being interrogated as we speak. But the evidence we have points to the same group that did the California power grid bombing. The explosives used have the same markers as those used in California. At this time we believe Islam's Fire is responsible, but we are still gathering evidence and talking to those who planted the bombs."

"Thanks, Jean, please keep me informed."

Carl made his way to the restroom where he sat for a few minutes as tears rolled down his face and the realization that he would never see Ann again set in. As he gave in to grief his body began to convulse with sobs. Twenty minutes passed before he regained control. He washed his face and vowed to never lose control again.

When he returned to his seat he turned to the window and thought about Islam's Fire. Anger began to surge through him. He made a promised to Ann he would find those responsible for her death and he would kill them all. By the time he met Ann's father at the airport he was fully in control again. Grieving had been replaced by a deep seated desire for vengeance. Carl made a vow to himself that Islam's Fire would be consumed in the fires that they had ignited.

30

Early on the day of the subway bombings in New York, Rossman had made his way to Massachusetts where he rented an apartment in South Boston. Before he left New York he had driven his car to a deserted dock and pushed it into the East River. For all practical purposes, Simon Rossman no longer existed. He had assumed another alias for which he had a driver's license, passport, credit cards, business cards, and social security card. When he reached Boston he purchased a new disposable phone. He placed only one call, to a number in Paris.

The new phone number and the area where the call originated were noted by the CIA. The call to a number that was under surveillance so close to the attacks in New York insured that it immediately received the highest level of review. The suspected area that Rossman had fled to was passed on to the FBI's Task Force on Terrorism and onto the desk of Jean Peters. The FBI's response was immediate. Hundreds of agents flooded into the Boston area. They interviewed every student from an Islamic country multiple times and every Imam from surrounding mosques. Rossman's photographs both altered and unaltered were circulated to the local Islamic community. None of the Imams or people interviewed recognized Rossman. Some of the students said that they may have seen him at the student union from time to time but were not sure.

The FBI's manhunt caused many of the Islamic students to quit school and go back to their home Countries because they thought they were being persecuted because of their faith. Others left because they had been recruited by Rossman and were now frightened.

Rossman's photograph was on every TV newscast and newspaper as being wanted for questioning regarding the blackout on the West Coast and the bombings in New York City.

Rossman realized he needed to get out of the Country. He decided to drive to the small town of Clayton, New York to make the crossing into Canada. He was apprehended late that evening by the border patrol. He was held in custody in an undisclosed location for fear that he would be killed before he could be put on trial.

The President wanted a trial so that the world could see radical Islam for the danger it presented to the world.

The next day another message appeared in Al Jazeera:

The brave believers of Islam have struck another blow against the infidel in their homeland. No longer can those who war against Islam ignore our demands. No longer will they rape Islamic lands with impudence, stealing our resources, and defile our holy sites. No longer can the Western crusaders ignore our demand that they leave Islamic lands. No longer will they feel safe in supporting the Jews in Palestine. No longer will they feel safe in their own homeland.

Should the infidels persist in their efforts to destroy Islam and subjugate Islamic people, they will fail. They now know that Islam's Fire will continue to strike them until the crusaders leave Islamic land.

The Jewish state created by the Western crusaders will not be tolerated. The Jewish state is an abomination and must be wiped from the face of the earth.

The day is near when Palestinians will be free in their own land.

31

The President had read the morning briefs and called Director Rice, asking Rice to join him for breakfast.

"Good morning, Dick, have some coffee. Can Sam fix you a little breakfast?"

"Good morning, Mr. President," said Director Rice as he sat down and poured himself some coffee.

Sam said, "I can fix you some poached eggs and toast. You are going to need fuel in you if you are going to get a good start on the day."

"Okay, Sam, you talked me into it."

"Okay, Dick, what are we doing about this terrorist organization, Islam's Fire?"

"As you know we caught one of the cell organizers trying to cross into Canada. He is being kept in isolation but he's not talking. We are tracing his movements hoping that he managed to leave something behind that will give us clues as to who the leader is or where he lives.

"We think a Mr. Parviz Jalili is the money man for the organization and that he is living in Paris. This information is based on a phone call program we have been working. We believe he is the man Carl and Ann Lukin found in Zurich. We have a few telephoto shots of him, and now that Ann is dead, Carl is the only person who has actually laid eyes on him. So I am sending Carl to Paris to see if we can find him."

"How is Carl holding up after the death of his wife?"

"He returned to the Farm after Ann's funeral and buried himself in his work. He doesn't socialize much, he runs miles each day, studies twice as hard as before, and buries his anger. I almost feel sorry for the leaders of Islam's Fire when Carl finds them. He is not going to be satisfied until he kills everyone responsible for Ann's death."

"I hope he can satisfy his vengeance so that he can get back to a normal life. What else do we know about this organization?"

"We believe the leader of Islam's Fire is living in Islamabad, Pakistan and that the planning is done there. We've located three training camps in Pakistan's rugged mountain areas. The mountain areas are governed by local warlords and operate independently of any Pakistani government direction. There is some question as to whether the Pakistani army is even capable of successfully taking on the warlords, and so long as Islam's Fire continues to pay off the warlords, they are left alone.

"The Pakistanis are not about to let our troops go in and clean them out and they are reluctant to take any action themselves. We believe their reluctance is out of fear that such a raid will set off a revolt within their country. If we send in troops to clean out the camps it will be viewed by all Pakistanis as an invasion by America, and Islam's Fire's goals will appear justified and its terrorist actions will have been vindicated.

"Our options are rather limited. We can put pressure on the Pakistani government by cutting off support and encouraging sanctions by other nations unless Pakistan does something. But those actions are hard to get and difficult to maintain.

"Second, we can cut the head off of the snake, so to speak, and hope the movement will die out, but that may or may not work.

"The third possibility is to capture the leader and bring him back here for a trial. The problem with that is it will incur the wrath of the Pakistanis if we go into their country and kidnap one of their citizens as part of the rendition program.

"Finally, if we put the leader on trial it just gives him a platform from which to speak and challenges Islam's Fire to carry out more attacks. In essence, he becomes a martyr to rally around whether he is convicted or not.

"We already have the terrorist who is responsible for the blackout on the West Coast and the bombings in New York. We can make our case to the world during his trial. Furthermore, with Rossman we have a great deal of evidence to support our case. For the leader of Islam's Fire we only have supposition at this point, no real hard evidence."

"Dick, it sounds like you're advising that we just kill the money man and the leaders of Islam's Fire, and take a strong diplomatic position with Pakistan regarding the training camps."

"Yes sir, I guess I am. Diplomacy may work with regard to eliminating the training camps but I doubt that it will do much to encourage the Pakistanis to take action against Islam's Fire. The Pakistanis don't want the training camps either. They are as much of a threat to Pakistan as they are to us."

"You are probably right, Dick. Okay, let's get this done before they have a chance to regroup."

32

The Director started the meeting with, "Sorry to drag you out of training camp two months early Carl, you can finish up when this project is completed. The President wants those responsible for the bombings on the West Coast and New York City put on trial. The FBI has Simon Rossman, the man responsible for the recruiting and organizing of the terrorist cells in California and in Princeton. But he is not the head of Islam's Fire, and we want the top man in the organization dealt with. Aaron, why don't you tell us what we know or think we know."

"Okay, here is what we think the organization looks like. At this time our analysts place the Islamic students, and others, as worker bees at the bottom rung of the organization chart, they are the expendables. The madrassas are turning out new radical students all the time. It is not difficult for terrorist organizations to fill their ranks with radical young men or impoverished people that have nothing to lose. The only requirement is some training and a sense of purpose, which the madrassas and training camps provide.

"Next up on the organization chart are the recruiters and organizers. We know that Rossman was on this level but we don't know how many others there are. Our phone program has turned up interesting numbers in France, England, and Denmark plus two other U.S. numbers, and we are continuing to track them. At this time we think that there are at least eight cells operating in the United States and Europe. Two new recruiters and organizers are here in the United States and at least three cells, and possibly a fourth. Rossman had organized one on the West Coast and we believe two others on the East Coast. One of which was destroyed after the New York City bombing. The FBI is still trying to locate the other East Coast cell. They think it may be in the Boston area.

"The next level appears to be the management level with our friend Mr. Parviz Jalili as the money man, and the leader, whom we believe to be the person in Islamabad we haven't identified as yet. There are probably three or four others at this level but we aren't sure of that at this time.

"We have passed on to our allies the names of the students we know about. Along with their fingerprints, the suspect telephone numbers, and any cryptic phone messages that we have recorded. These have gone to the appropriate agencies we trust in the Countries that I have mentioned. Hopefully they will be able to connect the dots in their respective Countries.

"The FBI is still interrogating Rossman and other cell members we have captured, and hopefully we'll get more information soon."

"Okay gentlemen, where do you suggest we go from here, Carl, Aaron?"

Carl said, "Our only real leads are Professor Parviz Jalili and the telephone numbers. I think I have to go back to Zurich and learn all that I can about our Professor. Anything that might give us an indication as to how he lives his life, his habits, likes, dislikes, friends, and hobbies."

"I already see differences between Islam's Fire and Al Qaeda and a number of similarities," added Aaron, "the focus of Al Qaeda seems to be targeting military and government targets, ships, military barracks, and embassies in an effort to force out the American presence from all Arabic countries, either through direct confrontation or terror bombings. They're also using terror tactics against our allies in an effort to stop support of our efforts.

"On the other hand, Islam's Fire seems to be targeting the civilian population rather than governmental installations in an effort to create an atmosphere of fear in the Countries that are seen as crusaders against Islam. Examples are the bombings in California, New York and the Marriot in Islamabad. There may be other attacks that fit into this category and have been attributed to Al Qaeda or other terrorist groups rather than Islam's Fire.

"The people that we know about in Islam's Fire seem to come from well-to-do families, not the average working class, rather the educated and professional ranks of society. They seem comfortable, and even prefer to live and operate in Western societies. I believe that over the years they have gotten used to a Western lifestyle and really don't want to give it up. I think we will catch these people in Western cities and not in the mountains of Pakistan. They have led much too comfortable lives to now be satisfied living in caves.

"Al Qaeda draws its troops from all classes but the majority seem to be the poorer and undereducated. They are religious zealots and fanatics with little to lose in life. The idea that they will receive their reward in heaven seems far better than their continued lot in this life. If you have nothing, and nothing to look forward to, then life is not worth living, so why not give in to Muslim ideology that promises the rewards in the afterlife?

"I think Islam's Fire is just getting started and they will continue to target civilians in the U.S. and Europe. If this is true, then Parviz is probably in France as the telephone calls seem to suggest. I believe the calls to the U.S. and other Western countries are directed to terrorist cell organizers.

"There is one thing that Islam's Fire and Al Qaeda do have in common. They both need money to operate their training camps, buy equipment, transportation, supplies, and the other things necessary to make an organization function. While they have private and governmental sponsors, they also receive support from Islamic charities, such as Lashkar Taiba and HAMAS, but it is not enough. They have increasingly had to turn to theft, credit card fraud, kidnapping for ransom, extortion, and drug trafficking, to name just a few of the methods they use as a means of supporting their activities.

"That's why Al Qaeda and now Islam's Fire have been involved in criminal activity and why Islam's Fire stole $985 million dollars from World Bank. The fact that the bank got most of their money back is going to put a crimp in their operations, but not stop them. I believe that Parviz Jalili is the money man. He is an economist and has some formal training in handling large sums of money, and he is bright enough to handle investments, banking, and currency investments.

"We have further indication that he is Islam's Fire's money man from some of the calls he has received. Although the calls are cryptic they all have one thing in common, they are all asking for money.

"Once we learn all we can about this man, we start looking for him in Paris. If we find him we keep an eye on him until he leads us to other members of the management group." added Carl.

"I agree with Carl," said Aaron. "There are probably two other cell organizers operating in the U.S. We don't have any idea how many cells they have put together. And I agree that we have to start in Zurich to find the trail of Parviz. Only this time we can call in the Swiss police, because Parviz took part of the five million that was stolen from the World Bank so he is now a common criminal. Since Parviz has skipped the Country, he already knows that we are after him, so the police can be as open as they want in asking questions, and Carl is free to work with them as a private investigator working for the bank. Or the FBI can fix Carl up with an ID. Once we learn all we can about Parviz's habits, we move on to Paris."

"This sounds like a plan. I hate to do this to you, Carl, so soon after losing your wife, but you will be going to Zurich as soon as we can get you some ID." said the Director.

"Sir, there is nothing in this world more important to me right now than killing these bastards." The anger in Carl's voice was palpable.

33

The plane had landed and Carl was heading toward the door leading to customs when two men approached, saying, "Mr. Carl Lukin?"

"Yes."

They introduced themselves as members of the Zurich police and led him to an office adjacent to the customs office. They asked to see his credentials and then asked if he was carrying a gun. When he said that he was, they told him he was not permitted to carry a gun on Swiss soil and asked for it, saying that it would be returned to him on his departure. Carl pulled the gun from his shoulder holster, ejected the clip and pulled back the slide, ejecting the bullets from the chamber, and handed the gun butt first to the two police officers. They walked out of the building to a Mercedes sedan parked at the curb. One of the police officers said they were going to police headquarters to meet the Chief of Police.

When they arrived, Carl was ushered into an office where a man introduced himself as Heinrich Gant, Chief of Police, and a second man, Sergeant Brinks. After some polite conversation Herr Gant said, "How can the Zurich police help the FBI?"

"I am investigating a bank theft of five million dollars. The money was wire transferred to the Credit Suisse Bank by the thieves. Part of that money was apparently withdrawn by a Professor Parviz Jalili. I have been sent to Zurich to find the Professor and recover the stolen money, and if possible, find out who besides the Professor was involved in the theft."

"Zurich police received a warrant for the Professor's arrest a few months ago but have been unable to locate him. The Professor has apparently left Switzerland and left no forwarding address," Herr Grant interjected.

"The reason I have been sent here is to learn all I can about the man, his habits, and his likes and dislikes. We hope that by building a profile of the man we can get an indication of where he might have gone."

"I wish you the best of luck. Sergeant Brinks will assist you all he can while you are in Zurich." Grant handed Carl back his gun, saying, "I trust you will not use this weapon on Swiss soil."

After thanking Herr Gant for his courtesy, Carl and Sergeant Brinks left the office and went out of the building to the parking lot. Sergeant Brinks said that he would take Carl to his hotel and that they could begin their search in the morning.

"It's still early, I would like to go to the University and get started, and go to the hotel afterwards, if you don't mind."

"Okay, then let's go."

At the University they went to the Economics Department and, after introducing themselves, asked to see the Economics Department head. They were led to his office, the sign on the door read Professor Peter Lund. Sergeant Brinks knocked on the door. A voice said, "Come in."

Carl and Sergeant Brinks entered the cluttered room and after introductions, Sergeant Brinks explained that they were making inquires about Professor Parviz Jalili.

"What is the problem? Is Professor Jalili in some trouble?"

"No, he is not in trouble. He might have some information that could help the Americans in an investigation."

"How long has Professor Jalili been teaching at this University?" asked Carl?

Professor Lund scratched his head and said, "Professor Jalili has been at the University close to thirty-five years, first as a student, then as an instructor, and now as full Professor. Parviz became a full Professor about fifteen years ago, but I would have to check the records for the exact dates."

"The secretary said that Mr. Jalili no longer works here, is that correct?"

"Yes, that is correct. Mr. Jalili failed to come to work about six months ago. We called his home but he did not answer. We checked with his landlady, several of his friends, and the young lady that he kept company with but no one has seen him. We finally had to terminate his contract and have one of the other professors take over his teaching duties."

"Could you please give us the names of his close friends at the University and the name of his lady friend?" asked Carl.

"Of course, but he really did not have many close friends here at the University. His girlfriend was a student at the University. She was in a car accident in her third year that somewhat disfigured her but she recovered and returned to school. She majored in economics where she met Professor Jalili, her name is Elena Schmitt. Most of the other people he knew were more in the line of acquaintances. He kept to himself, attended very few of the faculty functions. He taught his classes, kept regular office hours for his students, but other than that he seemed to spend his time writing books on economics. But I will give you the names of those that I know."

"Did Professor Jalili pick up his mail before he left? If not, we would like to see any mail that may have accumulated for him."

"I don't know if I should give you his private correspondence."

Sergeant Brinks spoke up, saying "We only want to look at the return addresses on the mail in order to identify people who might have more information on Professor Jalili's whereabouts. We have no intention of invading his privacy by reading his correspondence."

Professor Lund asked the secretary to bring in Professor Jalili's mail. Then he said, "You may use my conference table to look through the mail. If you have no other questions I have a few matters to attend to."

"Nothing else at this time, sir, thank you for your help," said Carl.

Carl and Sergeant Brinks looked through the mail but there was no personal correspondence. It mostly consisted of advertisements from publishers, office memos, and general advertising. The addresses of the publishers were noted so that they could be checked out to insure that they were legitimate publishing companies.

As Carl and Sergeant Brinks left the University, Carl said, "Let's make one more stop if we can find the address of his girlfriend, Elena Schmitt."

Sergeant Brinks agreed. When they reached the car, the Sergeant used the in-car computer to look up the address. There were thirty two Schmitts listed but only one was named Elena. The address was only a short distance from the University. They reached the apartment house five minutes later.

They entered the building and found the mail box for Elena Schmitt. They pushed the buzzer for her apartment but got no answer. They then pushed the buzzer for the manager of the apartment house, it was answered by a woman. They announced themselves and were buzzed in. The manager, an elderly woman, met them in the hall outside the door of the first apartment. They identified themselves, explaining that they were looking for Elena Schmitt.

The manager said, "Elena left for Paris this morning to visit her friend."

"Do you happen to know where in Paris Elena is staying?"

"Elena, such a sweet woman, she gave me the name of the hotel where she would be staying and a telephone number in case I needed to reach her."

"Can you give me that information? It's important that we talk with her."

"I suppose so," she agreed, then reached for her glasses, a pencil, and paper.

"Did she tell you why she was going to Paris?"

"She was going to see her friend, the Professor from the University. He is such a nice man. When he visits Elena, he often brings flowers or a box of chocolates. Elena is watching her weight so she sometimes gives me the chocolates. I'm too old to worry about my weight."

"I don't suppose you have a photograph of Elena, do you?"

"No, but she will be easy to recognize. She is a little shorter than the Sergeant and thin with blond hair and a scar that runs down her cheek and across her lips. She received the scar in an automobile accident when she was a young woman attending the University. She is very self conscious about the scar."

"Thank you, you have been very helpful."

Back in the car, Carl asked Sergeant Brinks to take him to the airport, saying he would fly to Paris that evening. Luckily, he had not checked into a hotel yet and his baggage was still in the car.

When they got to the airport, Sergeant Brinks offered to take him through security so he would not need to check his gun.

34

Before Carl boarded the plane in Zurich, he called Aaron Kovak. "I identified Parviz Jalili's girlfriend but she went to Paris this morning to meet Parviz. I have the address where she is staying and I'm on my way there now to find her and hopefully him. Have some help join me at the airport."

"Okay, I'll have someone meet you at the airport."

He cleared customs in Paris and entered the baggage area, then walked through the doors leading to the street. A beautiful young woman came running up to him, saying, "Carl, it has been so long." She threw her arms around him and kissed him on the cheek saying, "Come, Uncle John is waiting at the car, this way." With the young woman chattering about family they walked arm in arm toward a small blue car idling at the curb.

As they drove into town the driver introduced himself as John Cagen, Chief of the Paris station, and the young woman as Adriana Lignet a field operative. He said, "Aaron called a short time ago but did not give us much information other than your flight number.

He sent a picture of you and asked if we could pick you up and give you as much assistance as we could. So what can we do for you?"

"We need to find a woman named Elena Schmitt. She's in Paris to see a man named Parviz Jalili. We believe Parviz is one of the leaders in the Islam's Fire terror organization and Elena Schmitt is his long-time girlfriend. We don't know whether Elena is part of the terrorist group or if she was simply used as part of his cover. In either case, they have had a twenty-year relationship that's appears more than casual.

"Elena arrived early this morning and is staying at the Luxor Bastille Hotel, at 22 rue Moreau."

They drove to the hotel Luxor Bastille and scanned the surrounding buildings. Almost directly across the street was the Montmatre Clignancourt Hotel.

Carl and Adriana checked in as a couple and asked for a room fronting the street. They selected a corner room that looked down on the entry to the Luxor Bastille. Adriana and John left and were back within an hour. Adriana had packed a bag and John had gathered the surveillance equipment they might need.

That afternoon they spotted a woman who fit the description of Elena approaching the hotel. From the direction she was coming they were unable to see the right side of her face. Adriana called one of the team members who was sitting in a car parked on the street. He left the car and walked toward Elena, passing her on the right. He was able to see the scar clearly. Now that they had located her they had to find out in which room she was staying.

Carl decided to send a small basket of fruit with a card saying, "Compliments of the hotel." The basket was delivered to the hotel desk by a team member. The desk clerk in turn called a bellhop over and told him to deliver the basket to room 221, Elena Schmitt's room. Adriana, who was sitting in the lobby, got up and followed the bellhop and basket to the second floor, and noted the room number when the fruit was delivered.

That evening when Elena left the hotel to meet Parviz, a team slipped into the room and planted several bugs and a small video camera in the air vent. The camera was connected to a small transmitter able to send a signal that could be received anywhere within a radius of a half mile. While the bugs and video camera were being planted, Adriana and Carl followed Elena to a small grocery store where she bought meat, vegetables, and a loaf of bread. From there she went to an apartment house five blocks away. It looked as if Parviz was going to get a home-cooked meal that evening.

The following morning Elena and Parviz left the apartment, returning to the Hotel Luxor Bastille, where she packed her bag and checked out. They returned to Parviz's apartment and Elena settled in.

The closest apartment that Carl and Adriana could find to the one shared by Parviz and Elena was on the next street one block away. It was still within range of the bugs and video camera that would be removed from the hotel room and planted in Parviz's apartment. The apartment was not modern by any means but it did have a garage that opened to the alley behind the building.

At ten the next morning Elena and Parviz left their apartment and walked to a bus stop. They went to the Louvre museum and entered. Carl called John, saying, "It looks like Parviz is playing tour guide, their apartment should be clear for a couple of hours."

Within minutes a telephone van pulled up in front of the apartment house and two men got out and entered it. They found the apartment by looking at the names on the mailboxes in the lobby. Parviz Jalili was not listed but there was only one name on clean white paper, the rest of the name tags were beginning to turn yellow with age.

They entered the apartment, checking the books and papers to see if they could find a name to confirm that they were in the right apartment. On a table they found a copy of the Quran but they did not find anything with Jalili's name on it.

Going on the assumption that they had the right apartment they placed bugs that would pick up any sound in the living room and bedroom, and a bug in the telephone. They also installed two video cameras, one in the bedroom, and the other in the living room. The last item installed was a motion detector which was placed in the living room. Carl would be able to hear and see everything that was said and done in the apartment.

After installing the cameras and bugs the men took a thorough look at the apartment looking for details that were out of place or inconsistent with their surroundings. There were impressions on the carpet that indicated that the stereo cabinet that stood against the wall had recently been moved. They pulled the cabinet from the wall and found a briefcase behind the cabinet. In it they found $450,000 in cash and a laptop computer. They tried to start the computer but it would not boot up without a password. They could have gotten around the password by pulling out the battery and reinserting it, but the next time Parviz used the computer he would know that someone had tampered with it.

Before putting the briefcase back they photographed the computer from several angles along with the contents of the briefcase. They put the briefcase back behind the stereo, making sure to move the stereo cabinet back into the same carpet indentation.

They searched the rest of the apartment but found nothing else of interest. Before they left they photographed each room and any mail and documents they could find.

At four that afternoon Elena and Parviz returned to the apartment. Parviz said, "Elena, I have a business meeting that I have to attend. It should not take long, but when I get back we will go out to dinner."

A short time later Parviz left the apartment and walked two blocks to a main street and hailed a taxi, directing the driver to take him to the Paris Mosque.

The Paris Mosque is a beautiful structure with large central courtyards, fountains, and carpeted prayer rooms, one for men, and a side gallery for women. The courtyard is surrounded by a covered walkway lined with columns that are made of pink marble. In the center of the courtyard is a large fountain from which water cascades into a small pond. The walkways and the surrounding buildings are covered by intricate geometric designs in tile. Adjacent to the entry to the courtyard is a minaret on which the entire outside wall is covered with intricate geometric designs in mosaic tile.

Parviz took off his shoes and entered the large prayer room filled with men on their knees praying. He knelt on the floor and began saying his prayers. Soon another man entered, knelt next to him and began praying. When afternoon prayers ended Parviz and the man next to him lingered until they were the last to leave. They walked to an exit where they talked in hushed tones. Parviz then took a taxi back to his apartment. Both men were photographed as they left the mosque.

A short time after returning to the apartment, Parviz and Elena went to a nearby restaurant.

That evening, copies of all the photographs were sent to Langley where they were examined and added to the growing collection of information. The man Parviz had met was identified as Mohammed Aswat an Islamic political activist.

35

Carl and Adriana had the night and early morning shift to watch Parviz and Elena. Carl would wake up early and check the monitor to make sure Parviz and Elena were still asleep. Even though a motion detector had been installed in the apartment that would sound an alarm to wake Carl if anyone began moving in Parviz's apartment, he felt better if he could see them still in bed when he got up.

Carl's morning routine consisted of checking the monitor, starting the coffee then taking a quick shower. After he dressed he woke Adriana and kept an eye on the monitor while she took a shower and dressed. After Adriana had dressed he slipped out for a quick trip to the bakery for breakfast rolls and the newspaper. By the time he got back, John and Max, the two other team members, had arrived.

The difficult part of the monitoring occurred at night when Carl and Adriana were monitoring the apartment alone. If Parviz and Elena were having sex Carl and Elena would read a book or the paper. They did not want to be voyeurs on the intimate sexual relations of others, but they remained very aware of what Parviz and Elena were doing. Even though they were not watching the monitor screen, the sounds were very clear.

Carl was a tall, muscular and very attractive man, and Adriana was a young, slim, tall, very beautiful woman. To make things more difficult they were very aware of each other and privy to the intimate relations of another couple. Although they did not stare at the surveillance monitor, they were acutely aware of the frequent sexual activity that was taking place. They heard the sound of bodies move against each other and every sigh or moan.

Since Carl and Adriana shared the same small apartment they were very conscious of each other's sexuality. Carl had not been with another woman since his wife's death and Adriana was not a woman any normal male could easily ignore. Although he wanted to maintain a professional relationship with Adriana, it was extremely difficult in this situation, made worse by the sexual activity that they could hear and see.

The apartment Carl and Adriana shared had only one bedroom with two small beds. Although they did not share the same bed they were physically very close to each other. They could still smell the perfume or after shave lotion, hear the other person roll over, or the soft rhythmic breathing of sleep. They tried to keep a purely professional relationship between them but it was not easy, and as time passed it became more difficult.

The early morning, before the other team members arrived, was particularly difficult. As time wore on, they became more casual as they went about getting ready for the day. Sometimes Adriana would step out of the bathroom wearing only a bra and panties to refill her coffee cup, or Carl would be in the kitchenette in only his briefs fiddling with the coffee pot when Adriana came out of the bedroom wearing a very filmy robe that clearly revealed each curve of her near perfect body. Carl's body automatically responded to seeing Adriana and the result was clearly visible to Adriana. There was nothing that Carl could do except quickly leave the room. After a week of mutual frustration Adriana came into the bedroom and instead of going to her bed she pulled back the covers on Carl's bed and slipped in. Without a word Carl reached over and pulled her to him. For Carl their lovemaking was a way to calm his lust, but for Adriana it was both physical and emotional.

The days passed with Parviz playing tour guide, showing Elena the sights of Paris. One evening Parviz told Elena that he had some business to take care of. Thanks to the bugs, Carl and John were waiting. Earlier that afternoon Parviz had called a friend and arranged to have two men go with him that evening as bodyguards. They were to wait for him just outside the building at eight that evening.

Carl and John watched the monitor as Parviz removed the briefcase from behind the stereo cabinet just before leaving the apartment. He hugged and kissed Elena, saying that he would be back later and take her out for a late dinner. He then went downstairs where two thuggish men were waiting for him.

It was just getting dark, but Carl could see Parviz come out of the building and join the two men who had been waiting. After a few minutes of conversation, Parviz passed money to each of the men and together they walked toward a subway entrance.

Carl and John followed as the three men entered the subway and waited for a train that would take them to the outskirts of Paris. As the train made its way to the Eastern part of the city, the cars began to empty out and the station platforms were much less crowded. With each stop the crowd thinned and it became more difficult to blend in with remaining passengers. It was becoming obvious that Carl and John were not the usual subways commuters in this part of town.

Coming up out of the subway they found themselves in what was clearly not the best part of Paris. There were few working street lights, although some light escaped from behind the cheap curtains covering the apartment windows that faced the street. Most businesses were closed except for a small Algerian restaurant advertising couscous and falafel in the window, and two small coffeehouses. It was a decidedly seedy part of town.

Carl and John started to follow Parviz and the two bodyguards as they walked down the street and turned a corner. When Carl and John reached the corner the three men had disappeared. Carl and John began to walk faster hoping to catch sight of them at the next corner. As they came abreast of a dark alley, Carl heard a thud and felt arms grab him and pull him around, throwing him into the alley. John lay on the ground.

Carl didn't try to break the grip on his arms or fight his assailant. His reflexive action was to move with the flow of energy, not fight it. In doing so he hit the second man hard in the chest with his shoulder with enough force to knock him backwards to the ground. The first man, still on his feet, charged. Carl could see the flash of a knife in his hand.

Rather than try to run away as one would expect, he stepped into the man and used his forearm to parry the knife, forcing the blade to pass close by his left side. As the blade passed his side, he grabbed the man's arm with his left hand and pulled, lowering and twisting his body as he threw his assailant to the pavement. With a loud crack he broke the man's arm over his knee. There was the beginning of a scream as Carls fingers jabbed into the man's throat, crushing his larynx.

The second man had regained his feet and started to move toward Carl. Carl reached for the holstered berretta at the small of his back, brought his arm forward, and fired two quick shots into the man's chest. The man stumbled for a second then fell backwards.

Carl ran to John but could see that he was alright. He was getting to his feet and holding his head. John brushed Carl aside, saying "I'm okay, find Parviz."

Carl ran to the next corner but saw no one on the street. Parviz had disappeared. He returned to the alley and saw John going through the pockets of the two men. He found a small amount of cash in each man's pocket but no identification.

John took the money making it look like the two men had been killed in a robbery. There was nothing left to do but go back to the apartment and see if Parviz would return. They left the alley and started walking back toward the subway entrance, conscious of the silence. No one had opened a door, shouted, or turned on outside lights in spite of the gunfire.

Carl said, "We really stood out by the time we reached the last stop, they must have spotted us. We were led to that alley for an ambush. Parviz must have run into one of those buildings and out the back door."

They took the subway back to the apartment and waited to see if Parviz would return. He did not.

Parviz was a fugitive for a second time, and it was no easier than the first time. He was a nervous wreck, perspiration wet his face and shirt and he was breathing hard. He went straight to a train station and bought a ticket to London. Then went into a men's room, found an empty stall, and sat down and waited. After an hour his nerves started to settle down and the adrenalin began to wear off. He could think more clearly now.

He finally left the men's room and went to a kiosk in the station lobby and bought a razor, shaving cream, and magazine. Returning to the restroom he shaved off his moustache and goatee with shaking hands. Just before the train was to leave, Parviz boarded and found his compartment. Then sitting, he pretended to read his magazine while watching the other passengers as they boarded the train.

How had they found him? He had used an alias to rent the apartment and when he had purchased a prepaid cell phone he did not have to give his name or address. He had not used the name Parviz Jalili since entering France. The only thing he could think of was that they had found Elena and were watching her. As much as he cared for her he would never contact her again.

The train pulled out of the station and headed west. The last stop would be to transfer passengers to the electric train that went through the tunnel under the English Channel.

Not knowing what had happened to Parviz, Elena checked

police stations and hospitals, but found no trace of him. After a week of searching she finally decided to go back to Zurich. She had fallen in love with Parviz over the years, and his disappearance for a second time in a year shattered her heart.

The newspapers did not carry the news of the two dead men found in an alley in the Muslim section of the city. It was such a common occurrence that it was not considered newsworthy.

36

Director Rice said, "I have asked Special Agent Jean Peters from the FBI to sit in on this briefing with us today. I believe you have all met before. Carl, why don't you start?"

Carl brought the others up to date on his activities in Zurich and the events in Paris. He told them, "In my opinion, Elena Schmitt was simply a woman who was very self conscious about her disfigurement and had received comfort from Parviz. Over the years comfort had grown into love. Although Parviz might have developed some affection for Elena, she was more of a convenience for him, someone who could be discarded when she was no longer needed. I suggest that we keep tabs on Elena, but I doubt that Parviz will contact her again."

Aaron picked up the story, saying, "It has been a week since Parviz disappeared and we have only one lead. Two days after Parviz left Paris, a new phone number was used to call Islamabad from London. It's the first time that number has showed up. It's too much of a coincidence to be ignored. We will of course continue to keep track of the calls to and from all the other numbers, but it's my belief that Parviz went to London. I think it's time to brief the Brits on what we have and invite them to the party."

Jean jumped in with, "The Brits are certainly of a mind to listen to us and help in any way they can in spite of the manpower they are expending keeping track of their own suspected terrorist groups. Since the London subway bombing in 2005, they're very sensitive to the issue of terrorism. Having one known terrorist come into their country would be considered a very serious matter.

"London has a large Muslim population and has experienced a few episodes of civil unrest and terrorism at the hands of their own Muslim community, most of the radicals that have been identified as potential terrorists are people who were born and grew up in England. Many Imams are considered radical and believed to be recruiting people for Al Qaeda. Radical Imams have encouraged a number of Muslims to go to Pakistani training camps. The Imams have also been demanding that Muslims who break the law be judged using Sharia law rather than English common law. Of course, the English have not given in to that demand.

"The failure of the British to agree to this demand has further aggravated the Muslim community. Many in the law enforcement community have expressed the belief that it is only a matter of time before England experiences a major terrorist attack from their own Muslim citizens. The worst fears of the British police were realized on July 7, 2005, when eight men set explosives in the London subway system causing fifty deaths and a number of injuries. Five of the terrorists, all British citizens, were put on trial. It was thought that the rest of those involved in the bombing had died in the blast or left the city.

"As of now the British are trying to keep track of over two hundred suspected individuals or terrorists groups and having one more known terrorist leader in London is a situation they'll want to deal with fast."

The Director said, "It looks like we have to bring the Brits up to speed on our little problem and see if they can help. I'll call Alan Sheppard, the Director of MI6, and let him know that Parviz Jalili is believed to be in London." The Director then asked if Jean would be willing to join Carl early the next morning on a trip to England.

Jean nodded, saying, "Yes sir, I'll let my boss know."

37

It was close to 6:00 A.M. when Jean Peters and Carl boarded one of the CIA's Gulfstream-G5s. They landed at Heathrow Airport a little after five in the afternoon, British time, and were met at the gate by a man from MI5. After introducing himself as Inspector Jay Nash, he said, "Please follow me and we will avoid the boys at customs."

He lead them to a small room just before entering the customs area, and out a second door into a corridor that lead to the baggage area. From there they went out an exit door to the sidewalk where a car was waiting. With a smile he said, "I know that you are carrying weapons, but please don't shoot anybody unless it's absolutely necessary. It's frowned on and a God awful amount of paperwork if you do."

With a straight face Carl said, "We won't unless we can't get a decent cup of coffee."

That brought a chuckle out of Jay, who responded, "I'll keep that in mind."

The ride into town took about twenty minutes, with Jay pointing out various sights of interest as they passed. The car finally pulled into a courtyard where guards checked the car and the passengers' IDs. They were told to proceed to an underground garage in what was an otherwise typical non-inspiring government building. Jay said, "You can leave your luggage in the car if you would like, it will be safe. During your stay in London I will be available to drive you around. Both the car and I are available to you any time night or day."

They entered the building, had IDs checked again, and received visitor badges. They took an elevator to the top floor office of Alan Sheppard, Director of MI6.

There were several other people in the room, including Milton Howard, Director of MI5. After introductions they sat at a Conference table where Carl gave a brief description of events that lead them to Parviz Jalili, ending with the escape of Parviz in Paris and the belief that he had made his way to London. Although no one said it, it was obvious that the British were not happy to hear that piece of information.

Jean followed up with a description of the FBI's capture of Rossman and the ten terrorist cell members. She explained that they also had some evidence that three other cells were operating in the U.S. she ended with the telephone calls to the U.S. that connected Parviz to the U.S. terrorist cells and terrorist cells operating in Europe and the Far East.

Director Sheppard said, "Like the CIA, MI6's efforts are directed toward the gathering of intelligence outside of England. The responsibility of MI5 is to gather intelligence, and investigate terrorist activities within England. I believe the problem that you have presented us with falls within their jurisdiction. We work quite closely together so be assured MI6 will be watching this case, but Director Howard and his staff will be your principal contact."

Director Howard in a rather irritated voice said, "It appears we have another bloody terrorist leader in our midst."

He paused to think for a few seconds and said, "The easiest way to enter London from Paris would be by air or by train. With the photographs and surveillance film you have and the rather narrow time frame that he likely used to make his entry, we can use facial recognition equipment to review passengers from both train and aircraft. After we confirm that he is here, finding him will be a little more difficult. Will your boys at NSA be able to help?"

"If he uses his cell phone again we'll be able to narrow the search area to the cell phone tower he used, which is not going to help much. Unfortunately his phone doesn't have GPS location capability. If your people can work with NSA, we may be able to triangulate his position a little closer but I doubt it. Lacking a good technical solution, I believe it's going to take a lot of old fashioned police work. If we start asking too many questions we'll scare him off, he's sure to be a little edgy already after his escape from Zurich and Paris. We know he is a religious man so it's likely that he will start going to a mosque for prayer and to associate with other Muslims, so that will help," said Carl.

"There are several areas in London where those of Islamic faith have settled. Until we have something more concrete to go on it would be like looking for a squirrel in the forest," said Director Howard.

"Without help narrowing down the area, the best we can do is show his photograph to our people and tell them to keep their eyes open. We will also check with our confidential informants. In the meantime, Inspector Nash will work with you and be your liaison to both me and Director Sheppard."

There was not much that could be done until Parviz made a move, or was identified by the police or their informants. Inspector Nash offered to drive them to their hotel.

38

On the way to the hotel where Carl and Jean were staying, Inspector Nash explained that several sections of the city have large Islamic populations. "Although they've had a few problems in Muslim areas, for the most part the Muslims have tried to integrate into British society. Still, I don't think Parviz would have any difficulty finding lodging and support within the local Islamic population."

"Jean has to go back to the States tomorrow, but I would like to drive around and get a feel for the area if that is okay with you?"

"I can take Jean to Heathrow and then I'll pick you up at nine."

Carl was told that London had excellent public transportation so it was not necessary that Parviz live in any particular area to have access to a mosque or restaurants that catered to the Muslim population. But as Carl and Nash discussed the problem they came to the conclusion that Muslim communities and Mosques offered the best odds that that was where Parviz would be found. As a stranger to the city, Parviz would in all likelihood go to places that offered some degree of comfort, and he would want to live in areas where he would easily blend in with the local population.

The London Central Mosque was located near the Marylebone Station and the Baker Street Station and was easily accessible from anywhere in the city. Nash said, "The plan is to put plain clothes police near each of the entrances to the mosque and in the subway stations nearest the mosque.

"Each policeman will have several photographs of Parviz. Photographs that have been retouched to show him with and without a moustache or goatee, and with a full beard. Police will be in the subway station since they can be disguised as janitors or citizens waiting for a train. Putting surveillance on the entries to the mosque will be a little more difficult but not impossible."

For two days Jay introduced Carl to the city of London as they waited for Parviz to be sighted or a snitch to come forward with information. They didn't have to wait long. On the fourth day Parviz used his new cell phone to call Islamabad. The number was tied to a tower in Westminster, Central North London. Unfortunately the call was too short to get the needed triangulation but the police now had an area on which to focus their efforts.

During the second week of surveillance, police spotted a man that appeared to fit Parviz's description entering a mosque. He looked considerably different than the photographs. The man they sighted was growing a full beard and it was now almost a half inch long. Although his general appearance had changed, and he was dressed differently, Carl recognized him. In addition to his new features, the way he walked and carried himself added further confirmation that it was Parviz.

Parviz had a top floor apartment on the east side of the Regents Canal, a half mile from the Mosque. He now went by the name of Oussama Kassir.

That Friday when Parviz went to prayer, two members of MI5 slipped into his apartment where they placed listening devices in each of the rooms along with video cameras, after which they thoroughly searched the apartment.

They found the briefcase containing the cash and the laptop computer in the attic crawl space. After opening the computer case they disconnected the cable to the hard drive and connected a cable from a duplicate computer that had been supplied by the CIA. Within a few minutes they had copied Parviz's entire hard drive to their computer. After removing their cables, they inserted a small flat disk the size of a twenty-five cent piece next to the battery, connecting two leads to the battery for power, and a small ribbon cable to the motherboard. Before closing the computer case they photographed it, then returned it to the briefcase and put the briefcase back in the attic crawl space. The last thing they did was to photograph everything in the apartment. They left the apartment just fifteen minutes before Parviz returned.

The disk that had been placed in Parviz's computer was a small radio transmitter that would send every key stroke typed or message received to a relay transmitter located on a nearby power pole that re-sent the data to MI5 headquarters. The MI5 agents monitoring the signal from Parviz's computer could see everything that Parviz typed or received. A copy of the hard disk and a recording of all computer sessions were sent to the CIA and MI6 for further evaluation.

The plan now was to monitor all of Parviz's activities, his telephone, and computer work for the next three or four months. Within a short time the CIA, MI5 and MI6 had a good picture of the financial workings of Islam's Fire, including the names of donors, banks, account numbers, and transaction amounts and dates.

Although the stolen money had been retrieved by Dan Nakamura and Ann Curlin some time ago the leadership of Islam's Fire had not been told of its loss. Parviz handled all the cash and had been able to hide the loss. Using surplus money he had invested, and the continual influx of cash from supporters, he was able to continue operations. Parviz had been able to keep the loss a secret for the time being, but his surplus funds were running out. Once the leaders of Islam's Fire found out about the loss, Parviz's life would be forfeited and he knew it.

Businesses, individuals or charitable organizations would simply wire money to a numbered account in a bank in Switzerland. From there, Parviz would move the money to working accounts in various countries where training camps or cells were located. The leader of the cell could go to an ATM and draw out small amounts of cash, or go to the bank and draw out larger amounts if needed. Any excess funds that were received were invested by Parviz in stocks and bonds where they would stay, increasing in value until the time that the funds were required. That time was now. The portfolio that Parviz managed was quite impressive with a market value of over thirteen million dollars, but now, growing smaller each day.

Since Parviz held the purse strings, pilfering of funds was not a significant problem. If that were to occur, Parviz would simply not transfer any further funds to that account until the cell leader could account for the expenditures. If the cell leader could not, well, that was an issue that would be taken care of in a permanent fashion. In effect, Islam's Fire was run much like a successful business.

The information gathered by the CIA was shared with trusted security agencies around the world who would then watch to see who was drawing funds from the various accounts into which Parviz had transferred those monies. Within a relatively short time they were able to identify a number of cell members and leaders.

Where the information came from was always kept secret between the CIA, MI6 and MI5 organizations. All that other agencies were told was that the information was from a reliable source. If the receiving agency elected to ignore it, that was their problem.

When the CIA received a copy of the disk, they were able to immediately crack the passwords giving them access to e-mail and other correspondence. They found that the various cell leaders communicated with Islam's Fire's management through the use of e-mail. The e-mail addresses were hosted by small service providers and were owned by individuals using fictitious names and addresses. The e-mail addresses and passwords were distributed only to members who had a need to use the e-mail.

The computers that were used were clones of legitimate business computers, making it difficult to identify who was using them. All payments to the service provider were made in cash.

Sensitive information was sent by courier. This included budgets, data for specific operations, costs for operating a camp, plans for future operations, and other pieces of information that a terrorist cell needed to convey or ask. Innocuous information was sometimes simply mailed since its meaning would only be understood by the recipient. Seemingly simple innocent questions were e-mailed and always in code.

The use of the cell phone was rare, and only used to convey something urgent or time sensitive. The result was that it would sometimes be months between calls, and then they were cryptic and very short.

Communications from Parviz to other managers were held to a minimum. Important issues were discussed when the operatives could meet in person, which typically happened every three or four months. For this reason it was much more difficult to chart the organization's management structure.

Parviz had one immediate problem to solve, if he was to stay in England he would need a new identity. That meant a new birth certificate, passport, driver's license, credit cards, national health card, and business cards. He would have to find someone who could provide these items for him. To find a forger he began to visit the rougher sections of the city looking for Muslims who might know such a person.

On one of these trips, Parviz stopped for something to eat in a coffeehouse. It was not long before a man in shabby clothes, obviously down in his luck, approached him and with a foul breath asked, "Are you the bloke who needs an identity card?"

Parviz, looking up, asked, "Do you know where I can get one?"

"I have an address for a man who can make them for you for a price."

"Who is this man? Where can I find him? How much will it cost?"

"I don't know how much it'll cost you, that's between you and him. All I have is an address, and if you want it it'll cost you fifty pounds, take it or leave it."

With that he started to shuffle away.

"Wait, I'll pay." Parviz handed the man a fifty pound note and the man gave him a slip of paper with a name and address then shuffled quickly out the door.

One of the two MI5 detectives following Parviz got up and followed the man into the street for a few blocks then pulled him into an alley, slammed him up against a wall and asked "What did you give that man?"

When the bum hesitated, in a menacing voice the detective said, "Answer my question or you'll end up floating face down in the Thames River."

The man, believing he had been hijacked by a member of the London mob told him everything. The detective told him to forget their little chat if he wanted to live.

The man nodded vigorously and shuffled down the street as fast as he could go.

Parviz left the coffeehouse and went to the address given him. It turned out to be a small camera shop owned by a short, sleazy looking Pakistani who asked, "What can I do for you?"

Looking uncomfortable, Parviz said, "I need new identity papers. I was told I can get them here."

The shop owner studied him for a moment then invited him into the back room saying, "Tell me what you need."

"I need a complete set of identification: identity card, driver's license, health card, passport, and anything else I will need for a new identity. How much will it cost?"

"I do first class work. My price is one thousand pounds."

"That is too much, I'll pay four hundred."

After twenty minutes of haggling they agreed on a price of five hundred and fifty pounds. Parviz gave him two hundred pounds as a down payment, the information that he needed, had his picture taken, and said, "I will be back in three days with the rest of the money."

The detective following Parviz noted the address of the camera shop and then trailed Parviz home.

39

Carl hadn't been to the home he and Ann had bought since Ann's funeral. On his return from Seattle, he had returned to the training camp and then gone to England. But with MI5 keeping an eye on Parviz there was little for him to do in England.

Rather than wait in London until something happened he decided to return home. After landing at Dulles Airport he made a short detour to Langley to fill in Director Rice, John Gray, and Aaron Kovak on what transpired in London, then home.

He took his bags to the bedroom, returned to the kitchen where he found a beer in the refrigerator, then stepped out to the back porch and sat sipping his beer. He thought about Ann and how she loved the farm they had bought in the Maryland countryside. When his eyes began to mist he got up for another beer.

The next morning Carl awakened early and went for a run. When he returned he had breakfast and decided to take a look around the farm. He noted how much work needed to be done, fences needed repairs, painting, underbrush cleared, and yard work.

The house had 2600 square feet with a full basement. It sat back about 100 yards from the county road that fronted the property. The front portion of the property was heavily wooded with the back half of the property cleared for pasture except for a narrow wooded strip that followed a stream.

For the next two weeks he would rise at five, go for a run, have a light breakfast then work outside, repairing fences, digging postholes, painting and doing the things that needed doing around farm property. He didn't quit until after dark. By the end of the second week he had lost ten pounds and his muscles had hardened. The work was hard but therapeutic.

Ann's memory moved to the background and became less intrusive as the problems of tracking Parviz, and the other leaders of Islam's Fire moved to the forefront of his thoughts. He found that he missed Adriana's company. He was not in love with her, but she was there when he needed someone's touch.

Over the following week he made arrangements for Dan Nakamura to take over running the investigation firm. It was a good complement to the computer security business.

He hired a live-in housekeeper and made arrangements to have a sophisticated security system for the house and immediate grounds installed.

By the fourth week he was ready to rejoin the hunt for his wife's killers.

40

In the weeks following his visit to the forger, Parviz started to have the same feeling he had in Paris, someone was watching him. He began paying closer attention to the people who got on the bus when he did, and he watched the cars that followed the bus. He became conscious of the people entering the subway when he did, or people simply walking down a street. When he went to mosque for prayer he began to notice people who didn't quite seem to fit. After a few weeks he began to notice patterns. There always seemed to be a man getting on the bus with him no matter where he was going. It may have been a different man, but occasionally it would be a man that he recognized. When he walked to the mosque there would always be a car parked at the curb with a man inside. As time went by he began to see the same cars and faces.

He was being followed, he was sure of it. He didn't know how they had found him but they had. That afternoon he copied his computer hard drive to a DVD. After putting the DVD in an envelope and addressing it, he went to the mosque. He waited until there was a good size crowd in the prayer hall, made his way to some men that he knew and asked one of them to do a favor for him. When the man asked what the favor was, Parviz passed the envelope to him with some cash, and asked him to mail it. The man stared at him for a few seconds then nodded and took the envelope and slipped it inside his coat.

After prayers Parviz went back to his apartment, took the briefcase from its hiding place, and grabbed his overcoat. He didn't know if the apartment was bugged or not, but he needed privacy, so he took the overcoat and briefcase into the small bathroom with him. He carefully examined the walls, ceiling, cabinets, and anyplace else a camera lens or microphone could possibly be installed. When he completed his examination he turned on the water in the tub and sink, thinking that if he had missed a microphone the running water would obscure any sounds he might make.

He began shaking with fear but managed to calm himself. He opened the briefcase and took out all the cash that he could stuff into the pockets of his overcoat and jacket. When he was through he closed the briefcase, turned off the running water, and left the apartment.

The briefcase he carried now had only the few thousand dollars he could not fit into his pockets, and his laptop computer. He walked to the subway and took a train to central London. He noticed two men that he had seen before get on the train with him. His hands shook but before he left the train he removed the computer from the briefcase. When the train stopped he joined the large crowd on the platform surging toward the exit stairs. He dropped the briefcase next to a trash can and started yelling that there was a bomb.

Since the previous subway bombing, people were nervous about the possibility of another attack. It did not take much to panic the crowd. People began to run in every direction, and in the chaos Parviz pushed his way toward the exit. The two men that were following him were caught by surprise in the panicked crowd.

All they could do was watch as Parviz ran up the exit stairs to the street.

When he reached the street he turned left and ran. He noticed a bus on the next block that was boarding passengers and headed for it. He stopped by the bus's rear wheels, stooped, and placed the computer on the street in front of the wheels. When the bus moved, the computer would be crushed to a piece of twisted metal. As he stood up, one of the detectives saw Parviz and ran in his direction. Parviz saw the detective coming and in a panic dashed across the busy street. He didn't see the van that hit him.

When the detective reached him he was barely alive. The detective used his radio to call for an ambulance. While he was waiting he tried to talk to Parviz, but Parviz just stared up at him. Then he said three words that sounded like, "I see paradise," and died.

The police found the laptop computer that Parviz had placed under the bus. It was crushed. Any data that it may have held was lost. On the subway platform they found his briefcase with a few thousand dollars still in it.

A search of Parviz's apartment yielded nothing to tell them that he had recognized the detectives following him, or any evidence of his involvement with terrorism.

Although the authorities had enough information to begin rounding up terrorists and low level members of Islam's Fire, they did not have enough to identify the remaining high level managers that they really wanted, nor all the persons or organizations who were providing funds to Islam's Fire. The question then became one of, should they wait in hopes of gathering more information, or should they act immediately.

Discussions between the CIA and MI6 centered on the fact that Parviz had known that he was being followed, but no one was sure if he had managed to get that information to the other leaders of the Islam's Fire. If he had gotten the word out then the question they had to answer was, "Was he killed while trying to get away, or was he assassinated and his death made to look like an accident?"

Either way the terrorists would have no choice but to scatter like leaves in a windstorm.

If Parviz did not get the word out that he was compromised there was always the question of how much evidence he had left to be found by the authorities. Since the terrorist leaders would not know, it would be safer for the terrorists to scatter rather than take a chance.

It made no difference either way. The terrorists would close or move operations in fear that they had been compromised.

There was another question that had to be considered. Were there any planned operations so close to completion that the terrorists could simply move them up before closing down and scattering? The CIA, MI6 and MI5 did not want to take the chance that another terrorist attack would occur while they tried to gather additional information. The authorities had to act quickly on the assumption that there were other operations being planned that could be moved up in schedule. If they waited and there was another attack many people would die because of their failure to act.

Within hours the FBI moved in on two terrorist groups, one in Los Angeles and one in Chicago. The members of the group in Boston still had not been identified. But unknown to the FBI, most members had decided to leave the country when Simon Rossman had been captured.

When Jamil Kassir and Aza Hamza reached Pakistan after leaving the California power line bombing they had requested to be sent back to the U.S. to start new terrorist cells. They were viewed as two embers generated by the Islam's Fire attack in California whose fate it was to be blown on Allah's wind to the homeland of the infidel to start new blazes. Since it was obviously Allah's will that these two return to the United Sates, it would be wrong to refuse their request, the leaders decided.

The two had experience and the skills to function successfully at an American University. All they needed were new identities and academic credentials, and then to be accepted as students by two universities, it didn't matter which two universities. The two that accepted Jamil and Aza were the University of California at Los Angeles, and the University of Chicago. They were both swept up along with other cell members by the FBI.

When the FBI took the fingerprints of cell members they got hits on Jamil Kassir and Aza Hamza. They were both wanted for the bombing of the power grid in California and the resulting deaths of two hundred thirty-six people. Both Jamil and Aza, in addition to charges of terrorism, were charged with murder.

In the investigation that followed, the authorities discovered the plans for the Los Angeles group: to kill as many people as they could by placing bombs at sports stadiums, Disneyland, Marine World, and other places where large crowds would gather.

The Chicago plan was to bomb the power substations supplying the city with electricity in mid winter. They hoped to create the same level of chaos that occurred in California. Many would die of exposure and hypothermia before repairs could be made. Without power, heating furnaces would not work and the city would freeze before the power could be restored.

The goal of both terrorist cells was to inflict as much death on the civilian population as possible.

41

When Carl completed his training, Director Rice reviewed his training record and smiled. Carl did not know it, but Director Rice had plans for him. The Director didn't want to scare Carl off, but to instead, slowly reel him into the Agency. He knew that Carl had the potential to be one of the CIA's best assets and he was going to give him every opportunity to live up to his potential.

Carl had received some of the best qualification reports that the director of the training facility had ever seen. It was obvious that Carl's previous training had not been lost since he left the military. He stood out in the areas of self defense, weapons, interrogation, and critical analysis. He was significantly above average in classes covering interrogation, electronic surveillance and other subjects needed in the life of a CIA field agent. The director of the training facility forwarded his assessment of Carl's abilities to Director Rice with a personal note saying, "Hang on to this guy, he's good."

Carl, Aaron Kovak and John Gray met with the Director in his office. The question on the table was what to do next? Their primary lead had been killed in London.

Aaron said they had been reviewing the contents of Parviz's computer hard drive that had been copied earlier, and all the e-mail and transactions he had sent since arriving in London. Much of the e-mail had been in code and mailed using a computer at a cyber café or library. So there was no way to identify the sender other than by his signature, which consisted of a code name.

Aaron added they had found one item of interest in an e-mail that might be useful. "On two occasions Parviz said, 'I will see you at the conference.' We believe the "You" he was referring to is the leader of the organization. Parviz was a university professor of economics so it would not be unusual for him to attend conferences. It would be a way for Islam's Fire leadership to meet without attracting attention. Their attendance at an economic conference would appear quite normal, particularly if they were from academia and had legitimate reasons to be there. If they were properly dressed they could enter the conference center and simply go to a particular room for a meeting without being questioned or attracting attention.

"I asked the Zurich police to check with the University and get a list of the conferences that Parviz had attended in the past. They sent us a list of eleven. There is generally a conference on economics or some related subject someplace in the world about every four to six months. We had the FBI check with the groups putting on the conferences for a list of attendees. Six of them said that they don't keep lists of attendees longer than a year. Three said that they would not supply a list to the FBI since that would violate their clients' privacy. Two did send us their list of attendees and their addresses. At both conferences, there were eight men from Islamic countries that were possible candidates as members of Islam's Fire. Two were from Egypt, one from Syria, one from Jordan, two from Saudi Arabia, one from Iran, one from Islamabad Pakistan, and from Switzerland, our boy, Parviz Jalili. In my experience, people who attend conferences spend fifty percent of the time at conference functions and fifty percent at private meetings with other conference attendees. It would be ideal for the group we want to meet without drawing suspicion.

"The phones we have been keeping tabs on in Pakistan use cell phone towers that are in Islamabad, which would be consistent with the guy on the conference list. At this point, this is all conjecture but it could prove useful."

"Who is this guy from Islamabad?" asked Carl.

"He is Professor Yusef Azziz, a Professor of Government and Culture at International Islamic University in Islamabad. He doesn't have a record with us. But the Israelis have him on their watch list as well as a couple of others that appear on our list. They think Azziz is the mastermind behind a number of terrorist attacks in Israel.

"For instance, a Saudi, Mohammed Calid, is a rich minor prince who works at the Saudi Finance Ministry. His father is a known Wahabist, the most radical form of Islam, and has been known to give large amounts of money to radical groups engaged in attacking the Israelis. Both he and his father have called the Western culture decadent, but they are not above making frequent trips to Paris or London nightclubs, or going to Monaco to gamble. I would not put it past him to help finance Islam's Fire.

"Another interesting character is Ahmose Maswagi, who was picked up as a dissident by the Egyptians, and held prisoner for a year before being released eight years ago. Since then he's managed to get an education in Financial Management and a second degree in Economics. He teaches at a university in Cairo. The Egyptians are keeping an eye on him but he seems to be keeping his nose clean."

"That's quite a cast of characters," said the Director. "It looks as if we start with Yusef Azziz since the telephone calls seem to point to him as the man who controls the organization.

"The FBI and MI5 have scooped up a large part of their organization so they are going to be busy rebuilding it. This may be our chance to eliminate this group. Parviz left a list of all his accounts. Have forensic accountants come up with anything?"

"The computer techies are on it, but since all computer IDs have been cloned they pretty much have to wait until someone sends a message to the server so they can be certain they are tracing the right computer back to the point of origination. They don't often use the computers to send e-mail so it's a slow process to trace calls back to the members of the organization," answered John Gray.

"I think we should have a talk with Mr. Calid the next time he is in London or Monaco to gamble. We have to find a way to stop the financing of this group. Without money they won't be able to operate. If we can convince the Saudis to stop supplying money, our targets will be entirely reliant on what they get from Islamic charities or what they can steal." said Carl.

42

Mohammed Calid flew into Monaco six weeks later to spend a few days gambling and taking advantage of women who were willing to make themselves available for the right price. Mohammed considered these trips an opportunity to indulge himself with beautiful women, fine scotch whiskey, gambling, and good food, in that order. His Muslim faith was put on hold until his return to Riyadh.

He was ahead playing baccarat, winning a substantial amount, and his luck with women was even better. He had made the acquaintance of a beautiful blond who was charming, well educated, had a well toned body, and breasts that would challenge any dress designer. He was happy with the gambling and the night proved equally rewarding. She was expensive but she was very talented and athletic in bed.

The second night started off well, and he made the acquaintance of a beautiful French woman, a brunette named Adriana Lignet. As the evening wore on she suggested that they go to the dining room and have a late supper. They were seated, and had only a few minutes to chat over drinks, when a tall well built man entered the room and approached their table to say, "Hello Adriana, it's good to see you."

She looked up, and with a surprised look on her face said, "Mohammed, this is my brother Carl, may he join us for a moment? I have not seen him for some time."

"Yes, of course." he said as he rose to shake hands with Carl.

Mohammed's two bodyguards, sitting at a table across the room, stood up as if to come to his assistance, but Mohammed smiled and waved them off.

"By all means, please do join us."

Carl pulled out a chair and sat down, saying in perfect Arabic, "You are Mohammed Calid. You and your father are both well known by my organization and several others around the world."

"Oh really, I had no idea my reputation had spread that far, Carl. I hope it is not bad."

"Yes Mohammed, both you and your father's reputations are very bad, and something will be done about it if your behavior doesn't change, and rather quickly."

A startled look spread across Mohammed's face.

"Please do not concern yourself now, Mohammed, enjoy your meal. I am merely here to deliver a message and I suggest that you listen to the message very, very carefully."

"And what is this message?"

"We know that you and your father have been providing money to a terrorist group calling itself Islam's Fire. So far, your money has been used to kill thousands of people in the United States, England, Pakistan, and Bali. If you do not stop providing money to terrorists, all terrorists, you and your father will both be killed. This is not a threat, Mohammed, but rather a statement of fact. Please understand that we don't want to kill you but we will.

"Do not look so alarmed, I am simply delivering a message, you are in no danger here. If your bodyguards get a little too curious things could become difficult and embarrassing for both you and your family. Please be sure to pass this message along to your father. This is the first and only warning you will receive. The next time I or one of my friends meet with you, it will be to kill you and your father. Do you understand?"

Mohammed stared at Carl, digesting his words but remained silent.

"Please, Mohammed, I would like to hear you say that you understand so that there will be no mistake."

"I understand."

Carl and Adriana both stood, smiled, said 'goodbye,' and headed to the door.

When Mohammed stood, his hands were shaking. When the bodyguards approached, he told them to pack up everything, they were flying out that night.

From that time on, the only money that was wired to the Islam's Fire account came from Islamic charitable organizations or other benefactors that had not yet received a warning. Calls to the Calid family asking for support were politely listened to and then ignored.

43

The New Global Economy Conference was held in Cairo, Egypt, at the Diplomat Hotel Conference Center. Thirteen hundred people had signed up to attend. Many were from universities, some from private industry, and the rest from government. The global economy was apparently a hot topic.

The one delegate of most interest to Carl and Adriana was Yusef Azziz. The conference had just gotten underway and Carl was a paid attendee and Adriana again played the role of his wife. They were lovers who had studied each other's moods and were quite comfortable in each other's company. This comfort and ease with each other was obvious, which made their role as man and wife even more believable.

The day before, when they had registered at the hotel, they received a packet of material that included an agenda, a list of attendees that had pre registered, a tour program for the wives who had accompanied their husbands, a list of hotel amenities, and recommended sights to be found in Cairo. Yusef Azziz was on the list of attendees but had not yet registered at the hotel. Carl hoped that he was just late. Carl attended a few meetings to strengthen his role as a legitimate delegate, while Adriana did her best to become acquainted with the area around the hotel and the convention center itself. In the afternoon Carl went to the front desk and asked if Mr. Azziz had checked in yet. The clerk consulted his computer then looked up, saying that Mr. Azziz had checked in about an hour earlier.

Carl went to a desk and wrote a very short note that read, "John, meet me in the bar at 7:00, Mike." He folded the note in half, put it in an envelope and handed it to the desk clerk asking him to put it in Mr. Azziz's box. The clerk said, "Yes sir," turned and slid the envelope into box 7221.

Carl found a comfortable chair in the lobby with a view of the mail boxes, then using his cell phone placed a call to a number he had memorized. When it was answered he simply said, "Room 7221."

The answering party replied, "Okay, we got it covered," and hung up.

Carl pretended to read a newspaper while he waited. After three hours he called Adriana who had just returned from a walk through the local area. He asked her if she could come down for a few hours so he could have a break.

When she came into the lobby she had a book in her hand. She saw Carl and took a chair next to him. He leaned over to her, placed his hand on hers and said, "He's in room 7221," then got up and left. She waited a few minutes, then also got up and passed the desk on her way to the house phones. As she did, she noted the location of box 7221. After pretending to make a call she returned to her chair and sat down and opened her book. She was not there long when a man who had watched her come in approached her and tried to start a conversation. She told him that she was waiting for her husband. He left without any further attempts at conversation.

When Carl returned, he sat next to her and they carried on

a conversation as if they were a couple having a chat before going to dinner. An hour later another man came in and sat down. Carl and Adriana left to go to dinner while the newcomer watched the box.

Earlier in the afternoon a housekeeper knocked on the door of Yusef's room. When she received no answer she let herself in, then set about empting the wastebasket and dusting, she put a new ashtray on the desk and dusted the telephone while she put a bug in the handset. There were several books in English on a small bookshelf. The housekeeper added another one, only this one contained a very small video camera hidden in the spine of the book. The book could be opened and read without anyone realizing it held a camera.

When Carl and Adriana got back from dinner they again sat in the lobby. Their team member who had been watching box 7221 got up and left. They had only been there a few minutes when a middle-aged man, thin, of medium height with dark hair, and a light tan complexion, who appeared to be somewhere between fifty-five and sixty-five years of age, entered the lobby. At the front desk he asked for his key and received it and the envelope. He then opened the envelope and read the note. Looking confused for a second, he threw envelope and note into a trash can. Both Carl and Adriana studied the man. Adriana got a few photographs of him with the camera that was concealed in her purse.

Later that evening a man entered the hotel and took the elevator to the seventh floor, then down the corridor toward room 7221. He didn't notice the housekeeper approaching from the opposite direction pushing a housekeepers cart with extra towels and room supplies. As she neared him she took several photographs with the camera hidden between the towels on the cart. He knocked on the door to the room.

When the door opened he entered the room, kissed Yusef on both cheeks, and said "May Allah's blessings be upon you."

Yusef responded, "And you."

There were a few pleasantries then the conversation turned

to Islam's Fire. Yusef said, "Parviz is dead and all our people in America have been arrested except one cell on the West Coast. The rest of our people in England, France and Denmark have also been arrested. It will take some time to recruit and rebuild the organization. In the meantime we will have to find other ways to carry out our goals, but we can discuss that tomorrow."

The guest answered, "We have one person living in the state of Idaho who has infiltrated a group the Americans called "survivalist." The survivalists are a group who fear that America is being taken over by communists and blacks. They believe that if America is to be saved they must overthrow the government. The man we have there is a convert to Islam but still maintains his connections to the survivalist. He believes that the group can be guided into doing what we would like. But I have some misgivings about these so called survivalists. Perhaps we can use them to create a distraction but we can address that tomorrow as well."

"Of major importance is finding someone to take over Parviz's duties and re-establishing our system of distributing funds, but that will take some time to find the right person. These are things that must be discussed with the others.

"We will meet with Khan, Maswagi, Aswat, and Ujaama tomorrow at lunch. Khan is making arrangements for a lunch at an apartment not far from here."

The conversation drifted to a more mundane discussion of world affairs and then the visitor left a short time later.

When Carl met with the members of the team later that evening he asked, "Have we identified Yusef's visitor?"

"Yeah, he's Abu al-Masri. I sent his photograph to Langley, and they came back with a quick answer, apparently he is a well known troublemaker. He is an Iranian Imam who immigrated to England some years ago and has lately been living in New York. He's on everyone's watch list. He's a real radical, gives fiery speeches trying to incite the young Islamic men to go to Afghanistan and join Bin Laden. He appears to have been rather successful. Some of those that he inspired were involved in the London subway bombings and have been to a Pakistan training camp." said Dean.

"I guess we'll just have to wait and see if we can get ears on their meeting tomorrow afternoon. It's been a long day, everybody get some sleep, but let's keep an eye on our friend Yusef," said Carl.

Carl and Adriana left for their room at the Diplomat. They would take the first shift in watching Yusef.

The next day Carl and Adriana were in the dining room having breakfast, watching Yusef, when a man approached, whispered in Yusef's ear then walked away. Carl said, "I'm going to follow that man and see where it leads, keep an eye on Yusef."

Carl was back a short time later. He took Adriana aside and told her that the man he had been following had met two other men and then had gone to an apartment house on Madi el-Din, "We might be able to get laser ears on the apartment from the roof of a building a block west of there, Jim is working on it. I also told Dean to get a video camera and photograph everybody going in."

That afternoon Yusef left the Diplomat hotel. He wandered into several stores as if shopping then left through a rear door of a gift shop that catered to tourists, making his way to the apartment house on Madi el-Din. The apartment house was just across from Ezbekiya Gardens and diagonally across the street from the Cairo opera house. He entered an apartment that faced the back side of the building.

The room was bare except for a table and chairs that sat in the middle of the room. A small lunch had been set. Mohammed Khan, James Ujaama, Mohammed Aswat, Abu al-Masri, and Ahmose Maswagi were already at the table filling their plates and talking about the day's events. In deference, they all stood to welcome Yusef, after which they all sat down and resumed their conversation. Yusef joined them in the meal, adding his own comments to the conversation. When the dinner had ended, the plates were cleared and the caterers had gone, the meeting got down to business.

Abu al-Masri said that there had never been a war fought that did not, from time to time, lose a battle or experience a setback. He continued, saying that what won wars was perseverance in the face of adversity, and he cited the war in Vietnam as an example.

"From time to time, battles will be lost. At these times we must have faith in the words of the Prophet Mohammed, blessed be his name, as written in the Quran. If we follow his words we will win."

He went on bragging that he had helped Simon Rossman plan the bombings in the New York subway, and how bombings such as that would cause so much fear that the American people would begin to cower and lose faith in their government as they did during the Vietnam War. "When the American people are punished enough they will force their government to pull all its forces from Islamic lands and stop their support of the Jews." The others nodded at his words and praised him for his good work.

They discussed the guerrilla-style training that the Idaho survivalists were engaged in and some of the methods the survivalists had talked about to begin a war against the American government. After listening quietly for some time Yusef said, "Tell our man to leave the survivalists. Such groups are generally a bunch of buffoons who do nothing but bluster and strut about like roosters, and if they did take action they would be quickly crushed by the American government and our man would be crushed along with them. Tell him to go to Seattle, Washington, and join with Ujaama. He will receive his orders from Ujaama or Khan."

The conversation then turned to other matters. The question was who they would select as the new finance administrator. Yusef commented that whoever it was would have to have a good understanding of banking and the ability of law enforcement agencies to track financial transactions. Abu al-Masri mentioned the name of a third cousin, a devout member of the faith, who worked at a bank in London. He would approach the man to see if he was willing and capable. If so, he would arrange a meeting so they could question him more closely.

The meeting continued with discussions of possible targets in America, England, France, Denmark, and India. With each suggested target there was a discussion of the cost of the attack and the cost benefit ratio. That is, the cost versus the number of deaths that could be expected from an attack. The discussion then moved on to what outcome could be expected. Would the attack cause enough damage to topple the government, stop support of the Americans as it had in Spain, influence an election, or put enough pressure on the government to force them to remove forces in the Middle East.

They discussed the advisability of closer ties to Al Qaeda. If they formed an alliance with Al Qaeda, could that enhance their ability to get more funds or would they simply be absorbed by the bigger organization. Al Qaeda had a good supply of arms, munitions, and explosives. Could they expect to receive any of these resources?

The conversation then moved onto the subject of punishing American allies such as Germany, France, England, and Denmark. Would focusing attacks on these countries cause them to rethink their position regarding support to the American effort in Afghanistan? How many Danes would they have to kill to make them change their position?

Finally, the conversation drifted to day-to-day operations, such as recruitment of martyrs and operational needs. The opinion of the group was that recruitment did not pose a problem. As long as the madrassas continued to operate there will always be a good supply of the faithful willing to martyr themselves in defense of the Faith. It seemed that it was easier to get people to martyr themselves than it is to get money.

Their entire meeting was recorded by a laser listening device that used the plate glass window in the room as its microphone.

That evening Carl and the others met at the safe house. They all listened to the recording of the conversation. Carl grew cold with fury as he heard the group plan more bombings of civilian targets, bombings that were designed to cause the maximum amount of death and injury at the least cost. It was cold blooded and lacked any humanity. A cost of so many dollars was expected to yield so many deaths. If the equation did not give the desired result then alternative ideas for that country were considered. When they watched the video taken earlier, both Carl and Adrianna recognized Mohammed Aswat as the man Parviz met at the Paris mosque.

In Carl's mind the callous disregard for human life placed these men in the same category as vermin. The more he listened the more he felt the fury building within him. If he were to get the opportunity he would wring their necks with his bare hands and not think twice about it.

Without realizing it, Carl had moved closer to being the asset the Director had hoped for.

At the end of the recording Carl and the others sat for a few moments in complete silence. Then Carl assigned two team members to follow each participant. He assigned Jim, and Lorna, the Diplomat Hotel housekeeper, to follow Ahmose Maswagi. Lorna's ability to speak Arabic and her knowledge of Egypt could come in handy.

Lorna had changed into rather elegant street clothes and styled her hair, proving she was a very attractive woman who looked completely different than the woman in the role she had played earlier in the day. It was doubtful that she would be recognized.

Carl asked if she had her hotel master key with her. She said that she did, and passed the plastic card key to him. When she handed the key to Carl their eyes locked, and in that instant she knew what he was going to do.

He assigned Adriana and Paul to follow Mohammed Aswat. After listening to Aswat's voice they thought he had a French accent. Adriana's knowledge of France, and Paris in particular, would come in handy.

Carl said that he would not assign anyone to follow Abu Hamza al-Masri because he was a public figure and would be visible no matter where he went. To find him, all they would have to do was look him up on the internet to find a complete schedule of his planned appearances.

Because they had no other available staff, Carl said the he would follow James Ujaama to the airport and find out what flight he was on, then call for someone from the destination country to pick him up at the airport when he landed.

One of the team said, "Who is going to follow Yusef?" Carl answered, "Don't worry about Yusef, I know where he is going."

It was late when Carl and Adriana returned to their room at the Diplomat Hotel. Adriana said that she was going to take a long bath. Carl said, "Fine. I am just going to stretch out on the bed for awhile."

After a few minutes, when he heard the tub being filled, Carl got up and left the room. Using the stairs to avoid the security cameras he went to Yusef's room on the seventh floor. Using the key that Lorna had given him, he entered the room. He looked around and saw a light coming from under the bathroom door. Carl flattened himself to the wall next to the bathroom door and waited. When Yusef came out, Carl put his right hand over his mouth as his left hand reached across Yusef's head. Then he jerked Yusef's head up and twisted hard. A sharp crack signaled the second vertebra had snapped and separated from the spinal column. Carl wiggled his head from side to side to make sure the spinal cord was severed or badly damaged. Yusef's body went limp and sagged in his arms. Carl dragged him over to the sliding door to the balcony and dropped him to the floor. He picked a glass up off the desk with his handkerchief, and placed it in Yusef's left hand. Next he went to the minibar and removed three small bottles of whiskey. Opening each of one of the bottles, he placed them in Yusef's right hand, compressing the fingers around each bottle. He poured a little whiskey in the glass and the rest on Yusef's shirt and mouth. He then emptied the rest of the whiskey from all three bottles down the bathroom sink, running the water to remove any whiskey from the basin. He turned the room light out, opened the drapes and the sliding door to the balcony. Then, grabbing Yusef by his shirt collar and the seat of his pants propelled him onto the balcony and over the railing.

Carl returned to his room minutes later, undressed and climbed into bed just as Adriana was coming out of the bathroom. They heard the sound of sirens stopping at their hotel, prompting Adriana to ask, "I wonder what that's all about?"

Carl just smiled and said, "Yusef just jumped from his balcony."

Adriana stared at Carl as his words sunk in. She stood by Carl's bed, the thin nightgown she was wearing moving against her body, revealing all her body in detail, as the light from the bedside lamp highlighted her body through the sheer fabric. She slowly let the nightgown drop to the floor, and lay down next to him. She could hear his breathing and feel his heart beating a little faster than normal as she kissed him passionately.

Early the next morning Mohammed Khan went to room 7221, only to find the yellow police tape across the door. He stood there for a minute not quite sure what to do. He went to the front desk and asked the clerk what had happened to Yusef. The clerk told him that a terrible accident had occurred, that Mr. Azziz had died in a fall from the balcony late last night. The police had investigated and determined that Mr. Azziz apparently had too much to drink and then wandered out onto the balcony and fell, or jumped.

This last statement had caused the acid in Khan's stomach to back up into his throat. He knew that Yusef was a devout follower of Islam's tenets against drinking. He had never heard of Yusef having so much as tasted an alcoholic beverage. Obviously Yusef had been killed, but by whom?

Khan went back to his room and quickly packed. He was back at the front desk fifteen minutes later to check out. He stepped outside to get a taxi to the airport. A number of other conference attendees with baggage were waiting for taxis to the airport. No one seemed to be paying any attention to him. A taxi pulled up, the driver got out and ran around the taxi to open the rear door for Khan. Khan threw his bag in the back seat and climbed in. When the taxi reached the airport, Khan went to the counter to check in. Looking around, he saw many faces that he recognized from the conference but again, no one seemed to be paying him any particular attention.

He was booked on Delta 931, Cairo, Egypt to Chicago with a stop in New York to go through customs, and then on Delta flight 348 to Chicago. Carl noted the sign above the entry to the jet way that Khan entered when his flight was called. He called Aaron Kovak and gave him the flight number and destination. Aaron said he would pass the information on to Jean Peters. The FBI could follow him when he arrived.

Earlier in the week, Lorna the housekeeper had cleaned James Ujaama's room and had found his airline tickets that showed him booked on United Airlines 231 to Seattle, leaving Cairo at 8:00 in the evening. She passed this information on to Carl, who in turn relayed it to Aaron. When Ujaama's flight reached Seattle's SEA/TAC, two FBI agents were waiting to follow him to his apartment in midtown Seattle. The following morning he went to work at a warehouse for a restaurant food distribution company owned by his cousin.

Carl found a quiet corner and called Director Rice, saying that Yusef Azziz had committed suicide the previous evening. When Director Rice heard Carl's message he smiled, "Good man, Carl." He said, "Thank you, Carl, that's good news. Now we have only three more to go."

After hearing the Director, Carl knew he would not have much time to spend at home. He said, "I think our first priority should be those that are in the U.S. since they represent the greater risk. We can go after the others later."

"I agree, Carl, have a good trip home."

While Khan was on the plane he managed to shave his beard off which changed his appearance considerably. When Kahn arrived in New York he went through customs, then out onto the concourse where he managed to elude the two FBI agents assigned to follow him. He took a cab into the city and disappeared into a Muslim neighborhood.

The two FBI agents at O'Hare airport in Chicago met Khan's flight and reported to their supervisor that Khan was not on the connecting flight from New York. A check of the passenger list indicated that he had not boarded the flight in New York.

Director Rice called the President and told him that the leader of Islam's Fire had committed suicide in Cairo. He cautioned the President that Yusef's death did not mean that the organization ceased to exist, and that two of its leaders were now in the U.S., and that at least two terrorist cells were still active in the country. The FBI was following one of the leaders in Seattle, but the other one had eluded the FBI at JFK airport, and by this time was hiding somewhere in the City. He told the President that the emphasis was being placed on catching the two who were in the U.S. then they would go after the remaining two in Europe.

The recording made of the terrorist meeting was passed on to the CIA in Langley, who in turn passed on portions of the tape to Jean Peters. After hearing the tape the FBI increased surveillance of subversive groups in the Northwest, in particular, the Washington State area. The FBI also increased its efforts to infiltrate survivalist groups in Idaho, Colorado, and Utah.

The portion of the tape regarding Abu Hamza al-Masri's statement bragging about his role in the New York subway bombing was passed on to the Federal prosecutors preparing a case against Simon Rossman. The prosecutors were delighted to get it. An order was issued for the arrest and extradition of Abu Hamza al-Masri, who had left Egypt and flown to England.

44

Simon Rossman had been moved to a holding facility adjacent to the Federal courthouse, located at 225 Cadman Plaza East, New York City. He was in an isolation cell for his own protection and placed on suicide watch. A guard checked on him every fifteen minutes and the rest of the time he was monitored by a surveillance camera. A guard told him which way was east so that he could face Mecca while he prayed. He asked for and received a Quran to read. Five times a day he would face east, kneel, bow down, and say his prayers.

On the first day of his trial he was given breakfast and allowed to bathe and shave with a safety razor as a guard stood by his side. When he was through cleaning up he dressed in a business suit and was taken to Court room number two, where his defense attorney was waiting for him.

Other than the guards and his attorney, he was not allowed to associate with anyone. His wife tried to visit him once but Simon refused to see her. One hour each day he was led to the roof of the building where three wire enclosures twelve feet wide and fifty feet long had been constructed. They were intended to allow prisoners to get some exercise, sun, and fresh air. When Rossman used one of the enclosures he was the only prisoner there. The only other person on the roof was the guard who was watching him.

On the first day of trial the bailiff called the court to order when the judge entered the courtroom. Judge Cyrus Vance asked both attorneys if they were ready to go to trial. Both attorneys responded by saying, "Yes, your honor."

The courtroom was packed with prospective jurors and members of the press. The jurors had received a seventeen-page questionnaire earlier. The completed questionnaires had been returned to the court clerk, and each attorney received a copy.

The judge began with a summary of the trial and the expected time it would take. He asked if there was any reason why the prospective jurors could not serve. Hands shot up from eight of the twelve prospective jurors. He began questioning the jurors as to why they could not serve. Prospective jurors that had a medical problem that would prevent them from giving their full attention to the trial were released. If a prospective juror had a relative or knew someone who was injured in the bombing, or would endure financial hardship, they were also released. If the Judge felt that a potential juror could not put aside their personal bias, that person was also released.

When the judge had seated a jury panel the defense and prosecuting attorneys had their turns questioning the jury. Each attorney could challenge up to twelve jurors peremptorily and others for cause. Jury selection went on for two weeks, with the attorneys finally settling on a jury that both the prosecution and defense were equally unhappy with.

Each day during breaks, Rossman was taken from the courtroom to the bathroom and then an attorneys meeting room where he faced east, knelt, bowed, and said his prayers. Afterward he would meet with his attorney if necessary. The breaks were extended by ten minutes to allow Rossman to say his prayers without cutting into his attorney time.

On the first day of the trial, the judge asked the court clerk to read the indictment against Simon Rossman. The charges included crossing a state line to commit an act of terrorism that lead to the deaths of 662 people in New York, acts of terrorism on the power grid that affected California, Oregon, Arizona and Nevada, and resulted in 231 deaths, the loss of hundreds of millions of dollars worth of damage as a result of his acts of terrorism, and finally he was charged with importing and moving explosives across state lines for the purpose of committing acts of terrorism.

Throughout the entire proceeding Simon Rossman remained unemotional, his attitude verging on disinterest, only lifting his eyes when the clerk read the indictment. His wife and her parents sat stoically in the back of the courtroom. When the clerk finished reading the indictment the judge said that the prosecuting attorney could begin with his opening statement.

The attorney began listing the events that led to the blackout in the Western States, and the associated deaths. How Simon Rossman had recruited members of the terrorist cell, the smuggling of explosives that were used, and the capture of the militant students at the Mexican border, and finally all the events leading up to the bombing in New York City.

The trial proceeded with each student that had taken part in the bombings asserting that they were recruited by Simon Rossman, and were following his orders as members of a jihadist army. As part of a jihadist army, each asserted that they should not be tried in a Federal court but instead in a military court.

Following the testimony by the students of their role in the bombing, testimony by forensic experts on the explosives used was heard. Testimony by managers of power companies, Fire Department personnel, and other first responders followed. Police officers testified how secondary explosives were placed to kill those trying to help the injured.

The final piece of evidence was the tape recording of Abu

Hamza al-Masri bragging about how he and Rossman planned the attack in New York City.

Since it would be virtually impossible to find an unbiased jury that understood Arabic in New York City, the prosecuting attorney tried something that had never been done in a courtroom before. He had a verbatim script developed from portions of the recording of the discussion that took place in Cairo, Egypt. Then he had two professors of Middle-Eastern languages and two Arabic-speaking Imams testify that the script was an accurate word-for-word translation of the meeting. He then hired actors to play the parts of the men in the recording using the translated script. The actors duplicated the inflections in the voices, and delivery patterns of the speakers on the tape. The result was a dramatic and accurate re-enactment of the Cairo meeting.

The court spectators and the jury were spellbound by the re-enactment. The news reporters wrote furiously in an attempt to not only record what was said, but to also capture the mood of the courtroom.

The defense argued that the entire trial was illegal. That if a trial were to take place at all it should be in a military court, because Simon Rossman was an enemy combatant. Further, they argued he was in Princeton, New Jersey when the bombing in California took place and in Boston when the New York bombings took place. Finally, the attorney asked that Abu al-Masri be produced so that Simon Rossman could confront him. The court was told that a warrant had been issued for al-Masri arrest and he would be extradited following his arrest.

Simon Rossman refused to testify on his own behalf.

The evidence was so compelling that the jury only took three hours to come back with a guilty verdict.

At his sentencing hearing, Simon Rossman received 893 consecutive life sentences, one life sentence for each person who died as a result of his actions. He was sentenced to serve his time at the Federal Supermax prison facility in Florence, Colorado.

The following morning the newspaper headline screamed,

'Rossman is Guilty!' After following the story for the past month the news was anticlimactic and came as no surprise to anyone.

Simon Rossman's wife divorced her husband, and she and the children took her maiden name. Then they moved from their home in Sacramento, California to Las Vegas where her parents lived, hoping to avoid the stigma the Rossman name invoked.

The State of California and the State of Washington both issued warrants for Simon Rossman's arrest on the charge of murder should he ever be released from federal prison. He would have to stand trial for the murder of Ken Barkley, Al Genovese and Al Genovese's wife.

45

Carl sat in Directors Rice's office bringing him up to date on what they knew about Yusef Azziz. When he finished, he described how he felt on hearing Abu Hamza al-Masri bragging about his role in the planning of the bombing of the New York City subway.

"If I could have gotten my hands on Abu Hamza al-Masri or Yusef at that moment, I would have snapped their necks like dry twigs without any remorse. As it was, Yusef decided to jump off of his balcony, he just need a little assistance. I'm glad I was there to help."

The Director said that he was also glad that Yusef had decided to end his life. The Director had known that Carl had killed several men before, but in those situations it was kill or be killed. It takes a totally different mindset to murder someone. He knew he had the asset he wanted, intelligent, capable, and able to take action when it was needed. After a few a seconds, he said, "Carl, that was good work, unfortunately there are four other members of Islam's Fire that need to be encouraged to commit suicide, and then there are others in this world that are equally reprehensible. Have you given any thought to going to work for the agency full time?"

"Not really, I'd like to leave the arrangement as it is. I'm more comfortable as a consultant than as a full time spook. In fact, it seems my first assignment is almost complete. You asked me to find Parviz and the leaders of Islam's Fire. Both those assignments have been completed. Yusef Azziz and Parviz Jalili are both dead. Al-Masri will soon be arrested and extradited to the U.S, for trial. James Ujaama and Mohammed Sidique Khan are both in the U.S. and under the FBI jurisdiction. The last two are in Cairo and Paris and I will soon be going to each of those countries. That will basically wipe out the organization. So unless you have another consulting project that I am interested in, I would like to start doing some work around the house."

They discussed a few other subjects, and soon after, Carl left the office to go home. The Maryland countryside was beautiful at this time of year and he just wanted to be outdoors and away from people.

Two hours later, he had unpacked his travel bag and read his mail. Still feeling wound up, he went to the refrigerator and took out a bottle of beer then went out the back door to the porch where he sat and drank his beer. He stood and walked past the barn and into the pasture, along the creek, then back through the wooded area to the house. While he walked he thought about what had happened over the last year. He had recovered hundreds of millions of dollars stolen from World Bank, married and lost his wife, broken up a terrorist organization and killed its leader. In doing so he had saved countless lives. As he thought about it, he felt very satisfied with his accomplishments and profoundly alone without Ann to share his life.

Carl did not go in to the office for the next few days. Instead he worked in the garden, and spent some time at a hardware store buying tools for his workshop. In the warm afternoons he hiked around his property enjoying the sun and watching white tail deer at the edge of the wooded area. As he started back to the house one afternoon a noise startled him, and his heart rate immediately increased, a ring-necked pheasant had flown up at his feet. He realized that he was too tense. It was time to go into the house, put on some good music and try to come to terms with everything that had happened in the past few months.

46

Carl landed at Orly Airport in Paris in the late afternoon. Adriana met him as he came out of the baggage area. She gave him an affectionate hug, a long kiss, and clung to him a little longer than he expected. Two men that had been watching him stepped forward when Adriana broke away from Carl.

The two men introduced themselves as being from the DGSE (Direction Générale de la Sécurité Extérieure), the French equivalent of the CIA. They asked if they could have a moment with Carl. Excusing himself, Carl stepped to a quiet corner of the luggage area where they could talk. Carl explained that Adriana was a very close friend of many years. The two DGSE officers smiled and said that they were French, they understood such things. They asked if Carl would be available for a meeting with their Director the following morning to discuss Mohammed Aswat. Carl said that he was looking forward to it, and asked if eleven in the morning would work. They shook hands and Carl rejoined Adriana.

Adriana and Carl walked toward the passenger loading area

and hailed a taxi. Once in the taxi, they directed the driver to the hotel where Carl was staying. Speaking quietly Carl explained that the DGSE men thought that Adriana was his lover and he did not want to disclose that she worked for the CIA. She suggested that perhaps she had better stay in his room tonight.

When they reached the room Adriana explained that John Cagen wanted to meet him but something came up at the last minute. Adriana then filled him in on Mohammed Aswat's activities since his return from Cairo. Carl explained that he had a meeting the following day with the DGSE to discuss Aswat and he would pass along the information.

After they returned from dinner, Carl turned on the TV. He and Adriana listened to the local news regarding the student takeover at the University, and the incident with the Arabic kids being killed that day while running away from the police and the ensuing riots. Adriana said that Mohammed Aswat's activities would significantly contribute to the riot. He and his group had been stirring up religious and ethnic prejudice among the Islamic population since his return from Cairo.

Carl unpacked and went into the bathroom to brush his teeth, when he returned he crawled into bed. Adriana watched Carl enter the room and with a sigh got up to go to the bathroom. She used some of Carl's toothpaste to finger brush her teeth then washed the makeup from her face. When she returned to the room she turned off the light and undressed. Although the lamp had been turned off there was still enough street light coming in around the curtains to see to get around, and to clearly distinguish the silhouette of Adriana undressing and as she slipped between the sheets of Carl's bed.

The following morning Adriana was up early and was just finishing up in the shower when Carl awoke. When she came out of the bathroom she was fully dressed and made up. Carl was again very conscious of what a beautiful woman she was.

At eleven Carl entered the headquarters of the DGSE and was escorted to the Director's office. He was introduced to several of the Director's deputies. After polite conversation and coffee the Director said that they had received the CIA's report on the meeting in Cairo and were concerned about Mohammed Aswat. He told them everything he knew about Islam's Fire, the Cairo meeting and Mohammed Aswat and his activities.

Aswat had been spending a lot of time at student rallies, union meetings, and mosques giving fiery speeches about the unequal treatment of Islamic people in France. His speeches generally focused on the inequity in wages between the French workers and Islamic workers. How, even the children of immigrants that had been born in France were discriminated against. He hammered on the theme that even though they were French citizens, if they were Islamic, they were considered second class French citizens, and as second class French citizens they only received second class wages for first class work. He pointed out that if there were to be layoffs, Islamic workers were always the first to go.

In the sections of town where most of the Muslim population lived, the police often stopped men and asked for their identity papers without cause, which further caused the Muslims to believe they were being singled out for harassment and discrimination.

When two hundred Islamic students at the University started a student demonstration that took over University office buildings, it was like lighting a match while looking for a gas leak. The deaths of two boys that had run from the police was the match that would cause an ethnic explosion.

At four-seventeen in the afternoon, police were called to a construction site to investigate possible property theft. Three boys who had been playing football with others in a nearby lot thought that they were being chased by the police and ran. In their effort to get away from the police they jumped over a wall surrounding a power substation and tried to hide. Two boys died of electrocution and the third was shocked and badly burned. At six-twelve that evening a blackout occurred that affected the police station and a large part of the surrounding area. The police blamed the boys for shorting out the electrical power station. When word of this incident and the police involvement got out many people from the Clichy-Sous-Bois, a poor commune in the eastern suburb of Paris, joined the students in rioting. The rioting soon boiled over into the streets in the center of Paris. The riot increased in intensity because of years of discrimination that had been directed toward the Islamic population. The discontent that had been sown by Mohammed Aswat followers added fuel to the Islamic rage.

The riot lasted for five days, during which the rioters burned cars, battled police, and burned buildings. It was thought that the rioting could be contained to Paris, but it spilled over into surrounding cities. It was finally quelled when the President of France declared a state of emergency that allowed local authorities to impose curfews, conduct house-to-house searches, and ban public gatherings.

Aswat took advantage of the rioting to fan flames of discontent wherever he could. He would have put in motion his plan to place bombs in the Paris subway system but they did not have all of the explosives they needed, that portion of the plan would have to wait a few weeks. It was just as well, because of the warning from the CIA and the recording of the meeting in Cairo, the police were out in force watching tourist sites and transportation facilities in fear that Islam's Fire or some other dissident group would take advantage of the rioting to cause further damage.

Carl, John Cagen, Adriana, and other team members focused only on Mohammed Aswat. They were not distracted by the riot or the other police activities, they kept their eye on Aswat. After five days the rioting began to subside with only sporadic incidents across the city.

Adriana and one other team member were following Aswat when he entered a subway. Adriana followed close behind him. The train had just left the station and they were forced to wait for the next train twelve minutes away. Adriana hung back from Aswat. As she waited she thought of the deaths and damages that Mohammed Aswat and other members of Islam's Fire had been responsible for. As more people began to fill the subway platform she edged closer to Mohammed. By the time the train was within sight she was standing right behind him. Mohammed felt a strong shove at his back just as a train came into the station. He lost his footing and fell on the tracks directly in front of the train and was killed instantly.

Adriana and the rest of the crowd screamed and backed away from the edge of the platform. Adriana thought to herself, "You will not kill any more of my countrymen." She exited the subway and melted away in the crowded street. When police interviewed witnesses, some said he was pushed by a man, other said that a woman pushed him. Still others said that he simply stumbled. After hearing all the conflicting stories the police decided to call it an accident.

When she returned to the hotel, Carl was waiting. He looked into her eyes for a few seconds then took her into his arms and hugged her and whispered in her ear, "Let the DGSE deal with the rest of Mohammed's terrorist cell."

47

The following day Carl left Paris for Cairo. Lorna and Jim met Carl at the airport as he came out of customs. On the way to an apartment maintained by the agency they filled Carl in on Ahmose Maswagi's activities since the conference. Ahmose had kept a low profile since the conference, teaching classes at the University of Cairo, meeting with students, essentially keeping to himself and his work.

To all appearances, Ahmose was not involved in terrorist activities. He was in fact directing the activities of a group of young men posing as students who were trying to pressure the government to refute its recognition of Israel and disrupt Israel's economic connections with Egypt. Convincing Egypt's Islamic population that doing business with the Jews was anti-Arabic and anti-Islamic was becoming more difficult each day. As long as there was a peaceful frontier with Israel, and businesses were making money trading with Israel, America, and England, it was difficult to convince people to join a jihad.

Ahmose's dissident group focused on striking Egypt's tourist business as a means of disrupting the economy. To strike a blow at the government and Egyptian business, five car bombs ripped though the hotels of the Egyptian town of Sharm el-Sheik at one-fifteen on a Saturday morning, killing sixty-two people and injuring two hundred more. Most were Israeli, English, Russian, and Dutch tourists, and Egyptians workers. The damage was extensive. The Ghazals hotel was severely damaged by fire so intense that the walls collapsed. A second bomb severely damaged the Movenpick hotel. Although some tourists were asleep at that hour of the morning, many still packed seafront restaurants, sidewalk cafes or were shopping at the bazaars where additional car bombs were detonated. The number of deaths totaled forty-five with another two hundred injured.

This was not the only town that Ahmose's group had bombed. In October 2004 the towns of Taba and Shitan, one hundred miles northwest along the Gulf coast of Aqaba, had been subject to terrorist bombings in which thirty-four people died and many more were injured.

When Carl, Lorna, and Jim reached Lorna's apartment they discussed ways in which to neutralize Ahmose. Jim and Carl were in favor of the direct approach of simply killing him. It was Lorna that came up with the suggestion of framing Ahmose and letting the police take him out. They discussed ways in which this could be done and finally settled on a straightforward method of stashing flyers denouncing the Mubarak government in his apartment. Then having the Agency send a copy of the tape from the Islam's Fire leadership meeting and a copy of the conference registration to the police, thus providing Ahmose Maswagi's name and address.

The agency produced the flyers using a copy machine on cheap paper commonly found in Cairo. The copy machine was similar to copiers that could be found throughout the university where Ahmose taught. Once the flyers were produced they were sent to Lorna along with several other documents, including a copy of an e-mail from Parviz complaining about the cost of two of the operations that had gone over budget.

While Ahmose was teaching at the University, Jim, Carl and Lorna went to his apartment. While Lorna maintained a watch outside, he had picked the lock, a skill Carl learned at the CIA training farm, and entered the apartment. They placed the package of two hundred flyers on top of an armoire in Ahmose's bedroom. The armoire was tall enough that the packet of flyers could not be seen by anyone standing in the bedroom, you had to search the room to find it. The e-mail was placed among other papers in a folder in his bookcase. It appeared as if it had been picked up accidentally along with his other papers. They finished in less than five minutes and left.

When they returned to the apartment, Carl placed a call to Aaron at Langley. Then they waited. If the police did not pick up Ahmose they would have to take matters into their own hands.

Aaron sent a copy of the tape and a copy of the registration request, and a short report of their findings to the head of internal security in Cairo. Carl, Lorna and Jim were at a sidewalk café down the street from Ahmose's apartment when the police arrived. After a short time, Ahmose was dragged out in handcuffs and driven away. Fifteen minutes later other police officers came out carrying the flyers and the folder with the e-mail.

Lorna did not like to think of what was going to happen to Ahmose at the hands of the police but after listening to the tape of the business meeting at the conference, she felt no sympathy for Ahmose. She knew the world was better off without him.

To many, it appeared as if Islam's Fire had been destroyed but like the fabled Phoenix of mythology, it would again begin to rise from the ashes.

48

Three days later Carl was sitting on the back porch enjoying a cup of coffee in the cool of the evening when the phone rang. It was Jean Peters who, after a few pleasantries, asked Carl if he could be persuaded to take on another consulting contract. "If you are going to be home tomorrow morning I'd like to come out and talk to you about it and I would like to bring someone out with me."

"How about nine-thirty? I'll have a fresh pot of coffee made for you. I won't make any promises but I'll listen to what you have to say."

Carl was sitting in the kitchen drinking coffee when a black suburban drove up at precisely nine-thirty. Jean got out of the passenger door, and a tall black man climbed out of the driver's seat. When Carl met them at the door, Jean introduced Ron Johnson as her right hand man and the next in command of the Task Force on Terrorism. Carl offered them coffee and they sat at the kitchen table.

Jean started the conversation with, "I understand from Director

Rice that you have completed your current assignment with the CIA. Would you be open to a consulting contract to the FBI's Task Force on Terrorism?"

"It depends on what you have in mind, what rules I would be working under and whom I would be working for."

"What we have in mind is finishing up the Islam's Fire terrorist organization. We have two of the leaders, Khan and Ujaama, loose in our country. It is our belief that they are planning new operations. We know where Ujaama is but Khan got wind that we were tracking him .He managed to lose our guys at JFK airport when he entered the Country. The data base of non-desirable persons had not been updated with his name when he landed, the same with Ujaama.

"We know Ujaama is in Seattle working at the Dijon Restaurant Supply & Distribution Company. We think that with your experience with this group, you may be able to help in stopping whatever it is they are planning.

"The Seattle thing, whatever it is, was not discussed in any detail at the Cairo conference. It is almost as if the plans had already been approved and all they were waiting for was the right time. The go ahead was to come from Khan. Although no details were mentioned, I got the impression that it would cause serious loss of life.

"Our Seattle Office tells us that Ujaama is the dispatcher for the Dijon Company. It's his responsibility to insure that each truck is loaded with the right stuff and then make sure it reaches its destination on time,"

"What is his personal life like?"

"He frequently goes to a local mosque and he is taking evening classes at the University of Washington, in Seattle. He doesn't have a girlfriend and he has a clean police record. If you didn't know better he would look like a model citizen." answered Ron.

"Is there anything happening in Seattle that would be a good target or an event that would gather a lot of people in one place?"

"No, everything is pretty quiet, except for sports events and Pikes Market, which is always crowded.

"The University goes on spring break next week but there's usually a big influx of tourists at this time of year."

"I assume you have tapped his phones. It sounds like you have everything covered. But my guess is that if they are planning something big it will happen within a week, and probably not at the University."

"Why do you say that?" asked Jean.

"A couple of things Jean. The conversation we heard in Egypt had the sound of something imminent, they didn't say when, but listening to them you got the gut feeling that whatever it was would be happening soon and it would be huge. Probably not at the University, it's on spring break, no big crowds."

"Okay, if you are willing to consult for us we'll fly to Seattle this afternoon. You will have the same deal that the other agency gave you and you will be working for me. What's it going to be, do you want to join the party?"

"What time do we leave?"

49

During the flight to Seattle Jean received a message from the Seattle field office. It contained a transcript of a phone call to Ujaama that had been intercepted. She read the message a second time then passed it to Carl. The intercepted phone caller had said, "Have a happy birthday, James, and how is the weather?" The message from the Seattle field office went on to say that the telephone caller did not give his name. He just left the message and then hung up. The area code for the call was 917, a New York cellular number.

Carl let out his breath, and then said, "It would seem that whatever they are planning is on, probably within the next day or two."

"We'll double the number of agents in the area and keep the company warehouse and James Ujaama under twenty-four hour surveillance. If anyone makes a move we'll know about it."

Jean was sound asleep at the hotel when she received a call at one o'clock Monday morning. Three men had gone to the warehouse where they met with James Ujaama, they talked for a few minutes, loaded each of two vans with two fifty-five gallon steel drums, and boxes that looked as if they were fairly heavy. One van left the warehouse and headed north toward Vancouver, the other drove south toward Tacoma. It later turned north on Highway 18 toward Port Angeles. About twenty minutes later, a car driven by a man called Rahib pulled out and headed north toward Vancouver. Agents were following each of the vans.

"Ok, thanks for the call, I better call in some more people, it looks whatever it is they are planning is under way."

A couple of hours later, five other men arrived and loaded five more vans with what appeared to be the same cargo as the first two, two fifty-five gallon steel drums and heavy boxes. The vans left the warehouse at intervals of thirty to forty-five minutes. FBI agents followed each van. The last two to leave drove to pier 50 in Seattle, where the ferry to Bremerton and Vashon docked. The last van went to the Fauntleroy terminal on S.W. Barton.

The van that Malik was driving north toward Vancouver, Canada, stopped at the border crossing and was quickly inspected then released.

The FBI agents following the van were about ten cars back by the time they reached the border crossing. They were further delayed when they were asked if they were carrying weapons, and they answered, "Yes, we are" showing their credentials. They were told they had to wait until they were cleared to enter by the Canadian police. By the time the two agents explained what they were doing the van had gained a significant lead on them.

Eight minutes had passed before they were speeding toward Vancouver again with a Canadian police escort, trying to catch up with the van, but the van had taken the turnoff to the Tsawwassen-Swartz Bay ferry terminal. The police and FBI, unaware the van had exited the freeway continued speeding north.

The van arrived at the terminal just in time to be loaded onto the ferry. After parking the van, Malik started the timer for the detonators, got out of the van and hurried to the passenger deck then down the foot passenger loading ramp. He walked to the coffee/gift shop building. He bought two cups of coffee and two sweet rolls, and walked out to the parking lot where Rahib was waiting for him. Malik and Rahib sat in the car talking, taking sips of coffee, as they watched the ferry pull away from the dock and head toward Swartz Bay.

Carl and Jean were in the command trailer looking at maps of the Seattle area and the State of Washington, when Carl realized where the vans had gone. He told Jean to radio the following agents to stop the vans, "Don't let the vans get on a ferry, they're all carrying bombs. That's why they left the warehouse at different intervals. They had to take into consideration the different drive times to the ferry terminals. They wanted their timing to match the ferry schedule so that they could drive right onto the ferry without waiting in the parking lot, or at least minimize their waiting time."

Jean, grasping what Carl was saying, grabbed the microphone from the table. She ordered the agents following the vans to stop them and arrest the drivers. "The vans are carrying bombs, get them to a safe area fast!" They had only minutes to move the vans to an area where they would do the least amount of damage when they exploded.

Moving quickly, the agents stopped the vans and arrested the drivers, then moved the vans to the far side of the ferry terminal parking lots and told ticketing agents to lock the parking lot gates. They told the ferry boat captain to pull his boat away from the dock as quickly as he could. City police soon arrived and blocked the streets leading to the terminal. Within fifteen minutes of evacuating the area, large explosions shook the parking lots. The explosions were severe enough to blow large craters in the pavement and damage nearby buildings. A few people were injured by flying debris but there was no loss of life.

The ferry that left Tsawwassen Bay ferry terminal was not so lucky. The bomb exploded sixteen minutes after the ferry left the terminal. It tore a hole through the lower car deck destroying the engine room and killing the engineer and his helper. The force of the blast blew a hole in the side of the ferry and she began taking on water. The upward force of the blast destroyed the upper car deck and the forward end of the passenger salon, killing everyone sitting there. The fireball that blew through both car decks set cars and trucks on fire, and as they burned, their gasoline tanks exploded, spewing burning gasoline, turning lower decks into a blazing inferno.

Some of the passengers that were not killed outright tried to put on the life jackets that were stowed under the seats in what was left of the passenger deck. Others ran toward the exit doors in panic and jumped overboard.

Nearby pleasure and fishing boats on hearing the blast and seeing the smoke and fire, rushed toward the burning ferry. They began picking up what passengers they could. When their boats could not hold more, they threw whatever would float to the people who were still in the water to help keep them afloat till help arrived. Those that wore life jackets, could swim or found something to hang onto, managed to survive. The death toll exceeded one hundred and seventy.

The FBI arrested James Ujaama and his cousin who owned the Distribution Company, and the warehousemen that worked there. They confiscated all the records in an effort to see how they managed to get the explosives they needed for the bombs. They found that the owner of the business had bought a ton of ammonium nitrate, two hundred pounds of aluminum powder, and five hundred gallons of diesel fuel. Mixing these ingredients can create a very powerful explosive when detonated. They also had C4 plastic explosives that had been stolen from a mining operation. The C4 was used to detonate the ammonium nitrate diesel mixture.

While the FBI were arresting the drivers of the vans and raiding the warehouse, the car that had gone into Canada with the van was now headed back toward the U.S. border. At that time of the morning, the line of cars at the border crossing was relatively short. It did not take them long to cross back into the United States. Had they tried twenty minutes later the crossing would have been sealed while every car was thoroughly searched.

Three hours later, Malik and Rahib drove down the street in Seattle where the Dijon Restaurant Supply & Distribution Company had their warehouse and offices. From two blocks away they could see the flashing red lights mounted on the police cars parked around the warehouse.

They pulled to the side of the street and parked for a few minutes while they thought about what they should do. They were too alarmed by the police activity around the warehouse to come up with any detailed plan.

Rahib said, "The police know about us and the others. We have to get out of Seattle or they will kill us."

"Take the freeway and go to California. We can hide in a big city until we hear from the leaders."

"But first let's go to the apartment, we have to get our clothes."

When Malik and Rahib turned onto the street where they had been living, they saw two police cars parked in front of their apartment house with their red lights flashing. Malik said, "They are already here. Go! Go! Go!" They drove past the apartment house.

"They must know our names, they will have our clothes, and fingerprints, they have everything."

When they came to an on-ramp for the I-5 South they took it and headed toward California in silence. As they drove they listened to the radio. The newscast was devoted to stories about the sinking of the ferry earlier that morning by a large bomb that had been loaded onto the ferry in the back of a vehicle. The death toll was now estimated to be one hundred and seventy people. Interviews with some of the survivors described the explosion and the ensuing fire, the screaming they heard from the injured and badly burned passengers and crew, the sight of people as they jumped overboard, the ice cold water, and the loss of loved ones.

One woman described how she had to watch as her young son

and daughter drowned and she could do nothing to help. Malik and Rahib were both silent after listening to this woman's description through tears of anguish over the loss of her family. They had caused this attack against Canada and in any attack there was always death. The fact that they had caused the deaths of women and innocent children was not disturbing. After all, hadn't the Jews killed innocents in Lebanon and Palestine, and the Americans killed civilians in Iraq and Afghanistan? This was a jihadist war, and in war people died.

The newscast described the capture of the drivers of the other five vans and the leaders of the terrorist cell, Ujaama and his cousin. The report went on to say that the FBI and the Royal Canadian Mounted Police were interviewing the survivors in an effort to determine if the terrorists who had planted the bomb on the ferry had survived, or had martyred themselves in the blast. The newscaster reported that the terrorist cell was part of an organization called Islam's Fire, an Islamic group whose goal was to drive all foreigners from Islamic land, stop American support of Israel, and prevent foreign companies from exploiting the natural resources that they believed rightfully belonged to the Islamic people. Islam's Fire has been named as responsible for the bombing of the electrical power grid in California that lead to the power blackout of two thirds of the Country and the bombing that recently occurred in the New York Subway system.

It took Malik and Rahib thirteen hours to reach San Francisco. Much of that time was spent in silent contemplation of what they had done. The rest of the drive they talked about what they had to do. Get rid of the car they were driving, go to a large city with an Arabic population, find a place to live, contact the leadership for Islam's Fire and let them know what had happened, and ask for new orders.

They knew the authorities had their names or they would not have been at their apartment. They knew they had to get new identities but were not sure how to go about it.

If they wanted to live they needed to get to a city with a large Muslim community quickly, they needed to find help.

50

The FBI never located Mohammed Sidique Khan. After leaving the JFK airport, Khan had taken a cab into Manhattan, telling the driver he wanted an inexpensive hotel in a section of the city that had a large Muslim population. He would look for a more permanent address the next day.

The following day Khan rented a small apartment on 14th street and Fourth Avenue, in an area once called the Bowery. The area had been undergoing a revitalization resulting in a mixture of housing. Some old apartment buildings, others that had been renovated and new structures constructed. There was also a mixture of tenants some who exhibited wealth and many low income working class people. As the area underwent redevelopment, the working class began to move out as prices started to go up. But there were still some affordably priced, by New York City standards, rentals in the older buildings that had not yet been rehabilitated or replaced.

By the time the FBI had interviewed all the cab drivers that worked the JFK airport and found the one that had picked up

Khan, Khan had already moved out of the hotel and into his apartment leaving no forwarding address. The FBI put flyers up in the immediate area but no one reported seeing him. With new clothes, his hair styled in a more contemporary fashion, and his beard trimmed, he looked like a different person.

Once he had a residence, Khan began to search for ways to earn an income. Within a few days he found a job in a store that sold home furnishings. He was middle-aged and reasonably attractive. He could speak several languages fluently, and was obviously well educated. In an area that catered to a variety of ethnic groups, he was considered a talented and hard working employee.

Soon after renting his apartment he went into a store called "Your Office, Etc." where he bought a prepaid phone and rented a mailbox. That evening he wrote a letter to the headmaster of a madrassas in Pakistan who he knew was sympathetic to their cause. In the past he had supplied the names of students that appeared to have radical leanings and could be recruited to serve Islam's Fire. He sent the headmaster a short note that included his mailing address and telephone number. The note said that the organization that had been serving Allah had suffered a setback and that both Yusef and Parviz were dead. That he was rebuilding the organization and would continue to do Allah's work. With the assistance of the headmaster and his continued support, the infidel would suffer and Islam would one day prevail.

The first call he made on his new cell phone was to Ujaama wishing him a happy birthday. He smiled as he thought about what his message had set in motion.

Although Islam's Fire no longer existed as a viable organization, the vision of Islam's Fire was still alive and if the right leader could come forward it would rise from the ashes to again wreak havoc on the Western world. Khan knew that he, Mohammed Sidique Khan, was that leader. That he would resurrect Islam's Fire.

51

On the West Coast, three thousand miles away, Malik and Rahib had arrived in San Francisco, Looking very tired Rahib said, "We've been up since yesterday without any sleep and it is almost 10:00 P.M. We need to get some rest. Let see if we can find a youth hostel and rest until tomorrow then we can go on to Los Angeles."

"Okay, but first we have to get rid of the car. We can park it on some street and just leave it. It will be a few days before it is towed away. And by that time we will be gone."

They parked the car on Mission Street and left it. They considered themselves lucky that they had come all the way from Seattle without being stopped.

They entering a small coffee shop on Market Street and asked direction to a hostel and were told to go to Union square that there were several hostels in the area. After making inquiries at several places they ended up at a youth hostel on Geary just two blocks from Union Square.

The following morning they made their way to the Greyhound

bus station, bought tickets to Los Angeles, then went to the McDonalds that was situated in a corner of the bus station. As they sat in a booth and ate, Rahib asked, "What are we going to do when we get to Los Angeles?"

"We are going to find a mosque. Maybe the Imam will help us get a job and a place to sleep."

"If we cannot get a job we will have to steal the money if we want to eat, we are almost broke. I used the last of my money for the bus tickets."

"I am not worried we will find work. When we find someplace to stay we will write a letter to headmaster Chowla and ask for advice. He will know what to do."

When their bus arrived in Los Angeles, the two men found a phone book and searched the yellow pages for a mosque. They picked one that had part of the advertisement written in Arabic. Once they had an address they had to ask directions, and not realizing how far away it was they started walking. It was late at night before they finally arrived. The doors to the mosque were locked for the evening so they sat down by the main entrance and waited through the night for the Imam to arrive in the morning.

The next morning they were awakened by a man standing over them. They were disheveled and sore from sleeping on the concrete but most of all they were out of money and hungry. The Imam, after hearing the story they had concocted, felt sorry for them and gave them a few dollars and told them to go the restaurant down the street, get something to eat and to come back in two hours.

When they returned, the Imam told them that he had found them a job working for a landscaper who was one of the worshippers. "The job also comes with a room over the garage that you can use until you make other arrangements."

The Imam said that the landscaper would drive by later that morning to see if they were interested in taking the job. They expressed their thanks to the Imam for his help and asked if there was anything they could do for the mosque as a way to express their thanks to the Imam for his help. He put them to work hoeing weeds in the flower beds that surrounded the building.

Ray Anderson, who was the owner of the landscaping business and a convert to Islam, came by late in the afternoon. Ray said he would pay them two dollars above minimum wage and they could start work right away. He said he had a crew of eight. He asked if they could speak Spanish, when they said no, he seemed disappointed.

That day after work they told Ray they wanted to write a letter home and asked if it was alright if they used his business address. Ray said yes, a decision he would come to regret.

52

A month after arriving in New York, Khan found a letter in his mail box from the headmaster Chowla.

> *This letter is to pray for your continued good health and to offer you my condolences on the recent death of your family. Do not worry as your family is enjoying the gifts bestowed by Allah and are sitting at the feet of the Prophet. I have heard from your two brothers, Rahib and Malik, who will be calling you when they reached New York. Your brothers will help you through this time of sorrow and help you rebuild your business.*

At the same time the letter to Khan was posted, a second letter, addressed to Malik, was posted to the address of Ray Anderson's landscaping business in Los Angeles. In part it said.

> *Your brother Mohamed Sidique Khan has lost members of his family and is in desperate need of your help. He would be most grateful for your as-*

sistance if you could join him in New York. You can reach him by writing to his post office address or calling him on his cell phone when you reach New York

The question for Malik and Rahib was how to get enough money to make the trip to New York. Their wages provided enough to buy food and a few items of clothing but not enough to allow them to save anything. They decided that the only course open to them was to steal the money for the trip. With that in mind they began watching the businesses that could provide them with enough money and had poor security. They decided that the security systems in banks and savings and loans were too sophisticated to allow them to get away with a theft. Their focus then turned to bars, pizza parlors, and convenience stores.

They finally settled on a local bar. The owner would usually close the bar at two in the morning, do a little clean up, then leave taking the day's receipts home with him. The parking lot was not well lit, but the bar owner parked his car within ten feet of the rear door, and as a result, felt relatively safe. Malik and Rahib waited until Saturday night when the bar's receipts would be greatest. As the bar owner exited the building, Malik, who was at the end of the street began yelling. When the bar owner turned to look, Rahib who had been hiding behind the car, stepped out and hit the bar owner with a hammer. Rahib dragged the man to the other side of the car where he was not visible from the street and started to go through his pockets. He removed the money from the billfold and grabbed the canvas sack that had the day's receipts. Unfortunately, the bar owner was dead. He had been struck with enough force to crush his skull.

Malik and Rahib worked for another two weeks then told Ray Anderson that they had to go to New York to help their cousin who had lost his family in a car accident. They told Ray that their cousin had sent them the money for plane tickets and that they would be leaving the next day. The robbery had yielded twenty-six hundred dollars, which would pay for two tickets and still leave enough money to live on for a short time when they reached New York.

The following morning Ray drove them to the airport and wished them well. He said that if they needed work in the future to be sure and look him up. Four hours later Malik and Rahib were on a Blue Sky flight to New York City.

Malik and Rahib did not realize that the FBI was hot on their trail. The car they had abandoned in San Francisco had been towed to an impound yard. When the license plate was checked through the stolen car registry, it was found to be wanted by the FBI. It was not long before a forensic unit from the FBI arrived to examine the car. They found fingerprints belonging to Malik and Rahib who by this time had been identified as the terrorists who had planted the bomb aboard the Canadian ferry. A check of local hotels, mosques, bus, and train stations had turned up nothing. It seemed as if the FBI had hit a dead end. Then three weeks later the Los Angeles police submitted a fingerprint that was found on the billfold of a murdered man to AFIS (Automated Fingerprint Identification System) and got a hit for a man named Rahib Kalil who was wanted by the FBI on charges of terrorism.

The FBI began the search in Los Angeles by showing the Imams of the local mosques a Student ID picture taken by the University of Washington, and Washington State driver license pictures, as well as providing a physical description. It was not long before they came to the mosque where Malik and Rahib received help from the Imam. The Imam told them that he had called a member of the mosque, Ray Anderson, to see if he could help the young men with a job. Ray hired the two men and gave them the back room of his garage to sleep in.

Forty-five minutes later, they were talking to Ray Anderson who told them that he had driven the two men to the airport two days earlier. They had received a letter saying that their cousin in New York City had recently lost his family, and asking if they could come to New York City and help him run his business.

A forensic team was brought in to examine the garage and back room for any evidence that might be helpful in finding Malik and Rahib. The local police also joined the examination of the garage since Rahib was a murder suspect and they were hopeful of finding the murder weapon. The examination of the murder victim made them suspect that the weapon was a hammer-like tool, so it was not too long before they found the hammer with Rahib's fingerprint on the handle and the bar owner's blood on the hammer head.

Since Ray told Malik and Rahib that they could use his mailing address, the FBI searched the office for any evidence tying them to the murder or any scrap of paper that might have been used by Malik or Rahib to mail letters or may have been discarded by them.

The search by the FBI essentially closed down Ray's business office for two days. When the agents found nothing else of interest, the focus of the investigation switched to New York City.

53

When Malik and Rahib arrived in New York City they called the number that headmaster Chowla had given them. Khan answered the phone. Malik introduced himself and said that he had received the phone number from the headmaster of a school in Pakistan with instructions to call this number when he and his friend arrived in New York City. Khan gave him an address and told him to be there at seven that evening, not before.

Malik and Rahib wandered around Forty-second Street in Manhattan like thousands of other tourists. They were dazzled by the neon signs, stores loaded with goods and the throngs of people on the street. They had been to large cities before, Seattle, San Francisco, Los Angeles, but they were nothing like New York.

At six-thirty, they hailed a taxi and gave the driver the address they had received from Khan. Khan met them at the door, and after introductions they sat down in the living room and drank hot sweet tea with milk while Malik told Khan of their part in the Canadian ferryboat bombing and their escape to California. They omitted telling Khan about killing the bar owner and stealing his money. They did not want to be viewed as common thieves. Malik expressed pride in how they had evaded the police and was doubtful that anybody could know that they were in New York.

Khan listened to their tale and thought to himself that these two were very naive about the resourcefulness of the police.

Khan told them to shave off all of their facial hair and get haircuts, and then buy casual clothes more in line with what other people their age were wearing. When they were ready they would begin to gather the supplies needed for another strike at America.

"What is our new target?" asked Malik."

"The goals and aims of Islam's Fire remain the same, to destroy the infidel's economy through fear and the destruction of its economic infrastructure. The target I have chosen is the very heart of the country's finances, the New York Stock Exchange," said Khan. "Most of America's wealth is false wealth, it is not gold, silver, or other precious metals. The vast majority of America's wealth exists only as a number on some computer file. If you destroy the computer records you are destroying someone's wealth."

"I don't understand," said Rahib.

"Think of it this way Rahib. If, say, the Ford Motor Company is owned by thousands of different people each claiming a different number of shares of stock, and all the records of the share owners are kept on a computer at the New York Stock Exchange, and you are able to destroy that computer, then who owns the stock? Obviously the people who bought it, but who are they? Where do they live? How many shares of stock do they own? All of the names of the owners and the shares that they own are on the computers. Now multiply that by the hundreds of companies listed on the Stock Exchange.

"In that scenario, the owners of the stock could not buy more stock or sell their shares, and they could not be paid their share of the company's profits. Yes, eventually the computer files could be rebuilt from paper records, such as receipts or records maintained by the various stock brokerage companies, stock orders, and other paper documents, but there are millions of stock holders. It would take a great deal of time to rebuild the files and then the files would have countless errors.

"Thousands of people would lose their money. Since the stock owners would not get their share of a company's profits until the computer records were rebuilt the money could not be spent to buy the goods they want. The money would not be available in the economy. Since there would be less money to buy goods, companies that sell goods and services would begin to fail. There would be panic in the world economy."

Malik said, "Surely there must be a second computer with a copy of those records. They would not allow such important records to exist only on one computer."

Khan leaned back in his chair and said, "Yes, there is a second computer, it's called a mirror image back-up of the main computer. Every time a file is changed on the main computer a duplicate file on the back-up computer is changed. To be effective we must destroy both computers.

"We will begin by buying two delivery vans. Then we will load them with bombs and take them to the computer centers. The bombs must be large enough to destroy the buildings and the people working there.

"Malik, you and Rahib will take one of the vans and go into the countryside of New Jersey and buy all the ammonium nitrate fertilizer that you can from the local farm supply stores. At the end of each day we will drain the diesel fuel from the vans into barrels to be saved until we assemble the bombs. The following morning the first thing you will do is refuel the vans. We will detonate the ammonium nitrate bombs with explosives that we will take from a coal mining operation in West Virginia.

"It will take about a month to prepare for this attack. You must do nothing that will bring either of you to the attention of the police. You will start tomorrow by buying clothes and shaving, and then you will begin to visit automobile dealerships looking for delivery vans. If anyone asks why you want the vans, tell them that your cousin owns a small produce delivery business and wants to expand his business. Remember, the vans must operate using diesel fuel.

"Tonight you will stay here and tomorrow we will find you a small apartment."

Within the week they had found a small warehouse across the river in Hoboken, New Jersey, and purchased two used delivery vans. From then on Malik and Rahib were on the roads through the farm county of New Jersey buying small quantities of ammonium nitrate fertilizer and taking it back to the warehouse.

On one trip they found a salvage yard where they were able to buy the fifty-five gallon steel drums. At the end of each day they would drain most of the diesel fuel from the van and set it aside for later use, then refill the van's fuel tank the next morning. By the end of the third week they had accumulated enough ingredients for ten fifty-five-gallon drums. All that was left to do was obtain the explosives that would be used as detonators.

The last trip was to the coal mining region of West Virginia. Pretending to be looking for work, they talked to mine operators, miners, guards, and anyone else they could find who might know something about the operation and layout of the storage facilities. They explained that they had experience using explosives and were looking for a job. They finally found one strip mining operation that was removing the top of a mountain to expose the coal seam and was using a lot of explosives in the process.

On a Saturday night when the clearing operation had shut down for the day they were able to break into the explosive storage shed and take a large quantity of plastic explosive, primer cord, fuse, plus igniters with timers.

They were nearly back in Hoboken when they were pulled over by the police. Malik and Rahib turned to each other, not knowing what to do. They had been careful not to speed or break any traffic laws. When the State Trooper knocked on the window they didn't know if they should open the window or open the door and run. Finally, Malik rolled down the window.

The Trooper politely asked for his driver's license and vehicle registration. He told Malik that a tail light was not working properly and he was going to give him a fix-it ticket. He would have two weeks to get the problem repaired. "When it's fixed, have the garage where it was repaired sign the fix-it ticket and mail it to the address on the back of the ticket."

The trooper then asked how long Malik had been on the East Coast. When Malik said about a month, the trooper told him that he should have applied for a New York driver's license within two weeks of having moved to the state. Malik thanked him for the information, and the Trooper left. Both Malik and Rahib were physically drained with nervous tension by the time the Trooper drove away.

At the end of the shift, the Trooper turned in the fix-it ticket, information which now carried the Washington driver's license number, to the clerk at the office to be entered into the computer system. When the clerk entered the number, it came back with a message saying that Malik was wanted by the FBI for acts of terrorism, and provided a notification number. The same information appeared at the FBI's Task Force on Terrorism. Special Agent Jean Peters issued a BOLO (be on the lookout) for the van, but by this time it was locked away in the warehouse along with the second van.

When they told Khan about the police stop he became concerned and told Malik and Rahib that the vans were not to be driven again until they were ready to be used to deliver the bombs. For the next week, Malik and Rahib busied themselves repainting both vans with new signs reading, "Business Supplies Center." Delivery vans moving through the streets of New York delivering business supplies to the many business, including the Stock Exchange and its backup data center, would not be seen as unusual.

Next they had to actually build the bombs. Malik and Rahib had learned to build ammonium nitrate diesel bombs at the training camp, but it was a dangerous process under the best of conditions. And working in a poorly lighted warehouse was not considered ideal.

They first filled each of the fifty-five gallon drums three-fourths full of ammonium nitrate then weighed the drums. The next step was adding enough diesel fuel to equal ten percent of the weight of the ammonium nitrate. Once that was done they slowly stirred the mixture into a slurry. When it reached the right consistency they carefully added powdered aluminum. If they added too much or too little the bomb would not explode. The bombs were now complete. All they had to do was add a detonating explosive.

For detonators, C4 and blasting caps would suit their purpose and they had stolen enough C4 to make a hundred bombs. They pushed a blasting cap into the block of C4 and taped the ignition wires so that they could not be pulled out by accident. The last step was to tape the blocks of C4 to the drums. They ran the ignition wire to the front seat where it could be connected to the igniters. The timers on the igniters were set for a two-minute delay to give them time to run.

Then they set about making handheld bombs that they could throw. For these they used fuses and blasting caps. Inserting the fuse into the blasting cap and crimping the cap so that the fuse would not fall out, they inserted the cap into a block of C4 then taped the fuse securely in place. Now all they had to do was light the fuse, throw it and run. They would have about ten seconds before the blast.

Everything was ready, except they still needed the address of the backup computers. Khan decided that the only way to get that was to kidnap one of the New York Stock Exchange Information Technology managers and force him to tell them where it was located. Once they had that information they would have to kill him.

54

Getting the name of the IT manager was easier than expected. Khan simply walked into the lobby of the New York Stock Exchange and looked at the directory that hung on the wall. It listed the IT manager as John R. Bromely, and gave his room number.

The business offices and conference rooms of the Exchange were open to the public. The floor of the Stock Exchange was not. Khan simply told the guard in the lobby that he had a meeting with Mr. Bromely. He was asked to sign a log book, which required his name and the name of the company he represented. He gave a fictitious name and company and went directly to Mr. Bromely's office where he waited until a man he believed was Bromely came out.

When a man exited the office, Khan asked, "Mr. Bromely?" When the man said, "Yes," Khan said, "I would like to set up an appointment with you to talk about life insurance." Mr. Bromely scowled saying, "Talk to my secretary about appointments," turned on his heel and walked off. Khan waited until he had taken the elevator, then he also left the building. That afternoon Khan and Rahib were waiting for Mr. Bromely to exit the building. When he did they followed him to his apartment.

The next Friday evening Khan and Rahib took a taxi to an address a block from the Bromley apartment then walked back to the correct address. They waited until someone entered the building, then tailgating, grabbed the door before it could close. Studying the mailboxes, they found the apartment number for the Bromely's.

They took the stairs to the fifth floor and rang the doorbell. When Mrs. Bromely looked through the peephole, and asked who he was, Khan simply held up his wallet with a business card showing as if it were identification and said, "FBI, please open the door."

When Mrs. Bromely opened the door, Khan pushed his way in and before Mrs. Bromely could speak, he clamped his hand with a piece of duct tape over her mouth. Rahib came in immediately and taped her hands behind her back. Then making sure that the tape over her mouth was secure, they put a knife to her throat and walked her into the kitchen where Mr. Bromely was pouring two glasses of wine.

Mr. Bromely dropped the bottle of wine he was holding, letting it crash to the floor. "What the hell's going on?"

Khan put his finger to his lips indicating that Bromely should be quiet, making sure that he saw the knife at his wife's throat. Bromely did not move or say a word he just stared wide-eyed at the knife.

Rahib quickly put a piece of tape over Bromelys mouth and taped his hands behind his back. They tied Bromely and his wife to chairs, taping their ankles to the chair legs. They were unable to stand or move their bodies.

A quick search of the apartment assured the men that the Bromelys were alone.

Khan looked into Bromely's eyes and in a raspy voice said, "I will remove the tape from your mouth but if you scream I will kill your wife. Do you understand?"

Bromely nodded. Khan removed the tape from his mouth, saying, "All we want is information. If we get the information we want you and your wife will live, if we do not you will both die. Is that understood?"

"Please don't hurt my wife!"

Khan slapped him hard and repeated the question in a commanding voice "Is that understood?"

Bromely, with blood running down his chin from a split lip said, "I understand, what do you want to know?"

"That's better," answered Khan. "What is the address for the backup computer center for the New York Stock Exchange?"

"The backup center? Why do you want to know that?" Again there were two quick hard slaps. More blood ran down Bromely's face.

"You do not ask the questions. I will ask questions. Now tell me, what is the address of the backup computer center?"

"I don't know," said Bromely.

"Cut off one of her fingers."

A look of horror spread across Mrs. Bromely's face as Rahib cut through the tape tying her wrist to the chair. He yanked her right hand to the kitchen table and in one quick move cut off her little finger.

Khan put his hand over Bromely's mouth before he could scream. Then he said, "We are very serious. Tell me the address of the backup computer center or your wife will lose all the fingers on her hands, one by one."

Bromely nodded that he understood and Khan removed his hand from Bromely's mouth.

"It's across the river in Freeport, Long Island."

"Be specific, what is the address in Freeport?"

"In the business park, 10229 Elmont Street."

"Where is your cell phone? I will call them and if the

information you have given me is incorrect I will kill your wife. Do you understand?"

"I understand. I haven't lied to you."

"Cut the pig's throat." said Khan in Arabic.

Rahib stepped behind Mrs. Bromely and yanked her head back. With one quick slice of his knife he cut her throat. Khan did the same to Mr. Bromely.

Before they left they washed the blood from their hands and any blood splatter that had hit their clothes. When they were satisfied that they had cleaned up sufficiently they left.

55

Carl was getting ready to go out and see if the workmen who were putting in the new security system needed any help, when the phone rang. Picking up the phone he said, "Hello," and heard Jean Peters say, "Hello Carl, this is Jean. Are you available for a little consulting?"

"What do you have in mind?"

"We identified two of the people responsible for the sinking of the ferry near Vancouver and we believe at least one, if not both of them, are now in the New York City area. We think they have hooked up with Khan. Since you are the only person who has seen Khan in person, you could be key in this investigation."

"Yeah, I'm very interested. When and where do you want to meet?"

"Can you pack a bag and meet me at Andrew's in two hours?"

"I don't think that will be a problem. See you in a couple of hours."

On the flight to New York City, Jean filled Carl in on how they had traced Malik and Rahib to San Francisco and then to Los Angeles where they had murdered a bar owner. The matching of Rahib's fingerprints to those found on the murder weapon, and finally the traffic stop for a fix-it ticket in New Jersey, confirmed their findings.

"Any indication of what was in the van?"

"No, but we had an alert to a theft of a lot of explosives from a strip mining operation in West Virginia. We think Malik and Rahib stole the explosives and that's what they had in the van when they were stopped. If Malik wasn't hauling a large amount of explosives, why drive a van and not a car? We have a BOLO out for the van but it hasn't been seen since.

"The aim of Islam's Fire is to destroy the economy of this Country through fear and intimidation. Since Khan was one of the leaders, I'll bet he is going to hold to those goals. The big question is how would you go about destroying the economy of a country in New York City?"

The pilot yelled back into the cabin, "Agent Peters, you have a call. I'll patch it through to you."

Jean picked up the phone saying, "Special Agent Jean Peters speaking."

"This is Special Agent John Wilks of the New York City field office. We received a report from the city police of a double murder that you might be interested in. It looks like a torture for information, and a method of killing that is not often seen here. They called because of the unusual circumstances. A white male and his wife were found by their daughter when she went to their apartment to visit. Both victims were tied to chairs and had their throats slit from ear to ear. The woman also had a small finger cut off. Nothing appeared to have been stolen from the apartment and the victim's wallets were intact including cash and credit cards."

"Hold on a minute," said Jean.

Jean relayed the conversation to Carl. Carl thought about

it for a minute then said, "Ask him what the victims did for a living."

Jean asked Wilks the question and listened to the response. Then after repeating the answer to Carl she waited to see if Carl had any other questions, he didn't.

She thanked Wilks for the information, saying that they would be landing at JFK in about twenty minutes and they would see him at his office shortly thereafter. Then she hung up.

"That's got to be it. It fits the goals of the organization and it certainly would wreak havoc with the economy. They're going to try to blow up the New York Stock Exchange tomorrow."

"Why tomorrow?"

"First, they killed the manager on a Friday night or early Saturday morning so he wouldn't be missed at work. The longer they wait, the greater the chance that the bodies will be found and that the police will put together what they have in mind. The longer Khan waits, the greater the risk to their operation.

"Second, they will want to do it when they can do the maximum amount of damage and kill the greatest number of people. That would be Monday, when the entire staff is in the building and the traders are on the floor."

Jean thought for a minute then said, "That sounds logical. It would cause a financial disaster in this Country."

When they landed at JFK, Jean called John Wilks and asked him to have the head of the city's Anti Terrorism Task Force meet them at his office. She told him they would be at his office in forty minutes.

When they arrived the entire staff was called into the conference room along with police Captain Carducci, and a lieutenant Hutchings from the city's Anti Terrorism Task Force. Jean explained that she and Carl had reached the conclusion that the New York Stock Exchange was the target for a terrorist attack by Islam's Fire. It was their belief that the attack would take place on Monday, and that the method of attack would be a large bomb in a delivery van. Then she explained how she and Carl had reached that conclusion.

The police chief spoke up, saying that if they could get the license plate number of the vehicle, a computerized camera system at the bridges and tunnels coming into the city could scan all the license plates. If the vehicle was not already in the City, the system would notify police of the approaching vehicle when it tried to enter, giving them time to set up a trap.

"When the van is stopped you had better be quick or the driver will blow his load right there. These people are quite willing to be martyrs," said Carl.

Following the meeting, Jean, Carl and Wilks drove to the New York Stock Exchange. The building was locked tight for the weekend but they managed to rouse the watchman. After identifying themselves they asked him if anyone worked there over the weekend.

The watchman said the building was closed until Monday. The only people there were the cleaning staff and computer people in the basement.

"Take us to the computer room now, this is important."

When they found the shift manager, Jean introduced herself and explained their concerns. The shift manager blanched as Jean explained what they thought was being planned by terrorists.

When the shift manager calmed down, he told them that he had to call his management to tell them of the impending problem.

"Give me the call list and I'll call them, I need to talk to them anyhow," Jean said.

"What are the procedures in an emergency like this?" asked Carl.

"Our emergency plans require us to make backup copies of the files and then do an orderly shutdown of the computers. We're supposed to call our back-up computer center and let them know that we may be moving operations to their site."

"Where is this backup data center?"

"I don't know. Only the top managers know. It is kept secret for security reasons."

"Bromely would know where it is, wouldn't he?"

"Well sure, he's a top manager, he would know."

Carl took Jean aside saying, "That's why Bromely was tortured and then killed. Khan wanted to know the address of the backup computer center. There must be a second van involved. We've got to find out where the other data center is located and get some cops out there quick."

Jean told the shift manager that they needed to speak to the management people who would know where the backup site was located. She asked for their names, telephone numbers, and addresses.

56

Khan wanted their bombs to go off close to the same time. To ensure that the bombs were detonated nearly simultaneously, Rahib left the warehouse with his van several hours ahead of Malik. Rahib had to find Freeport, and then the address for the backup computer center.

The license plate on Rahib's van did not trip any alarms at the Holland tunnel. His van was just one of many making early morning deliveries to Manhattan businesses, but he did notice what seemed to be a large number of police cars as he exited the tunnel. The police seemed to give him an unusually long look, but did not stop him. He kept going east until he reached Canal Street, then he turned left. When he reached Delancy Street he turned right and headed toward the Williamsburg Bridge that crossed onto Long Island. He continued on Highway 278 then merged onto Highway 495. He continued east until he came to the Freeport exit.

On entering the town of Freeport he pulled to the curb and

spent a few minutes looking at his street map until he finally found Elmont Street. It was on the far side of town.

He checked the time, it was still early and he was hungry. He decided to drive past the entry to the business park and look for someplace to get breakfast. As he passed the business park he could see police cars had cordoned off Elmont Street about two blocks in from the entry. He tried to find another street that would take him around the blockade but couldn't. The business park had only one point of entry. The only thing he could do was create a diversion that would be sufficient to draw police away from the blockade. If enough police left the area he might be able to get through.

He parked. Deciding it was better to be prepared he went into the back of his van and removed several bricks of C4 that he and Malik had put together. The C4 could be used to blast his way through a roadblock if he needed to resort to that.

He drove further up Main Street until he passed a gas station about a quarter mile away. As he passed, he noticed a tanker truck and trailer unloading gas into the underground storage tanks. At the next intersection he made a left-hand turn and then pulled into the parking lot of a small store. He backed up and returned to the intersection and made a right turn. Reaching the gas station he pulled in and stopped next to the tanker truck and trailer unloading fuel. Rolling down his window and using the van's cigarette lighter he lit the fuse on a brick of C4. He tossed the block of C4 onto the truck's hose rack then left the gas station as quickly as he could. Ten seconds later the C4 exploded, ripping a large hole in the side of the truck's tank and sending hot metal ripping into the trailer. The gasoline in both tanks exploded. Burning fuel spread through the filling station, setting the cashier's building and cars near the tanks on fire. Burning gasoline spilled down the fill pipe to the underground storage tanks. The exploding storage tanks blew chunks of concrete and flames hundreds of feet into the air. Part of the gasoline truck crashed onto the roof of the strip mall next to the gas station, setting it on fire. The concussion from the explosion rocked the van as it sped down the street, nearly sending it careening into the cars parked at the curb.

Two men, a woman, and a teenager who had been fuelling their cars tried to run away but were knocked to the ground by the concussion and then enveloped by a wall of burning gasoline. The blond twenty-year-old woman, who was cashiering that shift, saw the explosion and the burning gasoline coming toward her but was too stunned to do anything except simply stand there and watch. Within seconds she too had died.

The blast was heard by the police guarding the computer center. They looked up to see the fireball rise hundreds of feet into the air, and burning debris begin to rain down, setting the roofs of a number of nearby buildings on fire. Believing that the terrorists had struck another part of town most of the police stationed at the blockade got into their cars and headed toward the burning gas station. A few minutes after the police pulled out of the business park, Rahib drove in and pressed the gas pedal to the floor. There were only two police cars left to block the street. The van continued to gain speed, finally ramming the rear end of one of the police cars blocking the street, sending it crashing into the second police car, but managed to keep going.

Instead of looking for the loading dock, Rahib drove straight through the front door into the lobby of the building before coming to a stop. Although badly injured, Rahib reached for the detonator that had fallen to the floor. He lifted the safety cover over the ignition switch and moved the switch to the 'Fire' position and pressed the timer start button. The timer began its two minute countdown.

People in other buildings went to the windows to see what had happened. Others came running from nearby buildings to see if they could help. The police at the roadblock came running down the street yelling for people to get back but no one listened, they were intent on helping the injured.

As police tried to remove Rahib from the cab, he smiled and

said something in Arabic. The blast almost flattened the entire building and killed all those that came to offer assistance.

The backup computers ran virtually automatically. As a consequence there were only six computer operators per shift, they were killed instantly.

Surrounding buildings were heavily damaged. The spectators that had rushed to the window to see what had happened were either killed by the blast and flying glass, or severely injured by flying debris. The buildings adjacent and directly across the street from the data center received almost as much damage as the computer center itself. The fronts of the nearby buildings disintegrated, killing a number of people in the front row of offices.

The target of the attack, the computer center, was buried under a mountain of debris.

57

Malik entered the Holland Tunnel unaware that the license plate of his van had been scanned and that police would be waiting for him. As he neared the tunnel exit he noticed that cars were beginning to slow down. Looking ahead he saw what appeared to be a wreck involving a car and another truck.

Police were guiding cars slowly around the site as they got ready to maneuver a tow truck into position. Malik's attention was on the scene in front of him and he didn't notice that the cars behind him had been stopped a hundred yards back. He continued watching the policeman that appeared to be trying to direct traffic around the wreck. Another tall husky policeman waved for him to stop so that the tow truck could be hooked up to one of the damaged vehicles.

The very large policeman who had stopped him, casually walked up to the driver's door smiling and saying that he was sorry for the delay, but that that it would only be for a few more minutes. Malik did not notice the officer had unhooked the strap over his pistol. When he was alongside the driver's door he yanked it open with one hand grabbing Malik with the other dragging him out of the van and throwing him to the street. Malik was so stunned by the surprise move that he could only scream something in Arabic. He found himself flat on his stomach on the pavement with the policeman's knee in the middle of his back and a gun pressed to his head. Within seconds, his hands were dragged behind his back and cuffed. Another man jumped into his van and began to move it to the far end of a parking lot a short distance from the tunnel exit.

Immediately two members of the bomb disposal squad pulled open the rear doors to the van and stood astonished at seeing the amount of explosives. They began the process of searching for timers or detonators. When they found the wires leading from the blasting caps to the front of the van they immediately cut them. There was an audible sigh of relief. The bomb squad started to go through the boxes to make sure that there were no other hidden detonators or timers. When the all-clear was given, the forensic team and detectives began to go over the van gathering evidence.

Malik was taken to one of the squad cars and bent over the hood while a forensic expert went through his pockets. He was told to strip to his briefs and given a jumpsuit to wear while his clothes were bagged. All his clothes and personal items would be thoroughly examined at the police lab.

When the evidence had been catalogued and photographed, Carl and Jean Peters were allowed to look at it. There wasn't much, a wallet with ninety-seven dollars, no credit cards, a piece of paper with a phone number and an address, a Washington State driver's license, and a student ID card from the University of Washington.

After he had gone through the wallet, Carl asked Malik in fluent Arabic, "Where is Mohammed Sidique Khan?"

Malik's head jerked up and he looked at Carl in surprise at

hearing the question in Arabic. Carl, more forcibly, again asked in Arabic, "Where is Mohammed Sidique Khan?"

"I don't know any Mohammed Sidique Khan."

"Don't lie to me. Khan is a leader of Islam's Fire. He is the one who ordered Ujaama to blow up the ferries in Seattle, and you to blow up the ferry in Canada. You are the coward that killed innocent women and children, and Mohammed Sidique Khan is the one who ordered the operation. Now where is Khan?"

Malik stared at this man who seemed to know all about Islam's Fire and its role in the Seattle bombings. He decided the best course of action was to not say anything.

Carl decided to try once more to shock Malik into talking. "Your friend Rahib is dead. His explosives went off by accident without causing much damage. So you and Khan are the only two left to brag about your criminal acts. For the last time, where is Mohammed Sidique Khan or should I just kill you now?"

Malik's head whipped around so that he was staring into Carl's face, and his eyes widened but he remained silent.

Carl walked out of Malik's hearing with Jean, saying, "Malik has not said anything useful. Our only hope is that the address and phone number in his wallet belongs to Khan. I think we should check it out."

Fifteen minutes later, federal agents and police surrounded the apartment building then went up three flights of stairs to the apartment listed in the address. They knocked but got no answer, knocked a second time, with still no answer. Jean ordered, "Break it down." One of the agents stepped back and kicked the door. The door jamb splintered and the door flew open. The agents poured into the apartment with arms extended holding guns. After checking all the rooms one of the agents yelled, "All clear" and Jean and Carl entered. The apartment was essentially bare. Khan was not there and they had no clue where he had gone.

Khan had packed his clothes and laptop computer earlier and stored them in a coin locker at Grand Central Station. Like a firebug who cannot help himself but instead is compelled by an inner need to wait around to see the flames and fire engines arrive, Khan wanted to see the results of the bombing. He knew that it was not a good idea but still felt forced to wait. He was not sure just how big the blast would be or how far away he would have to be in order to be safe. He knew that the area would be swarming with police after the explosion. The police would stop anyone who looked remotely Arabic. Profiling was not legal, but he knew that that bit of legality would be ignored. Still he could not resist staying.

As he stood next to his locker in an alcove full of lockers at Grand Central Station, thinking about the coming blast, his compulsion to see the sight continued to grow within him. Finally, he pocketed the locker key and walked out of Grand Central Station in the direction of the Stock Exchange.

When he was two blocks away from the Stock Exchange he could see that the street was blocked to all vehicle and pedestrian traffic. Many people standing there were complaining that they were not allowed to go to work but no one would tell them why. Others were complaining that the Stock Market was closed for the day.

As Khan stood there watching, the police began taking down the barriers and letting people pass through. As Khan watched the barriers come down he knew that Malik had somehow been captured or killed.

Carl and Jean drove toward the Stock Exchange on the very slim chance that they might spot Khan. Carl was watching the pedestrian traffic on both sides of the street. He told Jean to slow down so that he could get a better look. As they neared the intersection that had been blockaded the barriers were just being removed. Most of the crowd moved toward the area that had been blocked off. A few of the curious wandered in the opposite direction. As the car drew closer to the crowd, Carl yelled for Jean to stop. He jumped out of the car and started across the street.

Khan started to walk back toward Grand Central Station. Out of the corner of his eye he saw a car suddenly stop in the middle of the street and a man jump out. He looked vaguely familiar. It was obvious that the man was running toward him, trying to catch him. Khan started to run through the crowd on the sidewalk. A short distance ahead he saw the entry to the subway. He glanced back and the man was still running toward him. He took the stairs to the subway platform two at a time. When he reached the bottom he jumped the turnstiles and ran down the platform. The train had just left and the platform was almost empty.

Khan ran to the end of the platform and jumped to the track bed four feet below and continued to run down the dark tunnel. He could hear the footsteps of the man chasing him. Although the man didn't seem to be catching up, he wasn't falling back either. Khan started to gasp for air. Over the years he had failed to keep himself in good physical condition. He was fast becoming winded and running out of energy. He knew he could not keep this pace up much longer. He stumbled in the dark, regained his balance, and kept on running. The man behind him was closer now.

He had reached a darker section of the tunnel, but in the gloom was able to see what appeared to be an opening in the wall to his left. He ducked into it and found himself in a small alcove that was used to store track maintenance tools. He grabbed a shovel and prepared to swing it at the man following him. As Carl started to pass the alcove he felt the shovel strike his shoulder as pain radiated through his shoulder and down his arm and back. The blow sent him sprawling onto the track bed on his stomach. He felt pain again as the gravel scratched his face, and blood ran into his eye and down his cheek. He instinctively rolled onto his back as Khan stepped toward him with the shovel raised over his head.

Carl kicked out with his foot, hitting Khan in the knee and sending him over backwards. The shovel flew out of his hands.

Khan got to his feet and started to run down the track again but a sharp pain stabbed through his knee and it started to buckle under him. He shifted his weight and managed to keep his balance.

Carl tried to get back on his feet but his left arm was numb and of no use to him. He finally scrambled to his feet as blood on the side of his face trickled into his eye, making it difficult to see. He wiped the blood away and started after Khan.

The train tunnel had light fixtures every few hundred feet. The light was not enough to read by, but it was enough that you could see to walk in the tunnel without injuring yourself. Just as he neared one of these lights Khan stumbled and fell between the tracks. He was too tired and winded to pull himself up. The man who was following him reached him and stopped.

Khan in a wheezing voice asked, "Who are you?"

"I am the man who killed Yusef, and I am the man who is going to kill you," said Carl in Arabic.

Both men could hear the train approaching, and feel the column of air being pushed by the train as is it neared. Carl moved to the side of the tunnel. Khan just smiled and sat there.

The engineer saw the two men but it was too late to stop the train. The train hit Khan, decapitating him, and dragged the body another hundred feet farther down the tunnel.

Khan was dead. Carl began walking back toward the platform. He would leave this problem to be cleaned up by the FBI and the police.

58

Carl's shoulder and back ached. He knew that it was not a serious injury, nevertheless his shoulder muscles had been badly bruised and his arm was numb. At least his injury was not as serious as the ones suffered by Khan.

When he reached the platform, Jean was standing there with two transit authority cops. Carl reached up and tried to pull himself up onto the subway platform but couldn't.

Jean and a transit cop reached down and grabbed him by the wrist of his good arm, pulling him up to the platform. Jean, a worried look on her face, was asking, "Are you okay? Your face is bleeding."

"Yeah I am okay, just had my shoulder banged up a little and I scraped my face when I hit the ground. A couple of aspirin and a few band aids will take care of it. You had better call the coroner and a forensic team down here, Khan was hit by the train. I think the trainman probably called it in to the transit authorities but to make sure we get the right team down here you had better call in your people."

Jean stepped back and started dialing her phone. When she was through with her call she came back and asked what had happened.

"I started to chase Khan but he ran down the track. He waylaid me in the dark and hit me with something, I think it was a shovel, but I am not sure. When I fell he came at me again but I managed to kick him in the knee. He fell backward, got up and limped down the track. I got up and started after him. He was winded by the time I caught up with him, he stumbled and fell onto the track, and then the train hit him. He didn't make any attempt to get off the track before he was hit."

"Did he say anything?"

"He asked who I was."

"What did you tell him?"

"Nothing, I didn't have a chance before the train hit him." Carl didn't want to tell Jean what he had said. It would not have contributed anything to the case and may have raised some issues that he didn't want to get into.

Within minutes an ambulance was there along with fifteen of New York City's finest, including Captain Carducci, who immediately took charge. He told the ambulance crew to take a look at Carl's shoulder and face. The train victim was a case for the coroner. He sent four cops down the track to secure the scene. He then asked Carl to repeat his story.

A few minutes later the coroner was there with his assistant pushing the gurney. They were closely followed by the forensic team. Both groups proceeded up the track to examine and photograph the scene and pick up the body. Two detectives arrived within minutes and followed the coroner. Captain Carducci then organized a team of policemen to sweep the tracks between the subway platform and where the train had hit Khan. They were told to pick up every item or scrap of paper that did not belong in the subway in case Khan dropped or tried to throw something away.

When the forensic team returned to the platform they had removed and bagged Khan's watch and the contents of his pockets. Carl and Jean examined his wallet. They found sixty-two dollars in cash, a receipt from "Your Office etc," and a black and white photo of an older man with a beard and three young men probably still in their teens. The background in the picture appeared to be an older building with an unusual architecture. One of the young men in the photograph was Khan. There was no writing on the face or back of the picture. There were no credit cards but there was a folded paycheck from the "Household Furnishing Mart" with an address near Khan's apartment.

Also found in his pockets were thirty-one cents in change and a locker key. The handle of the key had "GCS 1242" stamped into the metal. One of the Forensic team members said that he had seen a similar key once before. The GCS stood for Grand Central Station and the number was for a locker. Carl and Jean said that they would go and find it. Captain Carducci sent Lieutenant Hutching with them with instructions to take Carl to the emergency room first.

Jean, Carl and Hutching were approaching Jean's car when Jean said, "Damn," and glared at Hutchings. She had parked at the entrance to the subway and followed after Carl. While they were in the subway she had received a ticket for illegal parking.

Two hours later, Carl was cleaned up with a couple of stitches just above his eye. He also had x-rays taken of his back, shoulder and arm. After the doctor had a chance to examine the x-rays, he gave Carl a bottle of Ibuprofen and put his arm in a sling. The doctor told him that he was going to be sore for about two weeks and not to try to use his arm for any heavy work, but to move it so the muscles would not stiffen.

When they entered Grand Central Station they had to ask a security guard where the lockers were. The guard said that there were lots of them in four locations on the lower level. He led the way to an alcove on the lower level that was lined with lockers. They were lucky that the first group they came to contained locker 1242, the one they wanted. When they opened the locker they found a small suitcase and a briefcase.

As they left Grand Central Station, Jean said that they would take the two items to FBI headquarters where they could be examined. Hutching suggested that it would be better if they went to police headquarters since that is where the body and the rest of the forensic evidence had been sent.

When they opened the briefcase they found a laptop computer, some cash, and an envelope with papers and receipts. They did not turn the computer on but instead sent it to a computer specialist who opened the computer case and extracted the hard drive, then made an exact copy of its contents. All examinations of the data would be made on the copy, thereby preserving the hard drive in its original state.

The envelope contained a receipt for Your Office Etc., a receipt for the purchase of two vans, a rental agreement from an agency in Hoboken for a warehouse, receipts for the purchase of fertilizer, diesel fuel, and aluminum powder, an apartment rental agreement, a letter, and fifty thousand dollars in cash.

The letter was written in Arabic. Reading the letter Carl said, "The letter is from a Mr. Chowla, headmaster of a madrassa in Pakistan. It is addressed to Khan. It says to not worry. His family is with Allah and sitting at the feet of the prophet." I believe he is referring to the leaders of Islam's Fire. He continued "It tells him to expect help from two brothers, Malik and Rahib. That they are currently in Los Angeles but would be joining him soon to help in his time of sorrow." That must mean help in rebuilding Islam's Fire or the attack on the stock exchange."

Jean and Carl both asked that photographs of all the evidence and a complete copy of the hard drive be sent to FBI headquarters and CIA.

Malik was still being held in a holding cell at the police station under suicide watch. Carl and Jean asked that he be brought to an interview room. The police were not taking any chances with a man who was willing to martyr himself. He was brought in by two large officers. His hands were handcuffed to a chain around his waist and he had a chain and ankle cuffs on his legs that forced him to shuffle when he walked. When he was seated he simply stared ahead, not speaking. Carl asked, in English, "How are you feeling? Are you hungry or thirsty?" Malik did not answer, he simply stared straight ahead. Finally, Carl leaned back and in a casual voice asked in Arabic, "Have you heard from headmaster Chowla recently?"

Malik looked at Carl and his eyes widened in surprise. He stared at Carl for a few seconds and asked, "How do you know about the headmaster?"

"We know everything about him. How you wrote to him and his response with a letter telling you to go to New York to help Mohammed Sidique Khan. He even gave you Khan's telephone number and address so that you could help him rebuild Islam's Fire. But Islam's Fire doesn't exist anymore, it is dead. You are all alone. No one will help you, no one will share your fate. Rahib is dead, Khan is dead, and Islam's Fire is dead. You have nothing left except what we give you. We know everything that has happened so all we would like is confirmation on a few points, and in exchange we will notify your family. At least it will be easier for them knowing that you are alive."

"I will tell you nothing!"

"That is truly too bad, life will be much easier for you if you confirm what we already know. There is no doubt that you will be tried and convicted. You know it, and I know it. We are a decent people, not monsters. We know what it's like to lose a son or daughter and the hurt that parents suffer. We could at least let your parents know that you are alive and well, but if you have no feelings for your mother or father you can just sit in a cell and await your trial. I really don't care, but I do feel sorry for your parents, they are innocents whom you obviously care so little for."

Carl started to get up and Jean rose to follow.

"Wait, I am hungry."

"Answer a few questions and you will be fed."

"What is it you want to know? I will not give you any information that will hurt my friends or Islam."

Carl started with easy questions. "I understand and respect your position, so let's start with your real full name?"

"Malik Karim."

"What is the name of your parents and where do they live?"

"My father is General Ally Karim and he lives in Islamabad. My mother's name is Anchu."

"That is not enough, how do I contact your father, give me his address."

"He is a General in the army, he will be easy to find."

"Where did you go to grade school?"

"Grade school? I went to Aga-Kan school in Islamabad, why do you want to know that?"

"We want to know everything about you. What was the name of the teacher who taught you to speak English so well?"

"My English teacher was Mr. Pyar Kardan."

"Where did you receive your religious training?"

"At a madrassa in Gilitt."

"Why Gilitt, that is in the North and far away from Islamabad?"

"I wanted to get away from my father."

Carl could see that Malik was becoming more at ease with the interrogation because of the non threatening questions. He switched to English for the next question.

"Do you have any brothers and sisters?"

"Why do you now ask questions in English?"

Carl smiled and answered in Arabic. "The lady is feeling left out and becoming unhappy. I want to sleep with her tonight and I want her happy and in a good mood."

Malik gave Jean an appraising look then grinned and said, "Alright, I will speak English. Yes, I have two sisters and three younger brothers."

Carl continued in English, "Why did you choose to go to an American university? Islamabad has a good university."

"Headmaster Chowla felt that I would do well at an American university and he provided the necessary papers that would allow me to enroll."

"Did you come to the United States alone?"

"No, the headmaster had papers for four other students but they were accepted at different universities. I never saw them again after we arrived in America."

"Has your father been helping you financially?"

"My father was against my coming here so the headmaster gave us the funds to get here. Once we were accepted at a university my father relented and began sending money."

"Did the headmaster continue to support you as well?"

"No, when my father started sending money the headmaster stopped."

"How did you meet Ujaama?"

"He came to the university to meet the students from Pakistan. As time passed we became friends."

"How did you become involved with terrorism?"

"I don't know what you are talking about. I am not a terrorist! I am part of a jihadist army. I was not a terrorist!"

"Come on, Malik, we know that you and Ujaama loaded the bombs, then you drove to the Ferry boat in Canada where Rahib picked you up. Then you drove to San Francisco, and then travelled on to Los Angeles, where you murdered the bar owner."

Malik yelled, "I did not murder the bar owner, Rahib did. I was on the street. All I did was yell and make noise. It was Rahib who hit the man with a hammer, he was supposed to knock him out but he hit him too hard, it was an accident."

There was a moment of silence. Carl continued in a soft voice, "Tell me how you found Khan?"

"The Headmaster sent us the address and telephone number for Khan. When we arrived in New York we called him. Can I have something to eat?"

"Just a minute more, we are almost through. How did you build the bombs here in New York?"

"They taught us how to use fertilizer, diesel fuel, and aluminum powder at the training camp in Pakistan."

"Who sent you to a training camp?"

"Headmaster Chowla."

"Who put together the plan to bomb the Stock Exchange?"

"Kahn did, he said that it would destroy the American economy."

Carl looked at Jean and then continued, saying, "The lady and I are going to step outside for a few minutes to get you some food. We will not be gone long." Carl and Jean stood up and walked out.

When the door had closed behind them, Jean looked at Carl and said, "Nice job of interrogation. How did you get him to switch to English?"

"I told him that you were getting bored and that I wanted sleep with you tonight. If we switched to English you would be happier and be in a better mood."

Jean stared at Carl in disbelief then started laughing.

Carl asked the officer standing outside the interrogation room "Is there a restaurant nearby where we can get the prisoner something to eat?"

"Yeah, about two blocks down the street there is a restaurant where they have takeout. A lot of the people from the station eat there."

"Can you take the prisoner to the bathroom if he needs to go?"

"Yeah, I'll take care of it."

"Thanks, back in twenty. By the way, can we pick up something for you?"

"Thanks for the offer, but no thanks, I've just eaten."

When Carl and Jean returned they placed a plastic container with a small green salad, fried potatoes, Salisbury steak covered in gravy and a bottle of water in front of Malik. They asked the guard to un-cuff his right hand. Malik had a hard time cutting his meat with plastic utensils and able to use only one hand. Carl had to cut the meat for him. While Malik ate, Carl asked more questions.

"Where did you get the material for the bombs?"

With some pride Malik explained how he and Rahib went into the New Jersey countryside to buy ammonium nitrate, and then mixed it with diesel fuel and aluminum powder. He explained how they mixed it by hand using wooden paddles they had made.

"Where did you learn to make bombs?"

"At the training camp in Gilitt."

"Where did you get the detonators and C4 explosive?"

"We took them from a mining operation in West Virginia."

Carl turned to Jean to ask, "Do you have any questions?"

"Not at this time but I am sure we will in the future."

In Arabic Malik said with a smile, "She is a happy person now, I hope you will remember that when I am put on trial."

59

The FBI checked the mailbox that Khan had rented, finding nothing there but advertisements. They would continue to monitor the mailbox for the next sixty days in the event that information was sent in before the sender had learned about Khan's death on CNN.

A check with Khan's employer brought nothing but praise for Khan. He was considerate of the customers and his ability to speak several languages was considered a real asset to the store's operation. The store manager said that he was considering giving Khan a raise in salary to ensure that he would not leave for another job. The fact that he was a terrorist came as a complete shock to the manager and the rest of the employees who knew him. They all thought that Khan was one of the kindest people they had ever met.

Using the receipts in Khan's briefcase, the FBI located the warehouse in Hoboken that was used to store the vans and make the bombs. In it they found the paper bags used to ship ammonium nitrate, five gallon containers that held the aluminum powder, and the steel fifty-five-gallon drums used to store the diesel fuel. The agents marveled at how lucky the neighbors adjacent to the warehouse had been. If the bombs had accidentally exploded while they were being mixed the whole area would have been leveled. A check with the manufacturer of the ammonium nitrate showed that the lot number stamped on the bags were not sent to a single distributor but had been sent to distributors all over the state of New Jersey and Pennsylvania.

The New York police had broken through the security passwords on the laptop computer and had been able to read the information. There were notations of expenditures by Rahib and Malik to pay for supplies, vans, rental of the warehouse and rental of their New York apartment. The files included plans for bombing the Stock Exchange, and the address for the back-up computer center. There was also an address for the Bromely's apartment. Khan was very organized. He would be able to account for every dollar. There was a lot of e-mail to others in the organization that provided some history of Islam's Fire. Most of the information the CIA already had. There was also a letter to other members saying that Yusef had been killed, and that Khan was now the new leader of the organization. Much of the information was not pertinent to Khan's activities while he was in the State of New York. It would not help the New York prosecutor in building a case against Malik, but would be of interest to the CIA.

Carl and Jean reviewed the various reports and reached the conclusion that there was no more that could be learned in New York City. It was time to head back home. He caught the next plane to Dulles airport. Jean stayed in New York City to oversee the completion of the file on Khan. As far as the FBI knew, Islam's Fire had been eradicated in the United States. All known members of Islam's Fire in America were in prison, awaiting trial, or dead. The only thing the FBI was sure of was that there would soon be a new organization ready take Islam's Fire's place.

60

Early next morning Carl called the Director and set up a meeting for later that morning. John Gray and Aaron Kovak were waiting when Carl walked in. The Director asked Carl to bring them up to date on the events in New York.

Carl gave them a description of the events leading to the bombing of the back-up computer center, shopping center and gas station by Rahib, the arrest of Malik and the death of Khan. He told them what Malik had revealed about Mr. Chowla, the headmaster of the madrassa, and how he supplied the names of students who he felt were promising candidates as terrorists to Islam's Fire, and possibly to others.

Aaron spoke up, saying, "The CIA analysis of the information on Khan's computer also bore out Malik's allegations. We found lists of student names and the schools they had been enrolled in, and that information has been passed on to the FBI. That's not to say all students on the list are terrorists, but only that they are good prospects for a recruitment into a terrorist cell by

Simon Rossman or others like him. I am going to suggest that the FBI interview each of these students to find out if they have been approached by anyone and whether they have been to a training camp. If they have, I suggest that their student visas be revoked. We don't need Islamic students that have received military training at a terrorist training camp running around a college campus."

The Director continued with, "Carl, I think you had better take a couple of weeks off to let your arm and back heal. After you are feeling better, pack a bag and take a trip to Pakistan to have a word with General Karim. You might be able to convince him to help us with Chowla and the training camp. The Pakistanis are a little touchy about our troops being involved in eliminating terrorists on their soil, particularly when it comes to religious teachers.

"Aaron, have your staff put together whatever information we have on General Karim for Carl. Also put together a report of Malik's activities, including his association with Mr. Chowla, the madrassas, and training camp that we can pass on to General Karim.

"Maybe we can convince General Karim that it would be in the best interest of Pakistan and the rest of the world if he took care of Mr. Chowla, and closed down the training camp that turned his son and other young Pakistani men into terrorists.

"Okay, gentlemen, let's pick this up when Carl's arm has had a chance to heal, and Aaron has some information on our good General."

For two weeks, Carl worked in the Lukin Investigation office performing a security analysis for two firms that were concerned about improving their physical security. He found the work boring after his experience in chasing down Islam's Fire leadership. In spite of uneventful days filled with meetings and report writing, the two weeks flew by.

He spent evenings at home, eating late dinners, sitting on the porch with a glass of wine, doing light chores around the house, listening to good music, and taking evening walks. Each day he exercised his arm and shoulder, and he almost had full use of both again. Each morning he would get up at five-thirty and run five miles, have breakfast and drive to the office. When he lay in bed at night he would think of Ann and on occasion Adriana.

Two weeks sped by much too fast, and then Carl received a call from the Director asking if he was ready to go back to work.

The Director asked John Gray, Carl and Aaron to meet in his conference room to go over what they now knew about General Karim.

Aaron started the briefing with a description of General Karim. "The General is a tough man in charge of the army in the Northern provinces. He appears to be pro-Western and very much a Pakistani patriot. Our people who have worked with him have found him to be likeable and fair. His troops are very loyal to him. He is a tough field commander, smart, decisive, and protective of his men, but quite willing to use his troops if he is convinced that the goal is militarily or politically worthwhile. He is a strict disciplinarian and he appears to be a moderate with respect to Pakistan's dispute with India over the Kashmir Valley. He believes that the Taliban present a serious danger to Pakistan and should not be allowed to control any part of Pakistan, including the mountainous regions. Our military people respect him.

"He's married and has five children. He has been married to his wife, Anchu, for thirty-four years. You have met his eldest, Malik. He appears to be a family man, he does not drink or chase women, he follows the tenets of Islam but is not a fanatic about religion. When he attends political functions he stays a short time, makes his excuses and goes home. He is not considered a man with political ambitions or a threat to any politician. He believes in a democratically elected government with the military subservient to the elected government.

"He appears to be the kind of man who might take action against Chowla and the training camp if he had the facts."

Carl read through the dossier on the General and the report on Malik that was to be given to the General. He complimented the excellent job that Aaron's staff had done. "If any document is going to cause the General to take action this is it. It's a convincing rendition of the facts."

"Okay Carl, if you are ready for another trip you can leave tomorrow. When you get there check in with the embassy. I'll call and ask the ambassador to throw a party or some other event and arrange for you to have a few minutes alone with the General."

61

Carl travelled by British Airways, landing in London and changing planes to Islamabad, where he was met at the airport by an embassy driver. As they drove to the embassy in the diplomatic enclave, at number five Ramna Street, Carl was struck by how busy the city was. There seemed to be people everywhere. Small shops or stalls filled the streets and appeared to be doing a thriving business. The character of the city changed as they drew closer to the diplomatic enclave. The small shops and stalls were left behind and the area took on more of the look of a Western city.

When the car arrived at the embassy Carl was led to the ambassador's office and introduced to Ambassador Collins. Ambassador Collins said with a smile, "So you are the guest of honor I'm throwing a party for. Good to meet you, Carl."

Carl said, alarmed, "I hope you are not throwing the party for me, Mr. Ambassador. My visit here is only to talk to one person."

"No, I didn't mean to alarm you, the party is for a congressman who sits on the Ways and Means committee. We had not planned to throw a party in his honor until Director Rice called and asked for my help in getting you an introduction to General Ally Karim. So it seemed to be the perfect excuse to get General Karim to come since the Ways and Means Committee will be looking at the appropriations dealing with foreign aid in which Pakistan will receive a share. You will be introduced as a member of our Military Attaché's office. We have a library that will be made available to you during this evening, and there will be a Marine at the door to ensure that you will not be disturbed. I hope you will not be discussing a subject that involves me or this embassy."

"No sir, I am simply delivering a message regarding his son who is currently in jail in New York City for murder and terrorism. We are not asking for any action from him but we are hopeful that he will close the terrorist camp that trained his son, and arrest the madrassa headmaster that guided his son and many others to lives of terrorism. If he chooses not to take action there is nothing we can do about it at this time."

"I see. Well, I hope your plan works. In the meantime we have a small apartment you can use tonight. My understanding is that you will be leaving for the States tomorrow."

"Yes sir, I see no reason to stay beyond tomorrow. If there is a change of plans I will move to a hotel."

"Very well, I'll see you tonight at the party."

At eight-fifteen Carl entered the reception hall wearing a dark blue business suit, white shirt and red tie. Looking around, he saw the Ambassador and his wife at the entry to the reception hall greeting guests. He joined the reception line and was greeted by the Ambassador, who introduced him to his wife. After chatting a few minutes the Ambassador whispered to Carl that the General was over at the bar with two aides.

Carl slowly made his way to the bar while he assessed the crowd. When he finally reached the bar the General was talking to two others. After a few minutes the General turned to Carl and said, "Good evening," in English.

Carl responded in Urdu saying, "Good evening, General, I hope you are having a pleasant evening."

With surprise registering on his face the general said, "You speak Urdu very well, have you been in our Country long?"

"No sir, I only arrived today and will be leaving tomorrow. Malik asked me to look you up if I had occasion to come to Pakistan."

Again surprise appeared on his face as he asked, "You have met my son?"

"Yes sir, I have some news about him if you have a few minutes. I can take you to the library where we can talk privately."

The General turned to his aides and said, "I'll be back in a short time." Turning back to Carl he asked, "Where is this library?"

Carl led the way out of the reception hall and down a corridor to the library door with a marine standing in front and entered.

The general noted the guard at the door. When he entered the room he asked Carl, "Why is there a guard on the door to this room."

"To ensure that we are not disturbed until you have had the opportunity to digest the information that I am about to give you."

"You said that you have spoken to my son. Is he well? I have not seen him for many years."

"I spoke to your son three weeks ago in New York City. He is well but he is being held in custody pending a trial. In the near future he will be tried and convicted for acts of terrorism and murder. The evidence is extremely strong and there is very little that can be done for him."

The General's face blanched and his hands shook.

"Perhaps we had better sit down while I tell you of Malik's activities."

Carl sat in an easy chair and the general sat on the sofa across from him. "As an act of rebellion against you, Malik entered a madrassa for religious training. Along with religion he and the others received a strong and steady diet of fanatical ideas. After several years of brainwashing, the headmaster of the madrassa, a man whom he trusted, suggested that he go to a training camp where he would receive military training and more indoctrination to the fanatical approach of serving Islam. Those students who were bright enough were given school transcripts that said they had received enough training that they were eligible to attend universities in the United States, England, France and a number of other Western countries. Malik was accepted at the University of Washington in the State of Washington. His name and those of other students and the names of the universities they attended were given to terrorist organizations. A recruiter named Ujaama befriended Malik at the university and suggested that he might want to join an organization called Islam's Fire, a terrorist group with cells in Washington, California and New York."

The General had not said a word during Carl's narrative but simply stared at him with an expression of shock and disbelief.

"The terrorist cell in Seattle, Washington is responsible for the bombing of the ferry boat in Canada with the resulting deaths of over one hundred and seventy people. You may have heard about the bombing and sinking of the ferry.

"Malik was the person who drove the car bomb onto the ferry. Malik and a friend, a man called Rahib Kalil then made their way to Los Angeles where they stayed for a little over a month. Once they found jobs and had a permanent address, they wrote to the headmaster of the madrassa, a Mr. Chowla, asking him to put them in contact with the leadership of Islam's Fire so that they would receive instructions on where to go for their next assignment. They received a response from Mr. Chowla telling them to go to New York and join a Mr.

Mohammed Sidique Khan. To get there they needed money, so they murdered a business owner, stealing his money and flew to New York. Khan instructed them to buy the supplies to build two large car bombs, which they did. Rahib and Khan then tortured and murdered the Information Technology manager and his wife for address of a back-up computer center. And in fact, Rahib did manage to blow up the back-up computer center and in the process killed a great many people, including himself. Malik was stopped while driving the car bomb intended for the New York Stock Exchange.

Khan was later killed while trying to escape. Malik is the sole survivor of the terrorist attack against the Stock Exchange and will stand trial for that attack. If he should ever be released from prison he will also stand trial for the murder in Los Angeles.

He will also stand trial in the State of New York as an accessory to the murder of the New York Stock Exchange Information Technology manager and his wife, and acts of terrorism that lead to the deaths of more than seventy people when the Back-up data center was bombed. Of course Canada wants to put him on trial for the sinking of a ferry boat and murder of 170 people."

Carl paused for a moment to allow the General to absorb the information he had just been given. After a few minutes of silence Carl said, "The case against Malik and how he arrived in his current predicament are documented in this written report, which has been prepared for you. It details the facts of the case and the evidence against him."

A somber-looking father sitting on the sofa asked quietly, "What can I do for my son?"

"I am sorry General, the evidence against your son is overwhelming and the crimes are too serious. There is nothing that you can do for Malik now. But you have the power to help many parents avoid the pain that you are feeling right now and save the lives of many young men."

In a soft voice the general asked, "How is that?"

"You can close down the training camp in Gilitt and make

sure Headmaster Chowla never has a chance to influence Pakistan's young men ever again."

Carl and the general sat there for a few minutes, neither spoke. Finally, the general stood, his body sagging. There was sorrow in his eyes. He said, "Thank you for coming to see me."

Also standing, Carl asked, "Is there anything that I can do for you?"

"Yes there is, please let me know when Malik is scheduled for trial."

"Yes sir, I will. There is an address in the folder that can be used to reach me should that be necessary."

The General walked out of the room, said goodnight to the Ambassador and started for the door. His two aides at the bar drinking fruit juice saw the General start to leave, put their drinks down and hurried out after him.

The following morning Carl left Pakistan for a two-day stopover in Paris and then a flight home.

62

The day following his meeting with Carl at the American embassy, General Karim called Falak Mabutto, Chief of Pakistan's National Police, and asked for a meeting with him later that day. Chief Mabuto was General Karim's first cousin and one of the General's closest friends. General Karim related the conversation he had had with Carl to Chief Mabutto over a cup of tea. Afterwards Chief Mabutto read the report given to General Karim.

When Chief Mabuto finished reading the report the General said, "I have been on the internet looking at newspaper articles from Seattle, Los Angeles, New York and Vancouver, Canada. All of the articles substantiate the information provided in that report. The headmaster of the madrassa in Gilitt has been teaching our young men to become radicals and then sending them for training in a terrorist camp. My son and your three sons have been the victims of his teaching and are now dead. He has to be stopped before more of Pakistan's young men are lost to us and other parents grieve as we do."

"Let me talk to the chief prosecutor and see what can be done. I will call you later this evening."

"Thank you, Falak. Regardless of what the chief prosecutor says, I intend to take care of the training camp. These training camps are for military training and are a real threat to Pakistan's security. I will wait to hear from you tomorrow afternoon after you have talked to the prosecutor."

The following afternoon Falak called General Karim to inform him that he had warrants for the arrest of Headmaster Chowla and a search of the school and the headmaster's home. And that the warrants would be executed later that night.

That evening the police arrested Mr. Chowla, and in searching his home they found correspondence from other headmasters who had submitted the names of students with radical leanings, suggesting they should be considered for the defense of Islam.

When the evidence gathered during the search of Mr. Chowla's home was presented to the prosecutor, he issued warrants for the arrest of the three headmasters who supplied the names of students to Mr. Chowla. All three headmasters were arrested a short time later and put on trial.

Unfortunately, Mr. Chowla could not withstand the interrogation process and died of a heart attack. Considering Pakistani prisons, he was the luckiest of the four.

The other three headmasters stood trial and were sent to prison for twenty years each, a term that they would not survive. The prosecutor presented the bombing of the Marriot Hotel in Islamabad as direct evidence that the training provided by the headmasters was a threat to Pakistan, as well as to other countries.

63

Following the arrest of Mr. Chowla, two Chinook helicopters, each loaded with forty battle-hardened troops led by General Karim, lifted off from a military airfield near Islamabad at three in the morning. Two hours later they landed in a grain field near Gilitt approximately three miles away from the training camp.

When the Chinook helicopters landed, the rear ramps came down and eighty fully armed soldiers disembarked. Each of the men was armed with an AR-16 automatic rifle, night vision goggles and a backpack with provisions for two days. Four of the soldiers also carried bags of explosives in addition to rifles. Their orders were to take no prisoners.

The camp stood against a hillside and faced a small mountain glen that served as a training ground. At one end of the open area was a small firing range. There were four mud brick buildings, one served as the camp office, communication center, and armory. One building served as a kitchen and dining and training room. The two remaining building were barracks.

After quietly killing the guards the troops simply advanced through the camp killing anything that moved. Six minutes after the attack started there was no one left alive in the camp. The troops then searched each body, removing any personal effects. Others searched the barracks and the administrative office for documents and equipment.

When the sun came up the troops began digging a trench to be used as a mass grave. Once they were done all the bodies were thrown in the trench and it was filled in. When that task was complete the buildings were destroyed with explosives. When the troops finished there was no sign that there had ever been a camp there except for the remaining piles of rubble from the destroyed buildings.

Later that day Carl received a nine word message from General Karim. It said simply, "The training camp and the headmaster no longer exist."

PREVIEW FROM
HEAT SEEKERS

1

An Unforgettable Voyage to Exotic Ports of Call That You'll Remember the Rest of Your Life.

The passengers who read that advertisement didn't know how prophetic that statement was.

The first leg of the journey took the Sea Traveler to Port Said, Egypt where the passengers had a chance to disembark for a few hours of sightseeing. Once underway again the ship joined a south bound convoy entering the Suez Canal. The eleven hour transit of the canal was largely boring because there was little of interest to see. Someone viewing the convoy of ships from the shore of the canal would see what appeared to be the ship's super structure, seemingly, gliding across the desert. From the ship's deck a passenger or crew looking at the shore would not be able to see any of the fabled wonders of Egypt. What greeted the tourists' eyes was an endless expanse of dull brown desert sand.

The passage through the Straits of Suez to the Red Sea had been without incident. Once they left the Canal a few passengers stayed on deck staring out to sea hoping to get a glimpse of the exotic land that they had heard about much of their lives. Unfortunately, they were far enough away from land that there was not much to see except the distant outline of the shoreline and the occasional dhow or flicker of light made by a cooking fire at a distant village.

The voyage of the Sea Traveler began in Barcelona, Spain. The itinerary for a twelve day cruise would carry them through the Suez Canal, into the Red Sea and the Gulf of Aden, with ports of call in Egypt, Yemen, India, and Pakistan. On the return leg Sea Traveler would pass through the Straits of Hormuz into the Persian Gulf stopping in Kuwait, Qatar, Saudi Arabia, United Arab Emirates, and Oman before returning to Barcelona.

The Sea Traveler was a medium sized cruise ship that was ideal for sailing to the more out of the way and exotic ports of North Africa and the Middle East. She was 610 feet long and designed to carry 536 passengers. Although not as lavish as some cruise ships she was well appointed and fast for her size.

The trip would take them through waters where a number of ships had been taken by pirates in recent years. International law precludes the carrying of defensive weapons aboard a cruise or merchant ship despite the real threat of being attacked by armed pirates. However, new technology provided a non-lethal alternative. The owners took the added precaution of installing two LRAD (Long Range Acoustical Device) units. Originally designed for the military and law enforcement, the LRAD could be used for crowd control and any situation where a means of nonlethal protection was needed. The LRAD were designed to issue voice commands in an emergency or emit a narrow focused loud beam of highly irritating noises to disorient a crowd. Sounds, such as fingernails on a black board, or the continuous beep of a smoke alarm, could be generated with enough intensity to be extremely painful within a range of 1500 feet.

There had been a brief stop in Yemen before the long run to Mumbai, India. The passengers had a few hours of daylight to relax and take in some sun before dinner, but for the crew, being on the Gulf of Aden brought a heightened degree of alertness. They knew that the Gulf of Aden had become a more dangerous place.

Within the past few years a large number of cargo ships, including a super tanker, a Russian freighter carrying a cargo of arms and ammunition, and a passenger ship, in addition to others, had been taken and held for ransom by Somali pirates. Even though the Sea Traveler was cruising over 150 miles from shore there was always the threat of being attacked.

Captain Mason Larken hosted dinner for special guests. He attended the entertainment in the ship's theater and prepared to visit the bridge, as was his custom, for a final check before going to his cabin. Captain Mason had retired from the British navy three years earlier. At 52 years of age, he was tall, with a slender build. He had a full head of light brown hair betrayed by just a touch of gray, giving him a distinguished look. The male passengers on the ship quickly learned to respect his naturally reassuring presence. The ship's female passengers simply considered him a very attractive man. The combination of his experience and his confident bearing made him the perfect choice as a cruise ship captain.

Early in the evening, Captain Mason noted his First Officer, Jack Muldoon, having a drink and engaging in intimate conversation with an attractive and shapely blond. In the crowd of mostly gray haired, middle aged, and overweight passengers typically found on cruise ships she stood out. Usually a young woman as attractive as she seldom traveled alone. Hopefully she was traveling with her grandmother rather than her husband or other male friend.

As was his custom each night Captain Mason made his way to the elevators that would take him to the bridge. As he stepped onto the elevator he met his First Officer. "Good evening Jack. I saw you entertaining that rather attractive blond at dinner. She seemed to be enjoining your company."

"Yes sir, this could prove to be a very interesting cruise. I am supposed to meet her later for a drink, then who knows."

As they stepped onto the bridge they were greeted by the Third

Officer, "Good evening Sir, everything is in fine shape, the weather is perfect, just a very light breeze out of the East, the sea is as smooth as glass, and the engines are purring like kittens."

"Thank you Mr. Kellum."

The Captain looked at the First Officer saying, "It looks like this is starting out to be a fine cruise. I think I'll go out for a smoke before turning in, care to join me?"

"Yes sir, I believe I will."

From the starboard bridge deck they could look down and see the light green luminescent glow emitted by microscopic sea life after being disturbed by the ship's prow. The green phosphorescence would gradually fade as it passed along the length of the ship only to reappear in the turbulence created by the ships propellers. Viewed from an aircraft overhead, it would look like a light green line that pointed directly at the ship before it faded back into the dark of the sea.

The moonlight was so bright that stars in that quadrant of the sky seemed to disappear. It was a peaceful, quiet, and calm night that could easily lull a person into believing that all was well with the world.

The Captain lit his cigarette and stared out to sea. After a few minutes he noticed what looked like four white lines in the water. Instantly he knew that he was looking at the moonlight reflecting off of the wake of four fast moving boats, "Jack, take a look at that!"

"Yes sir. I see them, they are moving pretty fast. Those aren't fishing boats. At the rate they are moving they'll be here in just a couple of minutes."

"You had better get on the LRAD unit, it looks like there's going to be trouble."

The Captain stepped back onto the bridge and told the helmsman to turn 30 degrees to port. He then reached the control panel and pushed the throttle to "Ahead Full."

He grabbed the intercom and pushed the button for the radio room. When he heard "Radio Room" he said, "This is the Captain.

Send a message that we are under attack by pirates and give our position. Keep on sending."

"Yes Sir, right away."

He then pushed the button for the crew quarters and the button that was labeled "Alarm." When the klaxon stopped ringing the Captain said, "This is not a drill; prepare to repel boarders. This is not a drill; standby to repel boarders."

Crew members that were in bed, reading, or playing cards immediately leaped to their feet, jumped into their pants, stepped into their shoes, and pulled on a shirt. They grabbed their life preservers and ran from their cabins, heading for the passenger deck. The crew's response was urgent but orderly. Captain Mason had drilled his crew until every man instinctively knew his responsibility and assigned station. Some crew prepared fire hoses that would be used to repel any pirate should they try to climb over the railing. Other crew members headed to the various doors in the passenger areas that led to the decks. They checked to see that there were no passengers on the deck then closed the doors locking them.

The majority of the passengers were not aware of the unusual activity that was occurring. Should a passenger ask what was going on they were told that a drill was being conducted and that there was no danger.

Minutes later the radioman called the bridge. The Captain answered "This is radio Sir, I just heard from a British cruiser about 60 miles east of our position. They said they're coming to assist but it will be about two hours before they can get here."

"Thank them and tell them we'll keep them informed."

"Yes sir, will do."

The four small boats were coming up fast, each appeared to be about 30 feet in length and looked to be carrying about ten people. A number of men had automatic rifles slung across their backs. A man near the bow had a grappling hook ready to throw while another man held a scaling ladder that had a hook on one end that could be placed over the railing.

The boats continued to move in fast. Suddenly, the boats

separated so that two boats could approach each side of the ship. At the rate of speed they were traveling, they would be alongside of Sea Traveler in less than a minute.

The Sea Traveler was now moving near its top speed. Boarding her from a small boat traveling at high speed would be extremely difficult and dangerous. Even so, the pirates could be seen getting ready to lift scaling ladders.

In an effort to get the ship to slow down, the pirates fired their AK-47's at the bridge but the fire was ineffective because of the up and down bouncing of their small boats. Several bullets ricocheted off the hull taking bits of paint with them but not doing any damage. Seeing the futility of their action the, pirates soon stopped firing.

The First Officer and two crewmen reached the LRAD units mounted above the bridge. They immediately put on ear protectors, uncovered the sound generating equipment, and switched on the power. They swung one parabolic audio lens toward the boats on the port side of the ship while the second parabolic audio lens was aimed at the boats on the starboard. The First Officer flipped the transmit switch and instantly a very loud screeching sound was emitted. The men in boats dropped their scaling ladders, grappling hooks, and weapons as they clapped their hands over their ears. This proved ineffective to stop the pain they were experiencing as they writhed in the bottom of their boats. The piercing sound seemed to come from every part of their skull.

The boats fell back and pulled away from the ship. Several times the boats tried to return to the ship but each time were turned back by the loud high pitched sound of fingernails on a blackboard.

The loud screeching noise forced the pirates to maintain a distance of at least fifteen hundred feet from the Sea Traveler. It didn't take long for the pirates to realize they were not going to be able to board this ship and they reduced their speed.

The Sea traveler was almost a half mile ahead of the pirates when a helicopter from the British naval cruiser approached. The Captain had just returned to the bridge deck to see what was happening when he saw the helicopter come in low, passing directly over the pirates before they realized it was there. As the helicopter came around for another look, a streak of light from a rocket shot up from one of the boats, hitting the helicopter. The missile exploded on impact. The helicopter instantly disintegrated in a fire ball and fell into the Sea

"Damn, they shot it down with a missile!"

The Captain ran back onto the bridge and reached for the intercom, pushing the button for the radio room he waited anxiously for the radioman to answer, "Radio Room. This is the Captain. Inform that cruiser that their helicopter was shot down with a missile a mile directly northwest of our current position."

"Yes sir, right away sir."

Returning to the bridge deck the Captain watched as a second missile was launched but this time it came toward the Sea Traveler. The missile had a heat seeking guidance system that zeroed in on the dining room, the warmest spot on the Sea Traveler. The missile exploded when it struck a huge plate glass window showering the dining area with shrapnel and glass shards killing two stewards that were cleaning up.

The blast ignited several small fires that were quickly extinguished by the automatic fire suppression system. The dining room sustained a good deal of damage from the explosion and even more damage from the overhead sprinklers. Water continued to cascade into the dining room until the fire suppression system was turned off. There was no structural damage to the ship and it was not in any danger of sinking or burning.

The Captain returned to the bridge and called the radio man saying, "Send a message to all ships in the area with our position and tell them we have been attacked by pirates. When they could not board us they fired a missile. We sustained some damage but we are in no immediate danger."

The response from the radio room was immediate, "Yes Sir."

When the First Officer returned to the bridge he spoke to

the Captain saying, "Shouldn't we go back to see if there are any survivors from the Helicopter?"

"After that explosion and the fall into the sea I doubt if there are any survivors, and we can't endanger the passengers. We've taken one missile hit already and they probably have more. No, we'll let the navy handle this problem.

"Check on the damage. Your girlfriend is just going to have to wait till later. Meanwhile I'll try and calm the passengers."

"Yes sir, right away"

The Captain, checking the charts, gave the helmsman a new heading that would take them directly to Mumbai. Mumbai had facilities that could make repairs quickly to Sea Traveler so the voyage could continue.

The passengers had heard the explosion and fire alarms ringing. They started to run to the lifeboat deck but the doors were closed and locked. Since there was no order to move to the lifeboats they were unsure of what to do. The corridors leading to the dining room were closed by fire doors. Their only other alternative was to move to the main salon. Within a few minutes of the missile strike the public address system announced that there was no danger, that there had been an incident and the Captain would be in the salon in a few minutes to explain to everyone what had happened. Some passengers returned to their staterooms to put away their life jackets, others continued to wear them and moved to the salon.

When the Sea Traveler sailed into the port of Mumbai the authorities were there in full force. Three navel officers representing the Indian navy, two officers from the National Police, a five man team of forensic experts, and two military officers attached to the British embassy were all waiting on the dock.

Although the Captain had made a full report over the radio he was required to describe the attack again and the actions that were taken. Following his presentation he and the First Officer, radio man, and other bridge crew were all interviewed separately and in great detail.

The bodies of the two dead crewmen killed by the missile were picked up by the Mumbai medical examiner so that they could certify cause of death. After the bodies were removed from the ship, members of the forensic team went through the dining room collecting every piece of metal, glass or other debris in order to determine where it came from.

Twenty-two hours later the ship was released for repairs and moved to a local shipyard where workmen advanced on the dining area like a swarm of ants.

At the expense of the cruise ship company the passengers had been moved to local hotels for the duration of the repairs, which were estimated to take three days. Although the passengers got an unexpected extension to their cruise they were not happy. Hotel reservations and connecting flights would be missed. They were resigned to the fact that there was very little they could do about it. The adventure of a pirate attack and a few extra days of vacation to roam around the city of Mumbai would certainly be better than an eight hour shore excursion. This was indeed a trip they would always remember.

The forensic team from the Indian Navel Science lab began shifting through the debris they had collected. Several pieces of metal, plastic and pieces of optical glass were found that simply should have not been found in the dining room of a ship. On closer examination, the debris in question was identified as the remnants of a rocket propellant tube, parts of a circuit board, and pieces of a glass dome which were later identified to be parts of a heat seeking missile.

A chemical analysis of blast residue indicated the presence of HBX, an explosive commonly found in the warhead of surface to air missiles. What everyone thought had happened was confirmed. The Sea Traveler had been attacked by pirates using a heat seeking missile. The big question remained. Where did pirates from the coast of Somalia get heat seeking missiles?

Within thirty six hours munitions experts from the U.S. and Great Britain arrived in Mumbai to examine the debris evidence in an attempt to identify who had manufactured the missile. The piece of circuit board that had been found had a partial part number consisting of eight digits that were visible. A check of manufacturers identified the circuit board as having come from the electronic guidance components used in heat seeking missiles made by the Martin Munitions Company in the state of Utah. The propellant and propellant tube appeared to be of Pakistani manufacture.

2

Within three days of the attack on Sea Traveler the FBI notified the Martin Munitions Company of the attack and of finding a circuit board with a part number that corresponded to the part used in the manufacture of Martin's heat seeking missile. The FBI called Jim Dunning, the CEO of Martin Munitions, to notify him that auditors would be in on the following Monday to audit the manufacturing process and to inspect records of missile sales, and parts inventory, and to identify how heat seeking missile parts had gotten into the hands of Somali pirates.

The Company immediately started an internal investigation. They were one of two companies that had contracts with the government to manufacture heat seeking missiles and the part number that was found was theirs.

The internal investigation included going through records to identify who had purchased the missiles since they had gone into production. Obviously the U.S. military were buyers, and they had licenses to sell missiles to a number of foreign buyers such as England, Germany, and Israel.

The FBI notified Martin Munitions that investigators would be coming the first of the week to find the source of the missile part and how it had gotten into the hands of pirates. In preparation for the coming investigation the company began researching their records to find the disposition of every missile that had ever been produced, sold, placed in inventory, or destroyed. Each sale to a foreign country required a EUC (End User Certificate) certifying that the buyer was the final recipient of the missiles, and certified that the missiles would not be transferred to a third party. Accompanying the EUC there was a DV (Delivery Verification) certifying that the buyer had received the number of missiles that Martin Munitions claimed had been sent.

The FBI would visit each country or organization that had received missiles to verify the existence of missiles, or review records of their use or disposal. It was frustrating to both Martin Munitions and the FBI when the audit found that each missile that had been manufactured was accounted for. None had been stolen or lost in transit, yet the missile that struck the Sea Traveler was a heat seeking missile using a circuit board manufactured by the Martin Munitions company.

The focus of the investigation finally came back to the Martin Munitions Company since it was believed that a terrorist group or a bunch of Somali pirates would not have the knowledge, skills, or resources to have manufactured the needed electronics guidance system or the ability to marry the electronics made by Martin Munitions to a missile manufactured in Pakistan.

Each step of the process was examined to ensure that the electronics could not have been stolen during the manufacturing process.

The employees were interviewed and their bank accounts reviewed. Those who were even the least suspect were given a more thorough investigation. Everyone at Martin checked out with normal financial histories. There were a few DUIs, and the normal money problems that one would expect to find in the general population but nothing severe enough to raise a warning flag.

After four months, the focus of the investigation turned elsewhere. Conditions at Martin Munitions began to return to normal. There was a feeling of relief that the investigators could not find a problem. Although the investigation was not over, the focus was shifted back to the end users and the records that they kept.

Another three months passed without incident. Then the USS *Nassau* (LHA-4), an ASW carrier escorted by two destroyers heading for the Mediterranean entered the Gulf of Aden. There were a number of radar targets in the area. Some were large enough to be commercial ships and others were presumed to be fishing vessels. As a precaution the task force commander had two recon helicopters out approximately 90 miles in front of the task force making sure the area was clear. They were at the maximum search range when they spotted what looked like boat wakes in the moonlight. As they drew closer they could see that the wakes were caused by four small outboard motor boats, each approximately30 feet in length. They looked as if they were headed toward a freighter that was about four or five miles away.

The pilot decided to go down for a closer look. As he passed over the boats they could see that each boat had about ten men on board. The pilot started to make the turn to come around for another look when a threat alarm sounded in the cabin, an instrument indicated an incoming missile. When the pilot looked out he saw a light and the smoke trail coming toward him from one of the boats.

The last transmission from the pilot was "Jesus Christ! That's an incoming missile!" Then there was only static and silence.

The task force had an approximate radar position on the helicopter but by the time they could get other aircraft in the area there was no sign of the helicopter or the small boats. The following morning a search of the area revealed a few pieces of debris on the surface. Members of the crew were never found. The only indication of what happened was the last transmission from the pilot.

The attack on the Sea Traveler and the loss of two helicopters in the same area from missiles caused the investigation to resume with renewed vigor. The investigators wanted to go over every record, manufacturing process, shipping method, and re-audit all of the end users. After another four months of effort they had to reach the same conclusion; all missiles and circuit boards were accounted for.

3

A short time after the completion of the second audit Jim Dunning was in San Francisco talking to Alex Pribich, the president of World Bank. After completing their business they left the office and went to the fiftieth floor of the World Bank building for a nightcap at a private club before calling it a day. Jim was telling Alex about the company's troubles associated with the investigation of the missile attack in the Gulf of Aden. "I am really concerned that Martin Munitions may be excluded from future government contracts if we can't find out how components manufactured by our company ended up in the hands of pirates in the Gulf of Aden. If we were to be decertified from bidding for government contracts we would be put out of business."

"You have a hell of a problem Jim. You may want to consider hiring your own investigator. Considering the risk to your company, I would want my own investigator looking into the problem. The bank has used Carl Lukin Investigations in the past with great success. With so much at stake you will need someone doing the investigating who is on your side. Why don't you give Carl a call? He's here in San Francisco. You might be able to talk to him while you're in town. If you like I can call him for you right now?"

"Yeah, why don't you. I have to get this problem resolved and soon. I don't think Federal auditors looking at records are going to solve the mystery."

The next afternoon Alex introduced Jim Dunning to Carl Lukin and his assistant Ann Curlin. After a few minutes of small talk, Alex left the room so that Jim, Carl and Ann could have a private conversation.

Jim described the events that began with the pirate attack on the Sea Traveler and the impact on the company if the source of the stolen circuit boards was not found. He explained his concerns about the ability to bid on future government contracts if this problem wasn't corrected soon.

After listening to the story, Carl thought how best to answer Jim's request, "From what you have said it sounds like at least a part of the rocket's guidance system was manufactured by your company. So, I guess the place to start is at your factory. If we are to take on this contract you are going to have to hire both Ann and myself. I am going to have to work in the unit that manufactures the electronics and Ann in the accounting unit, specifically, in the section that is responsible for tracking incoming inventory and outgoing product. Obviously some people will have to know who we are and why we are there but keep the number of people to a minimum and impress on them the importance of keeping the reason we are there an absolute secret."

"Yes, I can do that. I'll have to let the supervisors in each area know about you but they have been with the company a long time and have a lot invested in seeing the company resolve this problem."

"Ann and I will be in Logan, Utah within a week. We'll

rent an apartment and give you a call when we're settled in. That will give you a chance to figure out how you and your two supervisors are going to fit us into your work force and get the paperwork in order. Whatever you do it's got to look like we're legitimate new hires.

"One other thing, can you get me the employee records of all the people who work in the guidance system manufacturing unit?"

"I'll have copies of the employment records ready for you when you get to Logan."

4

Carl was hired as a parts inspector in the guidance system unit. His job consisted of measuring the various circuit boards to insure they were made to design specification and then placing them in an electronic testing device to make sure they functioned properly. Once the parts had been inspected and certified as having passed inspection they were moved to the parts room in the assembly area. The work load was not demanding which gave Carl time to move around the manufacturing and assembly floors.

Carl worked with one other inspector, an older man named Jake Lunemann. Jake was trained as an apprentice in Germany many years ago and had some eccentric habits. He arrived at work each morning dressed in a dark blue suit, white shirt, tie, and dress shoes, and wearing a black fedora hat. The first thing he would do on arriving at his work area was to change into a blue work shirt, khaki pants and crepe soled shoes. Then he would put on a white shop coat. He would wear his fedora all day, or he would place it on the corner of his work bench. His routine never varied.

He was friendly but not very outgoing; he did his work and did not engage in any of the usual social activities that one would find in a manufacturing setting. He didn't go out for smoke breaks although he would occasionally buy a cup of coffee from a vending machine. He did not engage in any of the card games that always took place at lunch time. He would eat the lunch that he had brought from home at his work bench and read his newspaper.

He was well liked but kept to himself. He spoke with a thick German accent, was always polite, and willing to help if something needed to be moved or lifted. He was considered a bit of an eccentric but that was attributed to his German upbringing. Jake had been with the company for many years and had had a number of opportunities to promote to shop foreman but had turned down each offer.

Jake was married and lived in a small house in Logan, Utah, with his wife of forty-five years. They had two sons, Hans and Fredrick. Hans lived in Salt Lake City with his wife, Callah, and two children, John and Albert. Fredrick had married and lived in San Francisco.

Jake was considered to be hard working and very competent in his job. He doted on his sons and grandchildren and spent as much time as possible with Hans and his family. Unfortunately, he was unable to spend as much time with Fredrick as he would have liked because of the distance to San Francisco. Frederick's brokerage business prevented him from coming to Utah very often. As a result Jakes attention focused on Hans and his family.

When Hans was twenty he had joined the Marine Corps for a four year tour. He had been posted to the American embassy in Algiers where he met and married Callah, a woman of French descent. They married within a year and when his enlistment ended they moved to Los Angeles, California.

Hans and Callah had two sons. When their youngest son, John, was ten months old he was diagnosed with cystic fibrosis. They were told their son's health might benefit from a dry climate and that the cystic fibrosis research facility located in Salt Lake

City would be able to help with his treatment. So they moved to Salt Lake City where Hans opened his own electronics and appliance store. Business was good enough to make a living but with demanding medical expenses they were barely scraping by and relied on financial help from his father. Making sure that they had enough money to cover the high medical bills for their son was always difficult and as he got older became a mounting problem.

Cystic fibrosis is an incurable genetic disorder. Hans and Callah knew that patients with this disorder typically died at an early age. Few lived to reach middle age, but with so many medical advances being made every day they wanted to prolong their son's life as long as possible in the hope that a cure would be found.

As a result, Hans and his wife continued to live in Salt Lake City although they would have preferred to move to California. Jake and his wife visited Salt Lake City to see their son and grandsons often and always managed to leave some money to help with medical expenses.

Hans' second son, Albert had joined the Air force and had been stationed at Elmendorf AFB, Anchorage, Alaska. Although Albert was close to his family and managed to visit his parents once a year, he wanted to get a degree in economics and live in San Francisco when his enlistment ended.

When Carl first started to work as an inspector, Jake was upset by having to share his job with someone else but he was told the company was concerned that there would be a problem if he were to become ill or have an accident. He was told that hiring a second man for the job was not a reflection on him but that management felt that having a second man trained to do the work was good insurance. The fact that Carl could speak German fluently made the situation easier to swallow for Jake. From that point forward most conversations between Jake and Carl were carried on in German and within a few days Jake warmed up to Carl.

Jake and Carl were responsible for inspecting a number of different parts, among them the circuit boards for the guidance system. The procedure required that when a batch of circuit boards came into the inspection area they were examined by either Jake or Carl. Circuit Boards that failed to pass inspection were tossed into a box for destruction at a later time. Periodically, the failed circuit boards were ground up into small pieces, and after being weighed, sent to a salvage company.

Since the precise weight of a circuit board was known, the total weight of the ground up circuit boards had to match the number of boards that failed to pass inspection. The company knew how many boards and components they had purchased, how many circuit boards had passed or failed inspection and how many were sent to salvage. They had a foolproof security system with respect to the manufacturing portion of the guidance system; or so they thought.

After about six weeks Carl began to notice a pattern. On the days that Jake worked on circuit boards he wore his hat as always to his work bench, but instead of wearing it during the day he would place it on a corner of the bench. During lunch he would handle the hat placing it back on the bench when lunch was over. After noticing this pattern of behavior Carl began to pay close attention to Jake and his hat.

When others had gone to the cafeteria or were eating their lunch and playing cards in the break area Jake, as always, ate alone at his work bench and read his newspaper. One day Carl noticed Jake fiddling with his hat at lunch. Nothing that would be noticeable if you were not paying close attention to the behavior of people; particularly those handling the circuit boards.

At the end of the day after everyone had left, Carl returned to the work area and examined the circuit boards in the failed inspection box. The tally was correct but one of the boards looked slightly different, not something that would stand out as wrong if you were not looking for it, but on closer examination it was just not the same as other boards. It had the same weight and the components looked right, but still, it was slightly different. After being ground up and weighed it would tally out correctly The light bulb in Carl's head flickered on when he realized that a good Martin Munitions circuit board had just disappeared.

That evening he was telling Ann that he thought Jake was smuggling good circuit boards out of the plant in his fedora hat. Carl thought that only one or two boards per month were being stolen because any more than that would have raised questions about the manufacturing process and invited a very close inspection of the entire process.

Ann thought about what Carl had said, "Okay, now that we know how they are being stolen what are we going to do about it?"

"We're not going to do anything yet. I want to know where the circuit boards are being sent once Jake has smuggled them out of the plant. Who does he sell them to and how do they get in the hands of Somali pirates?

"One other question bothers me; why does he steal the boards in the first place? He has been with Martin Munitions for more than twenty eight years. He's about ready to retire. Why would he risk his job and his pension for a few circuit boards? Money is the obvious reason, but after spending the past month talking to Jake I don't think that is the only reason.

"We have to look into Jake Lunemann's background. And find out where he is sending the circuit boards. I'll talk to Jim dunning and let him know what we have found and see how far he wants us to follow this trail or if wants to turn this problem over to the FBI.

5

That evening Carl called Jim Dunning. "I have some news that you need to hear and I think we need to meet as soon as possible." "Why don't you come to the office in the morning?"

"I don't think that would be a good idea, you know how gossip travels in a company. If someone were to see me going into your office my cover would be blown. Can you drop by Dunkin Donuts on the way to work, say at 6:30 in the morning?

"I don't think that would be a good idea either, a lot of the early crew stop off there on their way in. If you're free why don't you and Ann come over to my house in about an hour? We're having a few of the neighbors over for a backyard barbecue. No one from the plant will be here. I'll just introduce you as old friends from Sacramento. Dress is very casual, Levi's and loafers, bring a sweater or light jacket, it can get cool in the evenings. We can grab a few minutes to talk alone later in the evening when everyone has left or had a few too many beers to miss us."

When Carl rang the bell at the Dunning household he and

Ann were invited in and introduced as friends who were in Utah for a short time doing some genealogical research at the Mormon Genealogy Library in Salt Lake. When Carl was asked what he did for a living he said he worked for the State of California at the Department of Finance. It was assumed that Ann was Carl's wife and she did nothing to discourage that notion. Within a short time the subject moved to national politics, hunting, and fishing for the men, schools, and shopping for the women.

By 9:30 P.M. Carl and Jim were able to slip away to the library for some private conversation. Carl filled Jim in on what he had found. When Jim had heard the whole story he sat quietly for a few minute's thinking. Then he said, "I'm both mad and hurt that one of my own employees is screwing me like that. If this thing is not quickly resolved it could cost the company every government contract that it has. We would be bankrupt within a month and hundreds of good people, loyal employees, would be out of a job. I want to follow this to the end wherever it leads us."

"Do you want to tell the FBI what we have found?"

"No not yet. They have had a year since the attack on the cruise ship to find out what is going on and haven't found diddlly squat. Let's follow this lead as far as we can go then give them a complete package. If we go to them now they are liable to screw it up. What do we do next?"

"Your loyal employee Ann, is going to quit her job and do a little investigation on her own. She can follow up on the Lunemann family and find out why after so many years a once loyal employee has begun stealing from the company. Right now it just doesn't make sense. If we are lucky we may be able to follow the circuit boards to the point where they are being used to make heat seeking missiles."

On the way home Carl filled Ann in on the conversation, saying, "You're going to quit your job and investigate Jake's background. You know the routine, with special attention to his financial situation.

"Aren't we going to tell the FBI about what we found?"

"No. Not yet. Jim feels that the FBI has screwed up over the past year and doesn't want to get them involved until we have a complete package."

"What are you going to be doing?"

"I am going to try to get closer to Jake and make sure some surveillance equipment is installed that will catch him in the act.

"You'll probably need Dan Nakamura to give you a hand on your research. Give him a heads up in the morning."

Dan and Ann had become friends while working for the CIA. Dan had a Ph.D in computer sciences, had gotten tired of academia, and joined the CIA where his knowledge of the use of computers and operating software was vastly increased in the more unorthodox use of the technology.

Not long after joining the CIA he had attended a party at Georgetown University, had a little too much beer and had been induced to smoke a marijuana joint, something he would never have done had he not drunk one too many beers. The next thing he remembered was waking up in bed with a beautiful blond coed and a huge hangover. His tongue had grown fuzz and his stomach was doing flip flops.

By that evening he had recovered sufficiently to realize that he was going to survive and wondered if that was a good idea. By Monday morning he had returned to normal and reported for work. He told Ann about his experience and swore he would never do that again. All was well until the following week when he was required to report to the medical office. When he entered the office and gave the receptionist his name he was told to go down the hall to the room labeled Drug Testing. Gong in he was given a plastic cup pointed at a door marked MEN and told to pee in the cup then bring it back to the attendant.

The next day he was called into the department manager's office and told he had failed the drug test. He was also told if it were to happen again he would be terminated. Somewhat shaken by the experience he told Ann what had happened and swore that he would never smoke marijuana or take any other recreational drug again. Nine months later Ann decided to leave the CIA and join Carl's private investigating firm located in San Francisco.

Several months had gone by when Dan was again invited to a party at the university. During the course of the evening he had a few beers and was offered a joint which he refused. But he was inhaling enough second hand smoke that it registered in his blood stream and when he was tested for drugs the following week he failed and was summarily fired and escorted out of the building.

Soon after his dismissal he received a call from Carl Lukin who wanted to know if he was interested in taking a short term job. When Dan asked why Carl had called him he was told that Ann Curlin had recommended him. That was good enough for Dan, he said he was interested.

The job consisted of finding how a hacker had been breaking into a small bank. Within two days Dan had found a back door to the computer system that the hacker had used and identified the hacker. By the third day he had written a report and made a number of recommendations for improving the bank's computer security.

Within a short time Dan moved to Oakland, California and was working as a private consultant in computer security. The vast majority of his consulting contracts came from Lukin Investigations. Dan had moved from a private consultant to also being a personal friend of Ann and Carl.

6

Ann began her research of the Lunemann family by searching through public records, and obtaining credit reports from the major credit organizations: Trans Union, Equifax, and Experian. They all indicated that Jake Lunemann had excellent credit having never missed or been late on a payment. He owned only one credit card which was rarely used, and if used it was paid it off at the end of the month.

Her research revealed that he owned the house he lived in and was a cosigner for a home in Salt Lake City where his son lived. Ann canvassed Jake's neighbors saying that she was interested in buying a home in the area wanted to learn about the neighborhood. During the conversation a few questions about the Lunemann family always seemed to come up. The picture that emerged was that of a quiet couple who pretty much kept to themselves. There were no problems with any of the neighbors and they kept their yard neat. Although they knew all of their neighbors, they did not socialize beyond a casual "good morning" or "it's a beautiful day."

It was almost as if they were from a distant city and just passing through.

Ann followed Jake or his wife on their shopping trips, church, post office or to the mall. After a few days she had a fairly good picture of their shopping habits. On the day after payday at Martin Munitions she followed Jake to an ATM machine owned by Zion First National Bank where he deposited his paycheck. That information was passed on to Dan Nakamura.

That evening Dan was able to hack into the bank's computer system and access the Lunemann's checking and saving accounts. Other then the checking and savings account, Dan could find nothing else that belonged to Lunemann. No safe deposit box, CD's, mortgage or any other banking instrument. The following day Dan sent Ann an email listing six months of the Lunemann's banking activities.

A review of bank accounts revealed that there was very little in savings, and that Jake sent a check each month for a significant amount to their son in Salt Lake City.

At the end of the second week Carl and Ann had reached the conclusion that Jake Lunemann lived a very modest lifestyle and any extra funds they had were being sent to their son to help pay medical bills.

The focus of the investigation switched to Hans and Callah Lunemann. Ann began spending time in Salt Lake City looking into Hans Lunemann's lifestyle. Hans and his wife, Callah, owned a small home that was mortgaged to the Zion Bank of Utah. They also owned a small electronic and appliance store and an appliance repair business which did a modest business. The store and the repair business was their only source of income other than the money they received from Jake.

A search of public records did not indicate anything unusual. A review of the credit rating indicated that Hans had been late several times in payments to the Cystic Fibrosis Research Center but had managed to make late payments before they became delinquent and were turned over to a collection agency. Again what emerged was a family living on the financial edge. Their total life was dedicated to helping their son with his health problems.

Dan retrieved Hans' banking records and their son's accounting records from the Medical Center. What the banking records indicated was that all funds, including the money that Jake sent, that were not consumed by daily living expenses were sent to the Medical Center to pay for their son's medication and medical treatments. A review of the account with the Medical Center indicated that the medical bills were much higher than Hans' total income including the money that his father sent him each month. Every six or seven months a substantial amount was wired to Hans' account at the medical Center to cover any additional expenses and leave a positive balance to cover future medical costs. Six or seven months later the account would be depleted and more cash would be wired to the Medical Center. All the funds were wired from the Bank of Algeria located in Algiers.

It was becoming obvious to both Carl and Ann that the stolen circuit boards were being sent to someone in Algeria and the payoff was the money that was being sent to the Medical Center. Ann said, "I understand the need that Jake felt to help his grandson with his medical expenses, but the theft of the heat seeking missile circuit boards was not the answer. The missiles that the circuit boards have been installed on have already cost seven lives that we know about."

Carl and Ann met with Jim Dunning at his home in Logan Utah the following evening and told him what they had found. After discussing the findings Jim decided that Carl would go to Algiers to find the next piece in the puzzle. After considering what Carl had said Jim thought it was now time to tell the FBI what they had found. Once the FBI had verified the information the cloud over Martin Munitions would be lifted although they would have to update their security if they wished to continue their current contract and be eligible to bid on future government contracts.

Jim said, "I'll call the FBI in for a briefing in the morning. I'll let you know where and when we'll meet."

Jim called about 9:00 AM the next morning to say that the meeting with the FBI was scheduled for the next day at two in the afternoon in his office. Since the next day was Sunday, the plant would be closed except for a skeleton crew. He would tell the guards who was coming and to let them in.

The next day when Carl and Ann entered Jim's office they went through a second door to an adjoining conference room where five people were already seated. Carl and Ann were introduced to FBI Agents Mike Reynolds, Ann Blake and Special Agent in Charge Jean Peters. Jon LaCru, head of security for Martin Munitions was also there.

Jim started the meeting by saying, "Martin Munitions has hired Carl Lukin and Ann Curlin to see if the circuit boards were being stolen from the Martin Munitions or from a customer after the systems were shipped. Both Carl and Ann have been working undercover at the plant for the past two months and have uncovered the source of the theft. Carl why don't you tell us what you have found."

Carl started by saying, "I have spent most of my time in the circuit board manufacturing area working as an inspector. The job gave me the freedom to see the various processes used in making the circuit boards. What I found was that a parts inspector had been failing good circuit boards and substituting fakes in their place. As a result the tally of good and failed parts was consistent with all other records."

Ann picked up the story at that point telling everyone how she had researched the Lunemann family and eventually ended up looking into Hans' family in Salt Lake City. She had used her social engineering skills to talk her way into the Cystic Fibrosis Research Center and get a look at the medical records for John Lunemann. When she was asked how she got a look at the financial records she did not mention Dan Nakamura's role in her research, she simply said that she again used social engineering to talk her way into the accounting department.

She said that she knew what Jake was making at Martin

Munitions, and from what she could find out about Hans Lunemann it became pretty obvious that John's Lunemann's medical expenses exceeded their income. The medical center would receive a wire transfer for significant amounts whenever the Lunemann's needed money to pay for John's medical care.

Jean Peters spoke up saying, "That is not proof of payment for stolen circuit boards." It could just as well be a rich uncle trying to help the Lunemann's out."

Jim jumped in saying, "That is why I asked Carl to stay on this case till we have definitive proof. These people have brought into question the integrity of this company and by God I won't stand for it."

"Mr. Dunning, Carl and Ann are not law enforcement. Outside of this Country they would simply be tourists. They can testify to what they find in any prosecution but they have no power to arrest anyone inside or outside of this Country."

"Well if I am not mistaken Jean, the FBI doesn't have any jurisdiction outside of this Country either. And for the past year the FBI has investigated this case sixteen ways from Sunday and has yet to find anything. If it had not been for the work of Carl and Ann you still would not have any information and the integrity of this company would still be in question. There is too much at stake for this company. We have to follow through on this for our own protection. I understand your concerns and will insure that Carl and Ann keep you informed of any new information."

"I can't stop you but I have to keep another government agency informed and they do have an interest in what happens beyond the borders of this Country."

"I understand. Now what is our next step? Carl do you have any ideas?"

"The circuit boards have to get to Algeria some way. I believe that they are simply mailed to a family member or friend. No one would suspect a stuffed animal even if it contained a circuit board since many toys have voice mechanisms or mechanical devices to make them move. A small circuit board would be assumed to be part of the mechanized animal. I would suggest that the FBI and the Postal Service examine all mail going to Algeria from Logan or Salt Lake City particularly if it's a package.

"From what I know of Somalia it would be almost impossible to get an agent into the country to follow the missile to its final destination. The country has virtually no government. It's run by warlords who get the largest slice of any ransom that is paid. The pirates are poor villagers who get only a small piece of any ransom. It's a very closed society. Strangers would stand out, so the chances of putting an operative in that kind of a tight knit clan society where everyone knows everyone else would be impossible. The next best thing is to discourage them from using missiles."

"How would we do that Carl?" asked Jean.

"Each of these missiles has a proximity detection circuit. When a heat seeking missile locks on to a target it follows the heat source, making small corrections in direction as it moves toward the target. Most of the time the missile will hit the target dead on but sometimes the pilot takes an evasive action that the missile can't follow quickly enough and it will miss the target. As it passes the heat source, sensors immediately go black because heat can no longer be detected. At that time a signal is sent by the proximity circuit which detonates the explosive warhead. Normally, the missile is within feet of the heat source when the detection circuit goes black and there is enough explosive force to blow off a wing or rotor blades. If we reprogram the circuit to send a signal to detonate the warhead when the missile is launched, those nearby will be killed or severely injured. After a few premature explosions like that, pirates will give up using missiles."

"I can't give the OK for that kind of modification but I'll talk to FBI Director Riley about it. We should have our answer in a few days. If we find any good stolen circuit boards in the meantime we can hold on to them and blame the delay in delivery on the post office."

Carl continued, "Lastly, I will be going to Algeria. I hope that the FBI will keep me informed so that I am not flying completely blind while I am over there."

"It seems that the FBI doesn't have a choice but to keep you informed in this matter if we want to resolve this problem and get the bad guys."

"I'll also talk to Director Riley about that."

"We will also have a set of surveillance cameras above Jake's work station to catch him in the act of taking the circuit boards," said Carl.

Jim said, "I'll have engineering get busy designing the bogus circuit boards first thing Monday morning and our security people can install the cameras over Jake's work bench."